THE
WRITER

BOOKS BY MIRANDA SMITH

Some Days Are Dark

What I Know

The One Before

Not My Mother

His Loving Wife

The Killer's Family

The Family Home

The School Trip

The Weekend Away

THE
WRITER

MIRANDA SMITH

bookouture

Published by Bookouture in 2024

An imprint of Storyfire Ltd.
Carmelite House
50 Victoria Embankment
London EC4Y 0DZ

www.bookouture.com

ISBN: 978-1-83525-291-8
eBook ISBN: 978-1-83525-290-1

For Chris

ONE

My most recent mistake was thinking it was over.

It's been, what, nine months since I last received a note? Maybe a year. And yet, as I stand in front of the narrow mail receptor in my apartment lobby, the cold seeping through the glass door against my back, I see it.

There's no envelope or postmark, but it's tucked inside my mail slot. An index card with a single number—*10*.

For a moment, I try to trick myself into thinking it's nothing. Maybe it's a flyer for a local business, a piece of junk mail intended for one of my neighbors. But the box was empty ten minutes ago when I ran out to get a morning coffee. I'm sure of it.

When I turn it over and see that familiar symbol—a black heart—I know it's from him. Or her. Whoever has been taunting me for the past decade.

It's intermittent, of course, which makes it scarier. Every time I think I've outrun the past, one of these little black hearts turns up, usually in far more peculiar places. In the bark of the tree outside my childhood home, black paint poisoning the wrinkled wood. In my ex-boyfriend's car, alongside a pair of lacy underwear that didn't belong to me. More than a year ago, when I was working as a secretary at the MedSpa, I found one inside the front-desk tip jar, all the cash from that day stolen; I was fired that very same shift.

These hearts arrive when I least expect them, bringing chaos into my life. A message meant only for me, urging me to remember.

As if I could ever forget.

I look over my shoulder, frost turning into water droplets as the sun rises. There's no one outside, no one watching. And yet, someone must always be watching. That's the threat this flimsy piece of paper represents.

I crumple the card between my fingers, thundering up the stairwell. I close the door behind me, delighted by the clicks of the locks slamming into place. I'm safe here, unseen. Someone has been messing with me for years, but it's just that. They never openly confront me, so I won't give them the satisfaction of being scared now. I do what I'd intended on doing before I ran for coffee and checked the mailbox—settle up to the dining-room table, pull over my laptop and continue my morning writing session.

Not that I've had much success. For a writer, there's nothing more terrifying than a blank page, and I've stared at this white abyss all morning, the cursor blinking at me, waiting.

Write something, it says.

Write anything.

Man, you suck at this.

The most common question I get, on the rare occasion my hobby as a writer is mentioned, is: How do you come up with ideas?

People are hardly satisfied with my answer. I'm not even satisfied with it. Truthfully, I don't know where I come up with my stories, but I know the repressed trauma from the past decade beats against my insides like a drum, and writing is the only release. If I were to speak with a therapist, which I never have, he or she would likely point out a connection between my past and the dark subject matter.

Sometimes ideas flow freely, like a broken fire hydrant spewing creativity. My fingers can hardly keep up with the possibilities my brain rattles off. It's like I'm transcribing a movie that exists only in my head, sharing it with the page, and then, hopefully, the world.

Other times, trying to find a winning storyline is like sifting through hay in search of a needle. Every idea falls flat, every plot used. Being a writer can be dull, lonely and downright depressing, especially when there's no inspiration in sight.

It's important to point out that although I'm a writer, inside and out, I've yet to be published. I've yet to earn more than a couple hundred bucks from my craft, and I spent them on drinks celebrating the mediocre achievement. That's why I describe writing as a hobby. I'm doing everything right. Perfecting my skills. Allotting hours each day for projects. Sharing my progress with like-minded writers in my critique group, the Mystery Maidens. Years of trial and error—a much heavier emphasis on the error part—have brought me to this point.

I've completed an entire manuscript, and I'm even convinced it doesn't suck. *Night Beat* is a psychological thriller about a crime reporter who suspects her lover is behind a string of homicides. It only took three months to write that book, and I spent another six months editing it. Now I'm hoping a literary agent will agree that it has potential and guide me through the intimidating world of publishing.

Maybe then, I'll be able to call myself a writer without wincing.

None of that seems promising, however, as I stare at the blank page. Maybe it's because I've spent so many months focusing on *Night Beat* and nothing else. Maybe it's because now all I can think about is one day receiving that phone call from a renowned agent who believes in my book, and more importantly, my abilities. Whatever the reason, I've not been able to write anything worth saving for weeks, and I'm starting to fear that even if I do luck out with *Night Beat*, my inability to generate new ideas will leave me a one-hit wonder.

And now, the black hearts are back.

It's ironic, really, that I aim to write mysteries for a living, and yet I've never been able to solve this central one in my own life. I know what these hearts are supposed to represent. I just don't understand what the sender wants me to do about it. Nothing can change the past.

My neck makes a satisfying crack as I roll my head from side to side. I exhale slowly, amazed at how I can be exhausted from doing absolutely nothing. Because I work nights at Mario's Pizzeria across town, most of my writing sessions take place in the morning. It's almost ten and I've yet to write a complete sentence. I walk into the kitchen and start the coffee machine, hoping a second serving of caffeine will provide some inspiration. It's never as tasty as the boutique-made brew, but my budget can't justify more than one order from the shop in a day. The machine drips steadily, and I wait, the scent of potent coffee beans decorating the air.

My phone buzzes on the counter. Lazily, I swipe at the screen, half-expecting a text message from one of my co-workers begging me to cover a shift. Instead, it's an email from a literary agent I queried two months ago.

My heart starts beating faster, my mind going wild with possibilities. For a brief, wonderful moment, I imagine this is the YES I've been waiting for. Feelings of inadequacy and failure evaporate, even the anxiety from finding the black heart quiets, and all that matters in the entire world is this device in my hands, the opportunities it holds.

I open the email.

Dear Becca,

Thank you for considering Marcus Literary with your manuscript. Unfortunately, we will not be offering representation at this time, however, we wish you the best of luck...

I drop my phone onto the kitchen counter like it's something hot and I've been burned. No need to keep reading. At this stage, almost all rejection letters are the same. It wasn't even a personalized reply, just the same automated response sent to dozens of aspiring writers every day. All the publishing advice books insist rejection is an important part of the writer's journey, sprinkled with stories of uber-famous authors who tacked their rejection letters on the wall once making it big. If I followed suit, I could wallpaper my entire apartment with *potential lessons* that have led me nowhere.

Having abandoned my desire for caffeine, I return to the dining-room table, slumping into the chair beside my computer. My future, much like my current manuscript, is blank. Nothing in sight. Just a fragmentary story waiting to be finished.

I'm supposed to meet with the Mystery Maidens tonight, and I have nothing to show for the past week. I close the Word document and open Google. Social media is a black hole of distraction when I'm trying to write; however, sometimes scrolling local news sparks my curiosity, gets me thinking about scenarios that could potentially snowball into a story.

Whitaker is like most towns lingering outside a major city, caught somewhere between sleepy and urban. Never much excitement, but no shortage of crime. Over the weekend alone, there've been three arrests. One from a young man suspected of shoplifting at several Walgreens in the area. One arrest for domestic violence. One young woman arrested for driving under the influence. Sometimes, when I'm desperate, I find myself here, scouring the crime section in search of ideas. Or worse, I think with a shudder, maybe I'm simply searching for people whose lives are worse than my own.

Either way, today's selection is useless. If I were to investigate further, I'm sure there's sadness in each story, but not enough to spark an idea. My thoughts are interrupted by the image of fleeting black hearts. There's enough darkness there to inspire an entire series, but I'm not willing to go there yet.

I'm not sure I'll ever be ready.

I reopen the Word document, eyeing the screen like an opponent in battle.

The blinking cursor taunts me still.

TWO

Most people dread Mondays, and I used to be one of them. Things changed when I became a member of the Mystery Maidens.

Ever since I dropped out of college, I've struggled to find common ground with others. For so long, I was used to being alone, a prisoner to my past mistakes. Writing brought me comfort, but it couldn't cure my isolation from the world, and each time I received a black heart, I found myself retreating even more into my loneliness. That was until I found the Mystery Maidens, a group of like-minded, same-aged crime writers. For the first time in years, I had an opportunity to bond with others over a shared interest, and I jumped at the chance.

Once a week, we stake out the biggest booth at McCallie's Pub. Known for pretentious draft beer and pricy charcuterie boards, the place caters to the thirty-and-up crowd, a more sophisticated vibe than the dive bars scattered around Whitaker University.

Victoria, the mother hen of our group, is the first to arrive, sitting in our booth at the back of the room, wearing a pair of dark-wash jeans and a thick turtleneck. She sips a glass of red wine and raises her hand like she's hailing a taxi when she sees me.

"You're early," she says, making room for me to sit beside her.

"I'm off today," I tell her, unwrapping my heavy scarf and placing it in my lap. Usually, I'm late because I'm trying to finish a last-minute writing session. Thanks to my writer's block, I have nothing but time to kill on my day off, although I don't plan on telling the rest of the group that.

"I'm excited about today's meeting." Victoria unzips her messenger bag and pulls out her laptop. "This story is dying for some input."

"I'm sure it's great," I tell her.

Without a doubt, Victoria is the most talented writer in our group. She has a long list of published articles and short stories, even a few awards. Originally, she started Mystery Maidens as a critique group for her students over at Whitaker University, where she teaches creative writing. When she realized most college students would rather spend their evenings going to keggers than discussing craft, she sought out adult members online. April was the first to join, followed by Danielle, who recruited me.

A waitress comes over and takes my drink order—tequila and tonic with a lime wedge. Victoria sits across from me typing, her fingers rattling against the keys, like a pianist in the midst of composing a great symphony. My skin flushes with envy.

"Starting without me, I see," says Danielle, the next to arrive.

"Just adding some finishing touches," Victoria says. "I was telling Becca how I'm eager for some input. Something is missing, but I'm not sure what."

Danielle sheds her camel-colored trench coat and sits across from me, carefully unpacking her satchel. She's always exquisitely dressed, especially on days she's in court. She joined the group after Victoria started making posts about it online. As she tells the story, she was hesitant at first; her career as a lawyer keeps her plenty busy, but writing has always been a release for her, and she wanted to challenge herself.

"How about you, Becca?" Danielle asks. "Any good news from agents?"

"Nothing to report," I say, feeling defeated. The only thing worse than holding onto this feeling is having to express it out loud.

"Don't sweat it. You're talented. It's only a matter of time before you make it big, just keep focused," Victoria says, always the encourager. "Working on anything new?"

"I'm editing a few short stories while I'm waiting to hear back about *Night Beat*," I say, opening my laptop.

It's only a half-lie. I weeded through old documents to find an unfinished manuscript I could use today, although I doubt it will go anywhere. I'd rather show up with something terrible than admit I have writer's block. It seems rude admitting that to this group of accomplished women. They all have more on their plates than I do.

When Victoria is not on campus teaching, she's grading her students' work, yet she still finds time to churn out a new mystery novel every year and submit short stories to different literary magazines once a month. Danielle works as a defense attorney, for Christ's sake, but I've never once heard her complain about finding inspiration. And our final member, April, is—

"Sorry I'm late." April stops at the booth, out of breath. She has several bags hanging loosely from both arms. "Chase got held up at work, and right as I was headed out the door, Griffin spit up all over me."

"No worries," Victoria says. "We never get started until everyone arrives."

April smiles, nervously, and sits beside me in the booth. She starts unraveling her layers of clothing and bags. My nose scrunches when I get a whiff of Griffin's spit, which must have soaked through.

April is a stay-at-home mother of two. I can never remember how old her kids are, but they're both too young to be in any form of school. April's days and evenings are fully devoted to her family. She only carves out an hour a week for herself, and she shares that time with us.

"Don't worry about it," Danielle tells her. "You need this break more than any of us." She raises a hand, trying to get our waitress' attention. "And you need a drink."

"Some liquid courage to get the creative juices flowing." April smiles but there's no hiding the exhaustion etched on her face.

And then there's me. I had an entire day to do nothing, and I couldn't come up with a single idea.

"Who wants to go first?" Victoria asks.

"Me," I say quickly. Better to rip this Band-Aid off and start nursing the sting with booze. The story I've selected is something I wrote ages ago, back when I was still in college. It's a shitty story about a young woman who is convinced her nightmares can predict the future. I came up with the idea when I was deep into a Stephen King kick. It took several attempts, this story included, for me to realize King has an ease for the supernatural I don't possess.

Still, after I share it with the group, the other women are complimentary.

"Love the premise," Victoria says.

"It's different from what you normally write," April adds. "In a good way, of course."

"Really psychological," Danielle adds. "It reminds me of something Dean Koontz would write."

"Thanks, guys." I smile weakly, staring into my lap. It's not my best work and they're all too kind to say it. At least my turn is over, and I won't have to worry about sharing with the group again for an entire week. "It's been hard trying to find something new to write since I finished *Night Beat*. I've been searching through old folders, looking for anything that feels fresh."

"Same thing happens whenever I finish a large project. The brain needs time to decompress. That was a good pick," Victoria says. "You know, if you wanted to stick with it, the deadline for *Mystery Magazine*'s writing contest isn't until the end of the month."

"I'll think about it," I say. "Short stories have never been my specialty. It's more of a palette cleanser than anything."

Not only are our daily commitments outside of writing different, but so is the way we each approach our craft. Victoria self-publishes Christie-esque tales about little old ladies solving murders. Her work has a loyal readership, and she devotes the rest of her time to her creative writing students, something I respect.

Surprisingly, April writes horror stories. It's quite funny to think she copes with the hardships of parenting by writing about grisly, gory crimes. She says she needs something to balance out the constant stream of *Peppa Pig* and *Mickey Mouse Clubhouse*. Like me, she's just finished her first manuscript, and has submitted it to agents. She relies on her husband's income, so even though I know she'd be thrilled to get published, the stakes don't seem quite as high.

Danielle uses her legal knowledge and experiences in the court room to write high-octane legal thrillers. Most of her manuscripts revolve around detectives and attorneys. I can't help picturing Olivia Benson and the rest of the *Law and Order: SVU* gang every time she shares a new story with the group. If writing what you know works, Danielle will be a lawyer turned novelist in no time.

My genre is domestic suspense. I've always been drawn to books that focus on the everyday person's reaction to crime. Writing about serial killers and procedure doesn't do it for me; I'd rather write about the bagger at the grocery store who has a girl locked in his basement, or the agoraphobic woman across the street who thinks her neighbor is a murderer. It's the way the most obscure crimes can still weasel their way into a "normal" person's life that fascinates me.

Then again, perhaps the real reason I write about crime is deeper than that. It's a way for me to process my own experiences. When I'm writing, I can take back some of the control I lack in my real life, invent a different ending. It never fully erases my past, but it helps.

"So, what do you think?" April says, making eye contact with each of us. My eyes fall to the table, my cheeks blushing with shame. I've been so lost in thought, I hardly paid attention to what she just shared.

"I think it's brilliant," Danielle says. "An agent would be crazy not to request the full manuscript."

Ah, so April must have read her most recent query letter. Not only do we critique each other's stories, but our letters and submissions forms, too. We act as a confidence boost to one another when we need it most. And really, if it weren't for these women, I wouldn't have any support for my writing at all.

"Good luck," I tell her. "It really is a brilliant book."

April beams with pride, closing her laptop as Victoria begins reading her story, followed by Danielle. I try my best to listen, but inevitably, my thoughts trail away. It's intimidating listening to others, especially those I deem more talented than me. Some days it pushes me to be better. Other days, like today, it only highlights my own failures.

Before I know it, our hour is over, and everyone is packing up their belongings.

"Same time next week?" Danielle asks, her freshly mani-cured nails catching the light as she reaches for her satchel.

"Actually, I wanted to propose an idea," Victoria says, splaying her fingers wide. "Seeing as it's November, I thought we could add the pressure. Let's up our visits to twice a week for NaNoWriMo."

National Novel Writing Month. It's a popular challenge in the writing community where writers aim to write 50,000 words during November, the bare bones of a novel. I've never been successful at it, but other writers, like Victoria, swear by it. Her first self-published book was a byproduct of NaNoWriMo.

"I'm up for a challenge," Danielle says. "My best work happens under a deadline."

"April?" Victoria asks. "We know you have the most going on outside of writing."

"The hubs can handle the kids an extra night a week," she says, giddily. "I think it would be fun, and another excuse to get me out of the house."

Now, they're all staring at me, waiting for a response. I can't string a lousy paragraph together, let alone an entire novel, but I'm not going to be the one to opt out, not when the rest of them have found ways to make writing a priority.

"I'm in," I say, hiding my discomfort behind a smile.

"Let's meet at the same time this Thursday," Victoria decides, raising her wine glass. "Let the games begin."

We each raise our drinks and clink them together. As the dry, satisfying taste of tequila glides down my throat, I try not to think about the failures the following weeks could bring.

I bump shoulders and elbows as I make my way out of the pub and onto the street. The temperature has dropped, every exhale producing a cloud in front of my face. I'm about to turn in the direction of my car when I see something across the street.

A black heart.

It's sticking to a parking meter beside a lamppost, the falling light illuminating it perfectly. My own heart catches in my throat as I rush forward. A bright light stings my eyes as a car in the road slams on its brakes, narrowly avoiding me. The horn blares, but I continue forward, until my fingers are pressed against the cold metal.

My pulse slows. It isn't a heart, after all, merely a black smiley face sticker, the front of the forehead ripped off. I sigh with relief. At least that's one less thing to worry about tonight.

THREE

As I walk home, I search the area for anything that appears out of place, a rogue black heart intentionally left along my path. Nothing captures my attention, and when my paranoia dies, I find myself scanning the streets for inspiration, hoping the commotion around me will present potential story ideas. Whitaker is small, but lively. The main hub of activity is the twelve-block section reserved for WU, littered with bars and restaurants. It's after ten o'clock, which means there are just enough people crowding the cobblestone streets of downtown. Here, the business and residential districts are intertwined. There's a dessert shop beside a bar, and across the street from that is a two-story colonial I've always admired.

A young couple sharing ice cream on a park bench beneath the lamplight. A trio of men, their balance wavering as they leave one pub and head to the next. An old woman stands on her lattice-lined porch, just now taking down the rubber skeleton hanging on her front door.

Each vignette grabs my attention temporarily, but eventually falls flat. Coming up with an idea is never the problem. It's taking that idea and stretching it that becomes daunting.

With *Night Beat*, it was simple. I'd watched a *Dateline* episode that first sparked my interest. Just as I search the newspapers for inspiration, I do the same with all forms of media. Television shows and documentaries and podcasts—all serve as a kind of starting point for the strenuous marathon that is writing a novel. Most ideas, if they interest me long enough, morph into the same question: What if?

What if the person reporting on crime suddenly found herself investigating one?

What if she suspected the person closest to her was the culprit?

How would she use her background and experiences to combat that situation?

Writing *Night Beat* was a thrilling experience, one that's become increasingly harder to imitate. When a good idea strikes you, it's impossible to ignore. When a good idea evades you, that's when you really start to lose your mind. It's like I'm drowning in a sea of potential, and each structure I cling to for support turns out to be yet another piece of unsteady debris, making me sink further.

My body rattles at the sound of a blaring car horn. A young woman darts across the road in front of the car, holding up her hand in apology. The noise brings me out of my endless brain fog, makes me fully aware of my surroundings. I think of the black heart—what I thought was the black heart—on the parking meter. It turned out to be nothing at all, which wouldn't be the first time my paranoia has gotten the best of me. There's no denying that one was left for me in my mailbox, so it's only natural part of my brain will be searching for another message wherever I go. That's been the pattern.

The first time I received a note was the day I moved out of my college apartment. My things had been thrown into cardboard boxes. I stood next to the mess of belongings on the sidewalk, staring at the Christmas lights which decorated the lampposts, waiting on my mother to pick me up. She thought it was only for a holiday break, that going home would help *clear my head*. I knew I'd never come back to Whitaker University, not as a student.

I turned around, looking at the idyllic campus landscape, most beautiful in winter, and an icy shudder ran through my body. Too much had happened here, and I couldn't forget the wrong that had been done to me, just as I couldn't forgive myself for the wrong I'd done.

When Mom finally arrived, I hurriedly threw the boxes into her Suburban, eager to find warmth inside the car. As I pushed the last box into the trunk, it caught my eye. A single piece of paper with a black heart. Only a hurried sketch, I'd thought. Something that my roommate had added to my box by mistake.

It wasn't until another heart showed up on Christmas Day —the one carved into the trunk of my childhood home—that I noticed the pattern. Sometimes the notes come with a message, some more threatening than others. The most recent message is easy enough to figure out—*10*. It's been ten years since it happened, and maybe if I'd kept my promise, and never returned to Whitaker, my life wouldn't be in shambles.

Another blast of icy wind blows my hair away from my face. It's striking how quickly winter is approaching. It almost feels like that night I left campus all those years ago. By the time I reach my apartment, my fingers are stiff from the cold.

My apartment isn't much to brag about. In fact, the one I lived in as a student would have been considered an upgrade, although that place has long since been demolished. My current building's three-story structure only holds six units, so I rarely run into neighbors. The central location—my apartment is sandwiched between a coffee shop and a laundromat—provides just enough protection. I rarely feel scared or unsafe, even with the threat of an unseen stalker nearby.

I climb the rickety stairs that lead to the top floor and enter my unit.

The dining-room table is just as lonely and unwelcoming as it was when I left this evening. My half-empty coffee mug sits beside piles of notebooks, the pages littered with more ideas that never seem to stick. I think about the stories the other Maidens shared during our meeting, and that twisting feeling of failure returns.

Something clatters against the ground. A sound coming from the back of the apartment, toward where my bedroom is. My eyes dart over to the kitchen, my gaze landing on the knife block. Watch enough *48 Hours* and news reports, and your first thought is liable to be a defensive one when you hear a sound in the dead of night. And with the presence of the black hearts, whoever has been tormenting me all this time is back, and getting closer.

Cautiously, I make my way over to the kitchen, just as another sound, this time closer, lands. One of the bedroom doors opens with a creak.

"Shit, Becca." Crystal, wearing nothing but a towel, steps back, clutching her chest. "I didn't hear you come in."

"Didn't mean to scare you," I say, moving away from the knives, the pounding in my chest weakening.

"I thought you were working tonight," she says, wrapping the towel tighter around herself.

"Nope," I say, resting my messenger bag back on the dining-room table. "I had my critique group."

"That's right," she says, sitting in the armchair closest to the television. "It's been one of those days. I can't keep track of anything."

Truthfully, I'd half-forgotten Crystal was here. We've been friends for ages. She was my roommate years ago when we were in college. Thanks to her recently called-off engagement, she's reprised the role. I offered to let her stay in the spare bedroom until she gets back on her perfectly pedicured feet. It shouldn't take her long to find a place; Crystal works for one of the leading real estate agencies in the area.

"Busy day?" I ask, noting it's rather late for her to be taking a shower.

"That's an understatement," she says, kicking her feet onto the ottoman. "Endless showings. People think it's tough buying in this market; they should try selling. It doesn't matter how I spin it; smart deals are hard to come by."

"You're good at your job," I say. My mind conjures the image of a billboard on the I-40. It's advertising beautiful homes at competitive prices and features Crystal's airbrushed face. "If anyone can make a sale in this market, it's you."

"Thanks for the endorsement." She looks away, staring out the lone window in the living room. It must be difficult for her to waltz around beautiful homes all day then return to this dump. *My* dump. "It's not just work though. I talked to Thomas today."

Thomas, the ex-fiancé. He never really impressed me, although very few of Crystal's boyfriends ever have. I did think her relationship with Thomas might last, though. He was prone to chauvinist jokes and always had this dead-behind-the-eyes stare, but on paper he was a good catch. Handsome. Wealthy. Sociable. Those latter attributes were always important to Crystal, and I figured she'd overlook his undesirable qualities to make it work.

Imagine my surprise when two weeks ago she phoned and asked to stay at my place. She'd called off the engagement, and although making room for another person in my tiny apartment at the last-minute wasn't ideal, I couldn't turn her down. Her decision to leave Thomas and start over fresh demanded my respect.

"What did he want?" I asked.

She sighs, turning to face me. "He was giving me another

guilt trip about the wedding. Apparently, he's not told his extended family about the breakup. He keeps hoping we'll reconcile."

"And will you?" Crystal took a stand in moving out but tends to fold when the pressure comes.

"No. We want different things," she says, staring at her hands, at the finger where her massive engagement ring used to be. "All he talks about is moving upstate and trying to get pregnant. He knows I'm on the fence about even having kids, but he expects me to give in. If he's being this pushy before we walk down the aisle, what will he be like after we exchange vows?"

"I know walking away is hard, but it would be even harder a year from now," I say. "Five years from now."

Her jaw clenches. "It just sucks. You know, six months ago, I felt like I had everything figured out. Now, I'm starting over with nothing."

I move uncomfortably in my seat, the drab surroundings becoming more apparent with each passing second. Crystal's untimely fall from grace is my boring reality, the reality I've lived for almost a decade, and coming to terms with that fact is rather depressing.

"I didn't mean *nothing*," she says, having caught on to my reaction. "Obviously, I have you. It's just, the way you live your life is different from the way I've always lived mine. You're happy with so little."

Is that what people see when they look at me? A happy minimalist? It's certainly not how I view myself. I'm over thirty with no real career. No romantic partner. My closest friends are my old college roommate and the people I met less than a year ago at Mystery Maidens.

When I reflect on my life, the good and the bad, my failings and accomplishments, it makes sense why I am where I am. I think it makes sense why Crystal is here, too, although she's reluctant to admit it. It's impossible to outrun our pasts, even if she appears miles ahead. Neither of us really deserve a happy ending after the mistakes we've made.

"Sorry for being such a Debbie Downer." Crystal stands, tightening the towel around her once more. "I just need a good night's rest. I'll be fine."

"You always are," I say, taking my laptop out of my messenger bag.

Crystal is about to turn into her bedroom when she pauses. "How about you? I forgot to ask about your day."

"Uneventful. I lounged around the apartment most of the day before meeting up with the writing group at McCallie's."

"I think it's cool you've found people that are into the same thing as you," she says. She's leaning against the bedroom door, no doubt offering friendly conversation as a thank you for her free living arrangement.

"Yeah," I say. "Their feedback is really helpful."

Despite our long friendship, Crystal and I have very little in common, a fact that becomes more obvious each day we live under a shared roof. She never reads books. She's an early bird who works hard during the week only to go barhopping on the weekends. If I'm not working a shift at the restaurant, I'm back here, in this cramped apartment, writing unpublished stories that may never go anywhere at all.

Still, there's history between us. You can't find that with just anybody. No one will ever understand the harder parts of my life like Crystal. Our shared trauma bonds us to one another.

"Well, I'll leave you to it," she says, walking into the bedroom. "I know you creative types get your best work done at night."

The door shuts behind her, and I'm left alone. I stare at my laptop, waiting for the screen to load, trying to ignore the twisting feeling in my stomach. The phrase *Done is better than perfect* scrolling through my mind like a news banner. Too depressed to face the blinking cursor again, I check my email.

Another literary agent has messaged me.

Another form letter rejection.

Unable to shake off the humiliating feeling of failure, I lower my head into my hands. It's not just the rejection. It's my inability to come up with a new idea, too. It's being faced with the obvious talents of my peers at Mystery Maidens. It's witnessing Crystal's utter depression at having a life so like mine. These endless disappointments jangle inside my head until it's painful.

I wonder how many sentences of *Night Beat* this particular literary agent read before considering it an epic waste of time. Did she give it a chance at all?

After everything I've done, do I even deserve one?

FOUR

The alleyways are dark save for the lampposts overhead. The yellow light streaming down catches tree branches, casting claw-like shadows on the sidewalk.

The unmistakable sound of footsteps makes my heart leap into my throat. I turn around. Nothing but shadows and fallen leaves rolling against the pavement.

I walk faster, suddenly aware of the potential danger in the darkness.

Footsteps again. This time, more rapid. Someone is trying to match my pace.

Again, I turn around, but no one is there.

Still, something remains. A feeling, an aura, an entity.

I'm running now, my own footsteps pounding. The scenery changes, concrete swapped for wet soil, a carved-out gully in the ground beside where I stand.

Fingers clutch the back of my neck. I spin, wanting to face whoever is threatening me.

Still, no one. No face. No hands.

But I can still feel the fingers squeezing. The air leaves my lungs, the world around me turning slower, hazier...

When I open my eyes, my bed sheets are damp with sweat. My hair sticks to my neck. I've not had a dream so frightening, so vivid, in years. Around the time I dropped out of college, they were common, but that seems an entire lifetime ago.

I sit up straighter, putting a palm against my chest. My heart is racing. I reach for the glass of water beside my bed, but it's empty.

The living room is dark. In the kitchen, an overhead light illuminates the stove, casting shadows that remind me of the claw-like phantoms in my dream. I raise a hand to my neck, imagine I can still feel the unforgiving fingers around it.

My nerves are so rattled the sound of water hissing against the sink makes me jump. I fill a glass and begin chugging. Bad dreams are always unsettling, but there was something different about this one. A night terror, somehow bridging the gap between reality and the imagined. I'd hoped I'd never experience another one again.

I gulp the last of my drink and stare across the room. I'm safe here, far removed from my nightmares and my past, from the ominous black hearts that exist outside these walls. Nothing bad could ever happen here, in this drab apartment with the second-hand furniture and thick layers of dust settled into the corners. My life is boring, just as I always wanted.

In the dark, the blinking light of my computer charger captures my attention. I stare at the laptop, trying to conjure up the emotions I felt only moments ago. The adrenaline. The terror.

I sit, unfolding the laptop before me.

My heart still racing, I begin to type:

The Mistake by Becca Walsh

She thought she was special.
    She wasn't, not even worthy of a name.

He leaned against the paneled walls in the downstairs living room, watching each new arrival. Some faces he knew; others were strangers, invited to the party by the friend of a friend of a friend. Anonymity was a must with a hobby like his. If someone could pick out his face or his name, his plan would go to shit, so he was a fly on the wall, watching as the room around him buzzed, buzzed, buzzed.

When he saw her, he knew immediately she was the one. Something about the way she carried herself, careful politeness, afraid of making the wrong move, saying the wrong thing. She was a pleaser, willing to go along with anything and anyone to avoid being alone. The fact she had arrived without friends, was desperate to cling on to something familiar, helped too.

They found one another by the beer keg, and he offered to pour her a drink. She was hesitant at first, her eyes falling to her dress, the floor. But the more she drank, the more she opened up. Told him about herself. Her friends, her major. All meaningless details that did nothing more than build a rapport between them, made her trust him. Not that he needed her trust.

The pill he slipped into her second cup of beer would do the trick. Always had before.

His heart pumped faster as he guided her upstairs. He'd scoped out a room earlier, the busy partygoers barely acknowledging him as he wandered around the house. When the door closed behind them, he switched off the lights and felt like he'd entered another world entirely, one where he was in control of everything that happened next.

This was the thrill he was after. Always.

The girl fell onto the bed, her body limp, her eyes closed. He reached out to touch her—

The door burst open, bright lights filling the space. A trio of women entered the room, and it only took a few seconds for them to piece together what they'd almost interrupted. If only he'd remembered to lock the door.

Such a simple, costly mistake.

In a matter of minutes, more people appeared outside the room. Some were checking on the girl, others were attempting to confront him. He ran down the stairs, away from the party and the angry crowd that gathered around him.

Somehow, he got away, disappeared, never to be seen again.

Until another night, much like the first, when he went hunting at a bar. A beautiful girl walked in, and this time, her name was impossible to ignore. It rang off the tongues of her friends like a melody, a secret song reaching out to him.

Layla. Her name was Layla.

FIVE

My heart pounds as I stumble to my closet, searching for my apron.

I'd forgotten I'd picked up a day shift. Now that the Mystery Maidens want to meet two evenings a week, I need the extra cash, even if afternoons bring in less money. However, because of my late-night writing session, I slept through my three alarms, and run the risk of being late.

After I woke up from the nightmare, the intense aftershocks I felt from the terror stayed with me, allowed me an outlet to write. I sat in front of my computer until sunrise, feverishly typing out *The Mistake*—that's the tentative title, at least. The story begins with a woman narrowly escaping an attack but ends some place much darker; I'm still not sure how far I'm willing to take it. Whether it's a single story or the beginning of a larger project, I don't know. All that is clear is that for the first time in a month I sat behind my keyboard and words flowed freely. That fact alone is worth this morning's rush.

And yet, the dark content swirling inside my head disturbs me. I've written about murder and betrayal before, but never from the perspective of the killer. The ease with which the words filled the page is unsettling, even though part of me is thrilled to have moved past my writer's block. Perhaps the return of the black hearts has triggered something, unlocked a part of me I didn't know existed.

I hurriedly brush my teeth, minty foam dripping down my chin like a rabid dog. There's little time to do more than slick my hair into a ponytail. Although Mario, the owner of the restaurant, likes me, I can't push my luck by being late again. This is the most stable job I've had in a while, and I need to keep it.

This time last year, I was working at the MedSpa. The hours were good, and because business was booming, I received more than the standard hourly wage. It's one of the few seasons in the past ten years where things seemed headed in the right direction.

Any time I feel that way, a black heart is due to make an appearance.

My only responsibility at the spa was checking clients in for their appointments and finalizing their payments before they left. There was a tip jar for the massage therapists and estheticians where customers could leave cash, if they hadn't already added a gratuity on a card.

I'd been there for several months and was enjoying myself. One of the massage therapists had even piqued my interest about getting my own therapy license. I'd been researching classes, thought maybe I'd found a job outside of writing that could make me happy for the time being.

It had been a busy week, customers coming in around the clock for different services. It was near closing, and I stepped around the corner to use the bathroom. When I returned to the front desk, the tip jar was empty.

My first reaction was that one of the therapists had already come through to collect the cash, but they were all busy. I even questioned whether I'd already collected it and counted it for the day, since we were so close to the end of shift. I looked inside the jar, a small piece of paper resting at the bottom.

Written on the paper was a single word—*Fraud*. On the back, was that same black heart I'd seen over and over again.

I tried explaining to my boss what happened, but she couldn't understand how someone could simply take the money without me seeing, and there were no cameras to prove my side of the story. She believed I'd stolen the money, as she'd had trouble with workers in the past.

I almost told her about the black hearts, that someone had intentionally done this because they wanted me to be in trouble. Then I thought of the message left behind—*Fraud*. Showing them the note would only make me appear more guilty. In the past, I'd had problems with people believing me about the hearts; I couldn't take her judgement and pity on top of losing my job.

My phone buzzes, interrupting my memories. My stomach clenches, as I'm afraid it's Mario calling to see where I am. I'm even more upset when I see the true caller: my mother.

Normally, I'd ignore her, especially when I'm running late, but it's been more than a week since we talked, and I'm always afraid when she calls me out of the blue it's because she has some bad news to share. My grandmother has died or something equally awful.

"Good, I caught you," Mom says when I answer. The sound of birds squawking travels through the phone lines, and I can picture her now, sitting on the back patio of my childhood home, a cup of coffee with an extra splash of Baileys beside her, as she takes in the rural mountain scenery. "I've been so busy lately—"

"It's really not a good time," I tell her. "I'm running late for work."

"Really." Her pitch heightens. "You have a new job? Please tell me you're teaching again."

"No," I say, my chest aching as though I can physically feel her disappointment pressed upon me. "I'm still at the restaurant."

I never finished my degree at WU, so I'm not qualified to lead my own course, but last year, I started substitute teaching at different schools in the area. That built up my résumé enough to land me a secure job as a teacher's assistant. I only fell into the role because some of my former classmates had suggested it. Many literature majors end up in the classroom, and even though I didn't have my degree, I figured the job would at least buy me some time until I decided what I did want to do with my life.

I hated every minute of it.

The early mornings. The late afternoons stuck making copies in a cramped teacher's lounge. The constant rush of having to monitor the halls, the cafeteria, the bus drop-off. Most days I'd scarf down lunch and forgo going to the bathroom for hours at a time. It felt like I was a glorified, underpaid babysitter, and all the aspects of the job I thought I would enjoy—sharing my love of literature with bright young minds—was just a crock. Teenagers draw their inspiration these days from TikTok and YouTube, not Faulkner and Hawthorne. They care even less about writing; thanks to AI, they can submit a completed essay within minutes, and the instructors can't even tell if it's plagiarized or not.

With each passing day, it became increasingly clear I'd made a mistake by taking the job, until one day I broke down at work, rushed out the double-doors, and never looked back. See, in all fairness, the black hearts aren't to blame for every problem in my life. Sometimes, it's just me at fault.

"I assumed you only worked nights *there*." Her tone makes it sound like restaurant work is the lowest of the low.

"Not always," I say, slamming my car door closed and stabbing the key into the ignition. "I picked up some extra shifts to meet with the Maidens more this month."

"Maidens. Is that your little writing group?"

"Yes, it is."

"And how's that going?"

I exhale in frustration, silently cursing myself for answering the phone. Most topics with my mother are off-limits, but I particularly hate talking to her about my writing. She doesn't even try to hide her skepticism anymore. When I was still a college student, she at least pretended to support my dreams. Once I dropped out, she never missed an opportunity to remind me just how much of a starving artist I am. There was a moment of pride when I took the teacher's assistant position, but my mother's emotional support ended as abruptly as the job did.

It's yet another reason I hope *Night Beat* will go somewhere. I wouldn't dare tell my mother I've completed a manuscript and it's on submission; I'll tell her once the book is a done deal and watch her eat crow.

"Becca, are you there?"

"Sorry, Mom. Like I said, I'm running late," I say, searching the spots beside the restaurant for a place to park.

"It's almost eleven o'clock. Even a morning shift there isn't really the morning, now is it?"

"I was up late writing," I say. I won't provide further details than that, but it's important my mother knows I'm not a complete dud. "Is there anything you wanted?"

"Just checking in. You know, I'm visiting my sister at the end of the month. You're more than welcome to come. New England is beautiful in the fall, and I could loan you a ticket."

"Can't take off work, Mom," I say. "Busy here."

"Sounds like it." She pauses. For a moment, I think she's ready to fire off more questions. Then her tone changes. Her voice lowers, and she says, "I always worry about you this time of year. You shouldn't be afraid to reach out to me."

"You have nothing to worry about," I say between gritted teeth. "I'm fine."

"Ten years is a long time—"

"I have to go," I say.

By the time I exit my car and feed the meter, Nikki, the shift leader, is standing in the entrance of the restaurant, hands on her hips, eyeing me as I walk up the street.

"Sorry I'm late—"

"This is the third time this month," she says, as though she rehearsed this speech already. Her painted-in eyebrows make an angry M in the center of her face as she scolds me. "If you can't make it on time for lunch rush, I suggest you stick to the night shift."

"I said I was sorry," I say, but she's already stormed off.

As much as I felt out of place working in the school system, everyone is out of place here. Most people working in the restaurant industry are in transition. Students looking for some extra cash. People with more established careers that need to supplement their income. People, like me, who need to pay the bills while they're trying to decide what they want to do with their lives.

Nikki fell into the latter category until six months ago, when Mario decided to make her a shift leader. Now she uses what little authority she has to make my life, and everyone else's, a complete hell.

I avoid looking at my other co-workers as I dart to the back of the restaurant and clock in. When I approach the hostess stand to check my duties for the day, Mario is standing there, his expensive cologne peppering the air around him. He's tall, broad shoulders, his dark hair cut close to his scalp.

"Let me guess. Rough night partying?" There's that twinkle in his eye that lets me know I'm not in serious trouble.

"I wish I was that cool. I was up late working."

"Not here." He looks around the restaurant with a mix of exhaustion and pride. It requires a lot of work to keep a business running, especially in this economy, and Mario has always been an involved employer. "Don't tell me you picked up another gig."

"Writing," I tell him, proudly. "I was up half the night."

"Ah, the next great American novel. Well, I can't punish you for that." He starts to walk back toward the kitchen, then pauses. "But don't make it a habit, okay?"

"I won't."

"You already have your first customer," he says. "It was a special request."

The restaurant is mostly empty except for a high-top table close to the bar. Chaz, one of our regulars, sits there, staring at the sports highlights from last night's games. He's in his mid-thirties with dark hair and even darker eyes, a crisp button-down tucked into black slacks.

"Early for you, isn't it?" Usually, I only see him on night shift.

"I was going to say the same to you." He nods toward the hostess stand. "Nikki was bitching about you being late, and I told her I had to have my favorite server."

"Lame story." I fidget with my apron, avoiding Chaz's eyes. He's always friendly, makes a point to converse with all the staff, not just me, but there's an aura around him that always leaves me nervous. "How about you? What brings you in so early?"

"Worked all night. Figured I'd get a good meal before I sleep the rest of the day."

My eyes move downward, landing on his service weapon, which is secured inside a holster at his waist. Chaz is a police officer with Whitaker PD. He's one of the few customers who has tried to get to know me over the past year, mainly because he's here almost as much as I am. No wife. No kids. If he's not at work, he's either sleeping or fueling up for his next shift, which makes Mario's Pizzeria his local hangout.

"Any big happenings in Whitaker?" I ask, trying to keep my face neutral.

"Nothing too interesting," he says. "In my line of work, that's a good thing."

I smile again, my nerves writhing. Maybe it's Chaz's gun that puts me so on edge, being close to an object capable of taking a person's life. Or maybe it's the badge that bothers me. He always keeps it hidden away, tucked inside the inner folds of his jacket, which is presently draped over a barstool. I've never had the best track record with police officers.

"You ready to order?" I ask.

"I'll take the usual."

"Club sandwich and a Guinness on draft," I say.

"You know me too well."

I smile, relieved to be walking away from his table. Even though being around Chaz—all cops, really—makes me uneasy, I have to play along and act the part of the eager, wide-eyed server. That's how you end a shift with big tips: pretend to be someone you're not.

Hell, that's how I get through life in general, these days.

SIX

It's raining when my shift ends. I hurry to my car, wishing I could afford a vehicle that included a start button. How nice it would be to let my car warm up as I'm finishing my side work, so that by the time I sat behind the wheel, the interior would be fully heated and cozy. Instead, I press my fingers to the heater, hoping they'll loosen up before I drive home.

My apartment is only a few blocks away from Mario's Pizzeria. In the warmer months, I usually walk to and from work. The approaching winter makes me want to be outside as little as possible. As I pull onto the main street, I recall my various interactions throughout the day. The phone call with my mother, yet another reminder that I'm an epic disappointment. Nikki and Mario putting me in my place at work, even if the former is a lot ruder about it. Chaz, my well-meaning regular whose position as a detective always puts me on edge.

Police have always made me nervous. I think it's a power dynamic that's ingrained in us early on. The way a person's adrenaline spikes when they see a squad car behind them on the road, even if they've done nothing wrong. My discomfort with the police is more personal. Unfortunately, I've had more inter-actions with them than the average person, and it's never good.

I remember when I first went to them about the black hearts. It was right around the time I moved into my present apartment. The day the moving truck arrived with my belong-ings, I found an envelope attached to one of the boxes. When I opened it, there was a piece of paper with a single word—*Aban-doner*. On the other side, a black heart.

The fury that rose up inside me was immediate. Wherever I went, it seemed, these black hearts followed, and I was tired of it.

I wrote out a list of the various messages I'd received over the years, even detailing their chaotic aftermath. I wanted to make it clear I'd been ignoring these messages for far too long, and yet even when I'd changed addresses, the sender had somehow found me. There was nothing I could do to protect myself, but surely the police would have better resources.

The conversation was a complete disaster. The officer I spoke to was in his mid-forties, heavy bags under his eyes, a five o'clock shadow covering his cheeks and jaw. First, he suggested the black hearts were a figment of my imagination, said seeing the same image a dozen times over several years wasn't that significant. Then, he tried suggesting it was retaliation from an old boyfriend, someone I might have wronged.

When I pushed back, explained that these were targeted messages that were bordering on threats, he explained there was nothing he could do.

"If you find out who is sending these hearts, give me a name," he says. "Without that, we can't help."

Since then, a new sense of hopelessness has set in. These black hearts are consistent, but the pauses in between are long enough that it's impossible to prove who's behind them. The messages will keep coming, and there is nothing I can do to stop them.

I push away the memory of that conversation as I arrive home, exiting my just-heated car to return to the frigid night air. I rush to the front door and thunder up the stairs, relieved that the temperature inside the apartment is warm and inviting. On the fridge is a note from Crystal.

Gone out for drinks. I'll try not to wake you.

She kissed the card before she left, leaving the imprint of fuchsia lips that looked almost like their own dark heart. My body shudders.

As I change out of my clothes, my mind refuses to settle, replaying conversations I've had with different people about the hearts. The officer that brushed off the idea. I even tried telling my ex-boyfriend Jasper once, but he was skeptical. When I tried to mention them to my mother, she claimed I was the one at fault, said my stubborn head and pesky emotions were getting in the way of logic. By the time I crawl into bed, my heart is pounding in my chest, trying to release the frustration I've held inside for so long. No one believes me, and, sometimes, it makes me question how much I should trust myself.

Soon, other memories return to the forefront of my mind. Everything that happened before the black hearts started appearing in my life. Doesn't everything eventually come back to that same season of regret and despair? My body is exhausted from work, but sleep is no longer an option, my mind a live wire of memories and thoughts and tension.

Propped up against the pillows in my bed, I pull out my computer, and begin to write.

The Mistake by Becca Walsh

Layla no longer cared about the nightlife. She didn't care that her favorite song was playing, or that the bartender had just announced BOGO shots before last call. She didn't care about her friends, who were busy tearing up the dance floor, or that she had an exam scheduled for the next morning.

All Layla cared about was him.

Dark-haired and light-eyed, he hovered over her, his stance protective and inviting all at once. They'd spent half the night together, talking about life and laughing at the foolish antics of those around them. Somehow, the two of them were no longer like the hammered people huddled about; their interactions were elevated to a different level, confirmed by the warm feeling she felt in her chest whenever he smiled.

A fight broke out beside them. Two drunk men arguing about the most ridiculous of things. A pint glass was thrown, droplets of beer splashing across Layla's cheek.

"Are you okay?" His voice was all concern and caring. A napkin appeared in his hand, like magic, ready to wipe up the mess.

"Fine," she said. Nothing, not even spilt beer and broken glass, could dampen this fluttering sensation inside her, the one that had first developed when she started talking to him.

"Maybe it's time we get out of here," he said. His arms slipped over her shoulders like a jacket, protective and warm.

She practically floated as they left the bar, feeling as though she'd been saved from the dangerous and mediocre, and was headed in the direction of new possibilities. With him.

They continued walking, the winter air nipping at their cheeks. Still, there was that warmth. Layla could feel it spreading through her body, canceling out the harsh cold. And every time she dared to look up, to peer closer into his eyes, that warmth inside burned stronger, mighty enough to take advantage of her senses.

Layla was a cautious girl. A safe girl. She'd never met a stranger in a bar, never allowed herself such dalliances. It was her friends that took risks; she was the one to take care of them. Now responsible, capable Layla was living life for what felt like the first time, and she finally understood the rush of emotions that accompanied being in the present.

Everything around her was clear and in focus. The night. The feelings. Him.

She didn't pay much attention as they ventured further away from downtown, strolled toward the backside of campus. She was lost in the moment, in conversation, in thought. By the time Layla realized that it was only the two of them, nearing the end of a smooth paved road, which was soon overtaken by weeds and earth, her mind was elsewhere. The lampposts gone, there was only a sliver of moonlight falling down on them, and she thought of how romantic it would be if he kissed her now, in this precise moment.

He reached for her, his hands finding her pale, thin neck. Layla moved closer to him, leaning into his touch. It took several more seconds for her to realize he wasn't moving. That his grip was growing stronger, those long, perfect fingers tightening around her throat.

A flurry of thoughts went through her mind then.

This is a mistake. What is he doing? Why isn't he stopping? This must be a joke.

Why isn't he laughing? He's smiling. Now crying. Did I do something wrong?

Will anyone know where I am? Is this really happening? His eyes are darker now.

Did anyone follow us?

What will my mother think if she never sees me again?

This is all my fault…

SEVEN

I've returned to *The Mistake* story several times, adding to it and re-reading it, ensuring it's the high quality I believed it was when I woke up, frightened and afraid. I even teared up a few times: Layla's fear becoming my own, hoping against hope her pain was preventable.

My writing rarely provokes an emotional reaction, and yet, I don't feel overly enthusiastic about the progress I've made. It took a night terror to renew my creative spark, and the connection between what I'm feeling inside and what ends up on the page is frightening. *The Mistake* is different, darker. Part of me wonders if this newest story is testing my limits.

Once I arrive at McCallie's, I make my way to the back booth, happy to be a customer instead of a server after several shifts in a row. I take in the crowd, making mental comparisons between this place and Mario's. I wonder if I'd make more money in fewer shifts working at a bar as opposed to a restaurant, but then I think of all the chances Mario has given me. I'm lucky to have a boss who cuts me slack when I need it.

To my surprise, April is the only one here. A platter of cheese fries and ranch dressing sits in front of her.

"You're early," I say, sitting across from her. It's no secret April is always the last to arrive, usually due to some unforeseen crisis concerning her kids. "Already ordered, I see."

"Don't judge me." She pops another cheese fry in her mouth, licking her finger. "My husband showed up an hour earlier than expected, and I couldn't help myself. It's not every day I get a whole hour to kill."

The server arrives, leaving a glass of wine in front of her. "Is that your first?"

"Nope." She gives me a greedy smile. "Let's just say I'll be taking an Uber home."

"Let loose while you can," I say, unpacking my messenger bag. "Do you have anything to share this week?"

"Oh yeah, I've been working nonstop," she says. "It's like I've had an explosion of creativity since our last meeting."

I relate to how she feels. I've felt the same, but it isn't our meeting that sparked my inspiration; it was the dream. Or, maybe more than that, it's the reemergence of the black hearts and all the emotions they conjure inside me.

Danielle is the next to arrive, looking chic in a blazer and khaki chinos. "I hope your week has been more productive than mine," she says, sitting beside me.

"Are you talking about writing or life in general?" I ask.

"Both, I guess. Work is shit, and when that's a struggle, it feels like everything else is."

"That's usually what I say about my kids," April says. "At least I've got some help this week from the hubs."

"And you're taking full advantage of it," I say, clinking my glass against hers. I look at Danielle. "What did you work on this week, writing-wise?"

"I'll wait for Victoria to get here," she says, caving and stealing a fry. "After all, she's the professional. If anyone can help me, it'll be her."

The bar gets more and more crowded. It's soon a struggle to

see the front door. The waitress revisits our table, and Danielle and I order a second round—I'm not sure what round it is for April. The three of us dive into the enormous platter of cheese fries, and Victoria finally arrives.

"Sorry I'm late," she says, "but I promise I have a good excuse."

I turn to face her and see that she's not alone. There's another woman standing next to her. A much younger woman. She must be in her early twenties, almost a decade younger than the rest of us.

"Ladies, I'd like to introduce you to the newest member of the Mystery Maidens," Victoria says. "This is Marley."

"Nice to meet you, Marley," Danielle says, holding her drink in the air.

"It's a pleasure," April adds.

"I'm Becca," I say, smiling. It strikes me that, being the newest member of the group, this is my first time welcoming a new person. And I didn't expect her to be so young. I scan the rest of her appearance. She's wearing a thick cowlneck sweater and maxi skirt covered in flowers. Several scarves are draped over her ensemble, and a lightweight bag dangles from her right shoulder. Her hair comes down to her waist, tiny braids mingling with the untamed curls. A style that strikes me as unique and familiar all at once.

"How do the two of you know one another?" Danielle asks.

"Marley is the most promising student in this semester's creative writing class," Victoria says. "And she cares so much about her craft, she's agreed to join the Maidens."

"The more the merrier," April says.

"So, Marley, what do you write?" I ask.

"Mysteries. Like the rest of you."

"But what kind?" I say, scooting over to make more room for her on the bench. "Cozies? Procedurals? Thrillers?"

"Psychological thrillers, I guess," she says. "Really I just try to write whatever inspires me that week."

"And crime inspires you?" Danielle asks, a quizzical look on her face.

"It does us all, wouldn't you say?"

Marley smiles. It's the kind of expression that seems to brighten the world around you, draws you in. I can't help staring at her, taking in the other details of her appearance. The layered necklaces draped across her chest. The small tattoo of a bird on her left wrist. As I watch her, a strange heat climbs the back of my neck, my head swimming with drunken thoughts. But I've not had that much to drink, have I? From the moment Marley arrived at our table, I've felt out of sorts, like I'm meant to be somewhere else.

"Well, let's not waste more time," Victoria says, pulling a notebook out of her bag. "Before we share our stories, let's introduce ourselves. How about we go around and share our writing goals."

"I'll start," April says, carefully placing her glass on the cardboard coaster. "I'm just trying to carve out some time for me. Since having kids, my days revolve around them. And I'm fine with that. Really. But I've found writing gives me time to express myself. If I were to be published one day, that would be great, but it's really about time for me."

"I feel the same way," Danielle hops in. "I mean, I spent all of my twenties preparing for the job I have now."

Victoria leans close to Marley and says, "She's a defense attorney."

"That's impressive," Marley says, with a smile.

"Thank you." Danielle smiles tightly. "I love my job, but it comes with so much pressure. It really started to get to me, especially when I was in law school. That's when I started writing, and I find that it's the best way for me to cope with my stress. I can channel everything I'm feeling into what I write, and now that I'm part of a firm, I have a front-row seat to endless inspiration. It would be great to be published one day, but writing will always take a back seat to my primary career."

"I've been self-publishing for a few years now," Victoria says, "but I don't consider it my main job. I take pride in being a professor, would rather be a mentor than the next great novelist. I feel writing and teaching go hand in hand. Doing well in one field pushes me to succeed more in the other, and I've been able to provide valuable advice to my students over the years. Plus, my experiences on campus have helped shape my stories. I've been lucky to meet people from all walks of life, and that improves my writing."

"Well, you've certainly inspired me," Marley says. "That's why I'm here."

When it's my turn to answer the question, I lie.

I say something about writing giving me a sense of identity, the opportunity to walk in the various shoes of my characters... Blah, blah, blah. Truth is, I want to be a writer because I'm not suited for anything else. I don't have a primary career—a teacher, a mother, an attorney. What I want more than anything in this world is to be published, to finally feel validated for what I have to say. Get my side of the story out there, even if I do it through the actions and thoughts of my characters. I allow them to live the life I'm too afraid to have, force them to carry the pressure of righting my wrongs.

"Now it's your turn," Victoria says, looking at Marley.

Marley's eyes wander around the table, studying each of our faces. We've only just met her, yet she's already been gifted an intimate glimpse into all our lives. She knows our motivations, our desires.

"I guess my goal is to write the next *Gone Girl*," she says, punctuating that sentence with a cutesy shrug. I force my face muscles to not react.

"Well, you just might have that potential," Victoria says.

Again, I struggle to not react. Victoria, as a writer and a professor, must know how presumptuous Marley's answer was. What writer doesn't want an overnight hit? But it's a once-in-a-generation type of success. Most careers aren't a fast feat, rather a slow tedious journey.

"I'm curious now," Danielle says, leaning in. "Dare you to go first."

"Might as well jump off the deep end, right?" Marley clears her throat. She slips a hand into her knapsack and pulls out a short manuscript. "This is a story I've been working on. It's called *Rosebud.*"

She begins to read. Her voice is its own type of melody, soothing and calm, not an ounce of nervousness as she reads her work aloud to a group of strangers. When I first joined the Maidens, it took me two meetings before I worked up the nerve to share my writing. What it must be like to have Marley's confidence and excitement and... talent.

Despite my skepticism, *Rosebud* is a compelling story. It's about a young girl who grew up in an overly religious household, à la Stephen King's *Carrie*, seeking revenge on the youth minister who groomed her growing up. The plot is straightforward yet surprising. Her use of figurative language makes it come to life. As much as I try to find fault in her every word, I find myself sitting on the edge of my seat—literally—to hear what will happen next. When the story ends, my body is tingling with that sensation readers get when they read something spectacular, and I know *Rosebud*, and Marley, will remain imprinted on my brain.

My skin burns with jealousy.

"That was amazing," April says, clapping her hands together. "How long did it take you to write that?"

"I don't know." Marley shrugs her shoulders. "A week?"

"Seriously?" Danielle is just as taken aback. "It takes me that long to come up with a shitty outline."

"See what I mean?" Victoria, the proud professor, smiles. "She's a real talent."

"I'll say," Danielle says. "How old are you, if you don't mind me asking?"

"Twenty-one."

Another blow to my fragile ego. When I was Marley's age, I was going through the hardest, most uncertain time in my life. I wasn't writing literary masterpieces. I can't even do that now.

"You have to submit that somewhere," April adds.

"I've sent her a list of some different contests. If she keeps writing like that, the sky is the limit," Victoria says.

Heat climbs the back of my neck. I realize I'm the only person who hasn't said anything. I practically choke on the words as they come out: "You're talented, Marley. Great story."

"Thank you." She beams. "I've never shared my work with anyone besides my professors. I can't wait to hear what you've all written."

"I don't want to follow that," Danielle says, honestly. I feel the same.

"I'll go! I'm already drunk," April says, putting her laptop in front of her.

April reads the opening pages of a manuscript about a hell-bent wife slashing her husband's tires, no doubt a precursor for more slashings to come, followed by Danielle and Victoria sharing excerpts from their works in progress. When it's my turn, I still don't want to share. Hearing Marley's story seems to have erased all the confidence I had built.

Still, *The Mistake* is the only inspiration I've had in weeks, and I'm tired of reading old stories to the group, knowing they'll go nowhere.

"I've been working on this one the past couple of days," I say, clearing my throat. "I had a nightmare I couldn't shake, and I just started writing."

My mind returns to the dark streets, the lamplight above,

the shadows. A strange soreness develops in my chest, the sensation expanding with each breath. I haven't even started reading, and yet I'm already feeling emotional. My body's way of warning me not to continue.

"Ooh, that's what happened with the lady who wrote *Twilight*, right?" Marley says. "The whole thing came to her in a dream."

At least her comment forces me outside of my own thoughts and feelings. I stare at her, not knowing how to respond. That's the second mention of a book with a cult-like following. Are those the only novels Marley knows?

"That's right," April says, looking to me. "Becca, please don't tell me you're writing about vampires. The horror stuff is supposed to be my specialty."

"No vampires, I promise."

I begin reading *The Mistake*, and as I do, the emotions I felt during the dream return. The dread and confusion and fear. My body has a physical reaction to this story, perhaps warning me to leave it alone. I feel my throat closing in, my chest pulling tighter. By the end of the story, I realize there are tears in my eyes. I swipe at my face with the sleeve of my shirt so the others can't see.

When I finish, I look around the table, waiting nervously for their reactions.

"I love it," Victoria says. "I felt like I was right there with Layla. Chilling."

"It must have been a really messed up dream," Danielle says.

"It was."

"Is this the start of a new book?" April asks. "Now that *Night Beat* is out of the way, I know you're looking for something else."

"I'm not sure," I say. "Really, I was just so rattled, I had to get the story out of me."

"That's how I felt with *Rosebud*," Marley says.

For a moment, I'd forgotten she was here. When I look at her, she smiles with perfect teeth, her cheeks plump and blushing, but there's something in her eyes that doesn't quite match the rest of her face. An anger or sadness beneath her sparkling façade. Whatever it is, I don't trust it, and a twinge of anger rattles through me. I've worked alongside the other women for more than a year. They've become my friends, earned the right to hear my most intimate writings. Having Marley—a stranger—present feels like a violation.

When the meeting comes to an end, as she waves goodbye, I catch myself staring at the sparrow tattoo on her wrist. For the rest of the night, every time I close my eyes, that small, inky bird is all I see.

EIGHT

The last hour of work always moves slowest. I'm sitting in the breakroom waiting for my relief, Amanda, to show up. I'm praying she clocks in before I get sat another table, forcing me to stay here another half hour.

"You done with your shift?" Mario asks, hefting a tub of clean cutlery onto the table in front of me.

"Almost," I say. "Waiting on Amanda."

"At least roll some silverware, huh?" He says this with far more kindness than he would give to anyone else in the restaurant. Mario likes me. I'm not sure why, but I suspect it has something to do with the fact he has daughters. One just graduated WU with a degree in clinical psychology. The oldest is in her final year of veterinary training.

"Fine," I say, pulling the tub closer to me. The utensils gleam under the table light as I start sorting the knives and forks and spoons.

"I'll join you," he says. He grabs a thick stack of ironed table napkins and sits in the booth across from me.

"Sounds like you're only looking for an excuse to sit down," I say, raising an eyebrow.

He smirks. "Give an old man a break." He lowers his voice and leans closer. "And I won't tell Nikki I caught you back here on your lazy butt."

I roll my eyes. Nikki takes the job far too seriously, riding my ass all shift. She uses her limited control over other people to her full advantage, micro-managing every other person to make herself feel somewhat elevated. She forgets Mario is the boss and that being on his good side trumps everything.

"Out of everyone that works here, why'd you make Nikki a manager?" I ask.

"She's a good worker," he says. "I can trust her."

"She makes everyone's life hell."

"The place runs smooth, doesn't it? She'll lighten up after a while. Everyone leads with an iron fist before they find the best technique." He pauses. "Why? You think the job should go to you?"

"Gosh, no," I say, hoping my quick answer doesn't offend him. "Although I'd treat the staff better. That's for sure."

"But could you put in the late hours? The long shifts? Drop whatever you're doing because Amanda or whoever called in?" He waits, even though we both know my answers to those questions. "It's tough work, and Nikki has earned her role, even if she's not a peach all the time."

Mario is right. It's the problem that's followed me wherever I go, every job I have. It's not what I really want to do, and so I can't put my all into it. Then there are people out there who try their best at anything, whether they like it or not. Maybe that's the key to happiness or success, and the reason why both have evaded me.

"So, tell me about your latest book?" Mario says, rolling the cutlery into a napkin and tying it off in the center. "Are you working on the next Jack Reacher?"

Mario means well, so I humor him, but my stomach still clenches with anxiety. I hate talking about my writing casually.

"In between manuscripts at the moment," I say. "Sorry, no spies."

"Come on. That stuff's a lot more interesting than the other junk. All those housewives killing husbands and stalking people on trains."

I laugh. "I can't help those are the stories I like to write. Not to mention the stories that sell."

"Well, whatever you put out there, I'll be first in line to buy a copy, even if I shelve it and wait until the movie comes out."

I shake my head. "Maybe it'll happen one day."

"It will." He pauses what he's doing and looks at me. "You just have to believe in yourself."

A clanging mess of glasses hitting the floor interrupts our conversation. We both look to the front of the restaurant, although from where we sit, it's impossible to see who dropped what.

"Better check that out," Mario says. He exhales and stands slowly, stretching his back. "Shift's almost over, kid. Cheer up."

I nod, slowly rolling the silverware and making a clean stack of each new set. A frightening vision flashes in my mind of me doing this exact same action in ten years' time. Being a writer doesn't come with a clear career path, and the sad truth is, you can do all the right things and still never make it. I know a few people still paying off their creative writing degrees who haven't published a thing, and others who picked up writing as a hobby a few years back who are now bestsellers. It's impossible to know where I'll end up on the spectrum of success and failure, and the unknown is terrifying.

I think about Victoria. She loves writing, is the type of person who writes something every day, just because she needs a release for the words inside her. She has numerous degrees, has worked alongside some of the greats in the business, and yet, has still never found that success for herself. Sure, her cozy mystery series has some loyal readers, but it's not brought the commercial or financial success that most aspiring writers dream about. She's still teaching writing classes at WU, and although she claims to be happy with that job, there must be a part of her that wonders why she can't channel all that knowledge into success, why she can teach and not do.

April and Danielle are different. Each has their own priorities that aren't centered around writing—Danielle has her law practice and April her young family. Yet, even with those achievements, it's not quite enough. Something inside craves more, whether it's a creative outlet or the potential for future success. They struggle to find the time to write, but what they do produce is engaging and vivid. They're talented, but is that ever enough?

Reluctantly, my mind goes to Marley, the newest member of the group. I can't decide why she irks me so much. She's young and talented, embodies the stereotype of someone who becomes a bestseller on their first try. Maybe it's her flippant nature. The other Maidens, including myself, make it no secret that a lot of sacrifice goes into our work. Marley makes it look too easy, and I resent that.

Or maybe my distaste is because she feels so familiar. She reminds me of a time when—

"Becca, you back here?" Mario calls out. He's standing in the doorway, blocking the entrance to the main dining area.

"Yeah." I'm afraid he's about to tell me I've been given a new table, that I'll have to stay here that much longer.

"Amanda just clocked in," he says. "Get out of here."

My body relaxes. I gather the stack of newly rolled silverware and take it to the front. Today wasn't a particularly busy day, but I'm ready to return home and try to see what I can get done before this week's meeting. Really, I'm just ready to take off my apron and wash off the smells of frying grease.

It doesn't take long for me to tidy up my section and print off my checkout. I hand over my records to the shift leader, trying not to think about the small amount of money I made today.

"Lucky me," says a voice from behind. I stand to see Chaz sitting at the bar. "My favorite waitress is in."

"Not for long," I say, raising the car keys clutched in my hands. "My shift just ended."

"Bad timing," he says, perching onto a barstool. "Know anything new?"

"Same menu as yesterday," I say. I nod at the badge clipped to his belt. "Still keeping Whitaker safe?"

"Doing my best." He nods and gives me a mini salute with his forefinger.

I force myself to smile. "I'll catch you later in the week."

I walk out the front door, stopping when I feel the icy wind. It's easy to forget winter is approaching when you've spent the past six hours on your feet inside a heated restaurant. My car is right next to the curb. I flip through keys, finding the right one, when something catches my eye.

The right front tire is suspiciously low. I bend down. When I look closer, I see that's it's almost completely flat. I run my fingers against the rubber, finding a long gash.

"What the hell?"

When I walk back into the restaurant, Mario is behind the bar, a dishrag over one shoulder. He looks up at me and smiles.

"Back so soon?"

"Looks like one of my tires has been slashed," I say. "Cool if I leave it here until I can get it repaired?"

"Sure." He takes the dishrag off his shoulder and uses it to wipe his hands. "Need a lift home?"

"No, my apartment's only a few blocks away," I say, scratching the back of my neck. "Just not sure when I'll get a tow."

"Do you have a spare?" asks Chaz. He's sitting to my left, a full draft beer in front of him. "I'd be happy to change it for you."

"I don't," I say. Even if I did, I wouldn't go to Chaz, or any cop, for help. I don't like feeling as though I owe something to other people. "I'll have to order a new tire anyway and have someone install it."

"You say it's slashed?" Chaz continues, turning toward me.

"Looks that way," I say. "I don't remember hitting anything that could have done it."

"There have been a few reports of vandalism in the neighborhood. Local kids still wanting to do some damage after Halloween," he says. "You should make a report."

"It's not that big of a deal, is it?"

"It's a crime. I'll give you a lift to the station."

"I really just want to get home," I say, rubbing my forehead with my palm. "Can I do that after I call the tow truck?"

"Sure."

"I'd check the cameras for you," Mario says, "but they've been broken over a month and I can't get the guy to fix 'em."

"Don't worry about it," I tell him. "Like Chaz says, it's probably kids. I'm gonna head out."

I exit the crowded restaurant for a second time, feeling even more dejected than I did a few minutes ago. It's a good thing I live so close, but I'm not happy about the fact all the money I made today will go toward a tow truck, and I'll probably have to pick up an extra shift to pay for the repair.

Passing my car, I peer down at the useless tire, wishing I'd made a mistake, and that the large gash in the rubber has somehow fixed itself. My mind recalls April's story from last night, about the hell-bent wife who slashed her husband's tires. Dealing with the reality of the situation is far less entertaining, but I can't help thinking of the irony that mere hours after April shared her story, someone came along and did the same thing to me.

Talk about life imitating art.

My body stills, something on the ground demanding my attention. It's a piece of paper, near translucent and tearing thanks to the water puddled by the curb. I lift it, trying not to cause further damage, and stare.

It's a black heart, the colors running, the image crying.

I look over my shoulder, distracted pedestrians paying me no attention, let alone the damp litter in my hands.

My hand clumps into a fist, crinkling the shrinking paper until it's no larger than a nickel in my palm. I toss the wad onto the curb, leaving it where I found it, beside my slashed tires.

NINE

By the time I reach my apartment, my fingers are stiff. If I'd known I'd be stuck walking to and from work for the foreseeable future, I would have worn my winter coat. As soon as I get inside, I rush to the heating unit and turn it on full blast; I can deal with the hefty gas bill later.

Crystal is here. I can tell because the kitchen is a mess. Usually, the first thing she does when she gets home is pour a glass of wine and get ready for whatever social outing she has planned for the evening. I can trace her presence in the apartment like a hunter tracking a wild animal. Corkscrew on the counter. Coat thrown on the couch. A tube of lipstick on the bathroom sink.

The door to the spare bedroom swings open, and Crystal walks into the living room. She's wearing a short sweater dress and black over-the-knee boots. Her hair is pulled back with a trendy claw clip, and her eyes are heavily shadowed.

"What's on the agenda tonight?" I ask, suddenly aware of my frumpy jacket, warm but unfashionable.

"A work thing," she says, like she's spitting out a last-minute addition to a grocery list. She pulls a trench coat off the rack and shrugs it on. "We're celebrating our sales from this past quarter. Going to some new restaurant that opened downtown. Rocke-fellers. Have you heard of it?"

I shake my head, sitting on the sofa and pulling a blanket further up my legs to better conceal myself.

"You should come!" She says this like it's the most brilliant idea in the world. "I can't remember the last time we went out together."

I can, and I have to clear my throat to keep the memory from returning. "I'm working on—"

"Writing. Yeah, yeah," she cuts me off. "You're starting to remind me of Jack Nicholson in *The Shining*. All work and no play. It would do you some good to go out, see how the rest of the world spends a Friday night."

"Maybe next weekend," I say, knowing it won't happen.

Crystal knows, too. She huffs as she slings her purse around her shoulder. "Don't get me wrong. It's been fun living here, and I'm appreciative of your generosity, but I want to spend time with you outside these four walls. Just like the old days."

"The old days weren't always as much fun as you make them out to be," I say, regretting the quip immediately. It was too forward, too accusatory. I try to lighten the mood with my next comment. "Believe it or not, this is what I did every weekend before you moved in."

"That's not hard to believe at all." She wanders over, planting a kiss on top of my head, but there's a stiffness to her movements. My comment wounded her. "The world isn't as scary as you make it out to be. I wish you'd let me show you."

Her words echo in my head long after she leaves, creating resentment. Crystal hasn't had the black hearts following her for a decade, ruining her attempts to rebuild. My healing comes in the form of my characters, my writing. *The Mistake* has pulled me out of my writing slump, but I'd rather find a different story idea, one that isn't quite so haunting.

Before I begin, I scroll through my email. There's another standard rejection letter for *Night Beat*. I pull out the notebook with my handwritten log of my ongoing submissions, stabbing a long and deep line through the agent's name. An optimist would say rejection only opens the possibility for a new submission, but all I can see is failure flashing before my eyes, an intoxicatingly annoying neon sign.

I slam the notebook shut and pull open my Word document, wishing I could somehow channel the upsets from today into a dreary and dark story. Crummy work shift. Vandalized car. Another rejection letter. Inside, I have all the makings for a dark and twisted narrative, but I can't find a way to pull those emotions together, to turn them into something worth reading.

Before I know it, I've pulled up my latest manuscript, *The Mistake*. I'd promised myself I'd leave this story alone, that it was only a reaction to my night terror, but it's like this story has a life source of its own and its desire to be told outweighs my efforts to keep it hidden. As I read, the words tug on my heart and soul, bringing me back to the dark streets and the beautiful young woman left discarded in a ditch.

The Mistake by Becca Walsh

Had he planned to do what he did? That's a hard question to answer. On the surface, no. He'd let himself get carried away. His anger reacted before his logic, and now the girl was dead.

He rushed away from the scene, not even bothering to cover up the girl in the drainage ditch. She'd be found eventually, even if he did try to hide her body, an act that would only risk more of his DNA being left at the scene. No, it was better to run away, put as much time as possible between his escape and when the girl was found.

Back to the earlier question, had he planned to do this?

If he were being honest with himself, there had always been a part of him that wondered what it would feel like. He'd certainly worked his way up to this point, without ever fully committing the act.

The first girl he'd attacked in the forgotten room of some fraternity party. She was so inebriated, she only realized what was happening once he was nearly finished, and she was too weak to fight back. He'd been able to slip out of the house unnoticed and wasn't sure the girl even came forward about what he did.

With the second girl, there was more planning. He scoped her out at a club, carefully made his way over to her to strike up a conversation. It had been easy for him to slip something into her drink and offer her a ride home. By the time they reached his apartment, she was nearing unconsciousness; he wondered if she even remembered what took place after that.

Then, the mistake. The third girl had been a total disaster, and he'd narrowly escaped the angry partygoers who appeared upstairs, but sometimes a near-miss could provide the motivation needed to take on the next challenge.

Layla had been different. He'd noticed her right away, been drawn to her vibrant spirit like a moth to a flame. The moment he saw her, he knew he had to have her, but it was a difficult task. She wasn't as drunk as the other girls, and even though he tried, he wasn't able to slip her anything, not when the careful bartender was so close. So they'd left together, and he thought, maybe he could woo her on his own merits. She was clearly smitten with him; it couldn't be that hard to get her to do what he wanted.

And yet, once he touched her, he couldn't let go. He clung on tighter, much like someone who is drowning will unknowingly murder their rescuer. Before he knew it, she was dead. Her body absent of the vibrant spirit that first attracted him. He tried to wipe the memory away as he hurried back to his apartment, trying not to imagine what the scene would be like when someone stumbled upon her in daylight.

And yet, as he lay in bed, Layla haunted him. Her final words. The forever look in her eyes.

Unable to sleep, he remained still, waiting for whatever was to come next.

TEN

When I finish reading the latest part of the story, everyone around the table quietly claps.

"Very twisted, Becca," Victoria says, the bangles on her wrists clinging together as she applauds.

"Yeah," Marley says, her voice not as strong. "It's really dark."

"Why'd you start writing from the killer's POV again?" Danielle asks. "I figured you would have focused more on the crime."

"I don't know," I say. I'd not really thought of that myself. Why had I written the majority of the story from the killer's point of view? I wouldn't have guessed that perspective would come so easily to me. It makes the sudden rush of creativity all the more disturbing. "I guess I was trying to continue the suspense. Readers already know about the murder, but they must be wondering why the guy did it, right?"

"I think it's brilliant," April says. "I love getting inside a psychopath's head to see what makes them tick."

I quickly look back at the table, as though their stares are too bright to hold my attention. Despite my friends' praise, I'm not proud of this story. Everything about it—from the opening scene to my latest addition—feels wrong, and yet it's the only thing that holds my attention.

Marley's comment sticks with me. *The Mistake* is dark. Too dark. All the other stories we've shared this evening are light-hearted by comparison: a woman whose ex-boyfriend toys with her by sending letters to her friends; a man maimed in a hit-and-run; and a woman who finds out her father is a serial killer when she finds tokens from his kills in a garage.

Stepping inside the mind of a murderer and rapist is extreme, and even though I'm the one who wrote the story, I can't quite shake the macabre elements. For multiple reasons.

"I guess that leaves April," Danielle says, looking over at her. "You have anything new to share this week?"

"I do, actually," she says, her voice even more cheerful than normal.

I'm grateful for all the women in the group, but April especially. Nothing cuts through the dark subject matter like her upbeat demeanor, even if the story to follow is filled with psychological horror. Maybe it's because she's surrounded by primary colors and cartoons all day, but her personality is infectious, making it easier for me to forget the Layla story.

Before she begins her reading, I plan to tell her about my slashed tires. I won't mention the black heart I found, but I thought the group might appreciate the coincidence of her story from last week happening in real life, but April quickly turns her computer around, showing us all the screen.

"Originally, I did have a new story to share with all of you, but then I received this." Her voice is a near squeal, her fluttering fingers tapping against the screen. "I got an offer of representation!"

Everyone around the table gasps, except for Marley, who looks at our reactions with confusion.

"What's that?" she asks, her face so blank and dumb I want to slap the expression right off it.

"That means a literary agent wants to represent her work," Victoria says, kindly. "It's the first big step in getting published."

Marley's face lights up like a Christmas tree. She turns to April, all smiles. "That's great news. Congratulations!"

"It really is," Danielle says, clasping her hands together. "This is amazing. The first in our group to land an agent."

"I keep pinching myself," April says, her eyes darting from the computer to us. "When I first sent off my manuscript, I expected to spend months waiting on a response. I can't believe this is all happening so fast."

"Tell us everything," Victoria says. "We want all the details."

We listen as April goes into the story. It's not a big deal by most people's standards, but when you're a writer, this is the moment you fantasize about for years. Dreaming about that one Yes lessens the sting of the never-ending Nos. Seems to erase all the self-doubt and fear that comes along with this profession.

April says she was in the middle of school pickup when she received the email. "I had to refresh the screen a couple times to make sure I was reading it correctly," she tells us, her eyes bright with excitement. "We set up a phone call for the following day, talked about our plans and goals for the book, then she made the offer."

"Did you accept right away?" I ask, trying to sound more interested than jealous.

"Of course!" she says. "This was my dream agent, and all the others had been rejections."

"What did your husband say?" Danielle asks.

April blushes. "He was ecstatic. Sent me flowers the next day. And we're making plans to go out this weekend and celebrate."

"That's what you deserve," Marley says, waving her hand to get the waitress' attention. "Round of drinks on me."

The others hoot and holler, continuing to praise April and her achievements. My focus is set on Marley. Why is she the one buying a round of drinks? She's the newest member of this group. Hardly knows April or the rest of us. She didn't even understand the importance of receiving an offer of representation. She only picked up writing as a hobby. She can't possibly understand what it's like to pine after something for years, to wonder if it will ever happen.

"Are you okay?" April asks, squeezing my hand. Her voice is soft, so the others can't hear.

"Fine. My head's all over the place." I smile tightly. "I'm so happy for you."

"It's only a matter of time until it's your turn," she says. "If I can land an agent, I know *Night Beat* will, too."

I smile again, but this time I can't meet her eyes. April's kindness is appreciated. Unlike Marley, she understands that sometimes one person's success can only highlight another's failure. My happiness for April is genuine, and she's right. If she can make it, maybe one day I will, too.

"To April," Marley says, raising one of the champagne flutes the waitress brought to our table, her sparrow tattoo on full display. Her eyes are gleaming, waiting as each of us joins in on the celebration.

Reluctantly, I reach for a glass and repeat, along with the others, "To April."

The fizzy liquid slides down my throat, delivering a near-instant heady high. And yet, cutting through the fog of alcohol and celebration, I can't stop staring at Marley.

Wondering who she really is and why she's really here.

ELEVEN

Good thing my car is out of commission. I consumed more alcohol than I'd intended. The short walk home is more of a stumble, but it is early enough that there are still several pedestrians on the sidewalk, and the alcohol thrumming in my bloodstream keeps me warm.

I glide farther away from downtown, until the lights and sounds are distant. The streets here are dark, tranquil, and it's only now that the images of the black hearts return, carrying with them the unknown intentions of whoever is sending them. I should know better than to walk home alone at night, my head swimming with alcohol, my chest filling with fear. This is the exact type of situation that leads to danger—the exact type of situation I write about—and I'm in no position to be so risky. When my complex comes into view, relief washes over me, and I hurriedly type in the security code to the front door.

Inside, the apartment is a cluttered mess, and quiet.

"Crystal?" I call out, but there's no answer. As expected, she's probably out with co-workers, likely celebrating the achievements of someone else, same as me.

I could have stayed longer at McCallie's, but my head was

beginning to swim, and I wasn't sure I could stand another minute around Marley. Maybe it's the newness of her, her youth, but something about her gets under my skin, makes me feel like I'm longing to break free.

I slump onto the sofa, retrieving the remote to aimlessly scroll through what's on television. Finding nothing of interest, I turn it off. This overwhelming feeling of emptiness has plagued me ever since April shared her news. Perhaps even longer than that, if I'm being honest. I'm lonely, and the fact I've just left a gathering of people does little to ease that sense of loss.

I raise my phone, wishing there was someone I could call. But who?

When I dropped out of college, an immovable distance appeared between me and every other person I know. My mother is disappointed in my failures. Crystal is still in my life, but I assume it's because of pity more than anything. I don't have any real friends, only acquaintances I've met in my various jobs before moving on to the next. Nothing real, nothing important.

There's only been one serious boyfriend in the past decade. Without meaning to, my thumb finds his contact information in my phone, hovers over his name. Jasper. The alcohol coursing through my body dares me to call him. Maybe we could just catch up. Maybe he could come over so I wouldn't feel so alone.

You'll regret it, a voice from inside warns. A sober voice. Just as quickly, warring thoughts appear in my mind, reliving the good times in our relationship. We were together for nearly two years, my longest relationship by far. More than that, Jasper was my first adult relationship. We met on my twenty-seventh birthday, when I was having a miserable celebration dinner by myself at my favorite Chinese restaurant.

He appeared at my table wearing a plaid button-down tucked into jeans, dark-rimmed glasses resting on the bridge of his nose.

"Did you order egg rolls?" he asked, holding a plate in front of me.

"Yes," I said, confused, looking around the near-empty restaurant for my server.

"I think they brought them to my table by mistake." His gaze followed mine. "There aren't many people here besides us."

"Eating alone, too?"

"Yes," he said. "It's not as pathetic as it sounds, I promise."

"I guarantee you it's not as pathetic as me," I said, leaning deeper into the booth. "I'm dining alone on my birthday."

He pulled a face that was hard to read, part smile, part wince. "That is sad. Surely you aren't celebrating alone?"

I nodded. "And now you've taken my egg rolls."

"I'd be willing to share," he said, putting the appetizer on my table. "Consider it my birthday gift to you."

The entire interaction felt staged, a corny meet-cute from some romcom I'd never finish. Normally, I would have told the stranger to hit the road and take his contaminated egg rolls with him, but there was something about Jasper that made me pause my initial impulses. He was kind, nervous and safe. It was that safety that let me build a relationship with him, and for the first time in years, it seemed like maybe I was able to reenter the world as everyone else knew it.

Remember what happened next, that annoying voice inside insists.

It wasn't right away. Two years passed, and I fell in love. Jasper was about to move in when I found them in his car. A pair of lacy underwear that did not belong to me. Sewn into the fabric was a black heart, and beside it, a paper with a single word: *Cheat.*

I confronted him immediately, lacking all the casual cool that protagonists typically have in books and movies. I couldn't sit on the information, wait for the right time to confront him. I started a fight immediately, demanding to know who the underwear belonged to. Jasper, being the kind, decent person he was, folded immediately. He admitted to having slept with a random woman he met in a bar. Claimed to not even know how it happened. It was out of character, but she was practically throwing herself at him, and he just couldn't help himself.

He couldn't rely on the love I had for him.

He couldn't consider the fact we were about to move in together.

Just like that, Jasper was gone, and I was on my own again. Have been ever since.

Even though he begged for my forgiveness, and part of me did believe him when he said he'd never do it again, I couldn't move past it. When I wasn't imagining the man I loved in the arms of another woman, I was picturing the black hearts, which had managed to wreak havoc on my life once again. Could this woman and my stalker be the same person? If so, she was willing to go to extreme lengths to ruin the only solid romantic relationship I'd ever had. I begged Jasper to tell me what the woman looked like, asked him to look for her online, but he refused. He thought knowing the details would only injure me further. Shame he hadn't considered that before sleeping with another woman.

Now the black hearts have returned, twice in one week. The postcard in my mailbox and the scrap of paper beside my slashed tire. But why? I haven't been fired or cheated on, no huge life change like before. The black hearts aren't always threats, it seems; rather a way for the sender to remind me they're always near.

Anger and resentment fueling me, I drop the phone back on the sofa, determined not to give into my drunken feelings and call him. I'm annoyed I even considered it. I suppose people are all the same when they're tipsy and alone.

The living room is dark, the faint glow of streetlights outside the far window casting small shadows across the furniture. Across from me, on the dining-room table, my laptop charges, the blinking light drawing me in like a moth.

I walk over to the table and sit. The most recent addition to the Layla story is still pulled up on the screen. I read it, and without realizing, my fingers find the keyboard, and I begin to type.

The Mistake by Becca Walsh

If the murder had taken place in a different time, perhaps he would have gotten away with it.

Decades ago, people relied on eyewitness testimony, faulty fingerprints and the overwhelming pull of gut instinct.

Now, it's easy to trace a person's whereabouts. We're constantly being tracked by our phones and our watches and our cars. The police department were able to pull up the surveillance footage from the bar within a matter of days.

That's where they first saw him. Sitting beside Layla, engaging it what seemed like a flirty conversation. They witnessed the altercation between the two drunk men, saw the couple slip out of the camera's range without anyone noticing.

He'd known they would find him. There was the slightest hope that maybe he'd get away with it, but that was useless. He had taken it too far. A he said/she said scenario was easy to combat, but a dead body? It was only a matter of time before the trail led back to him.

First, there were the newspaper articles. FEMALE STUDENT FOUND NEAR CAMPUS. He'd gone to his scheduled classes, trying to keep up appearances, but he overheard the whispers. A girl had been murdered. Right outside the buildings where all the other students learned and ate and slept. She'd last been seen at a bar other students frequented. And then he heard about the video, and he knew his time was up.

When the police came to his dorm room, he opened the door with ease. It was useless putting up a fight. He'd been the last person with Layla, and there was no denying it. Still, he tried. He tried to say he didn't kill her, that he'd left her alone and someone else attacked her. But what were the odds of that?

After the other two girls came forward—the girl from the frat party and the other from the bar—his fate was sealed. Pleading out was easier than going through a trial; it saved his mother the pain of hearing the details.

Now, he sat on the flimsy mattress in his cell, staring at the cinderblock walls, the dull and dingy ceiling. This is what he deserved, he figured. He couldn't control his impulses, and now he was locked up like an animal. Another girl would never be hurt, by his hands at least. In time, maybe the world would forget about his crimes, forget him altogether.

Night after night, he sat in that lonely cell, replaying the events of that night and what followed. Justice didn't always look like the inspiring vignettes you see in the media.

Sometimes justice looked like this: lonely and dark.

TWELVE

My phone starts ringing before nine o'clock in the morning. The auto repairman has arrived to deliver my car. I stumble down the stairs, half-awake, wearing an oversized hoodie, pajama pants, and fluffy slippers.

The man is blocking the street, leaning against his tow truck, scrolling on his phone.

"You Miss Walsh?" he asks when he sees me approach.

"That's me," I say, pulling out my checkbook. "Thanks for coming on such short notice."

He nods. "It'll be two hundred," he says.

My arms fall to my sides. "The receptionist said one fifty on the phone."

"That's for a midday drop-off," he says. "It's before noon."

"Of course," I say. I can't give him attitude because the tire has already been fixed, and I never would have been able to do it myself. I write him the check, and hand it over, trying not to think about the extra fifty that will be leaving my bank account.

As I'm climbing the stairs to my apartment, my phone starts ringing again. My mother.

"Two phone calls in two weeks," I say. "What did I do to get so lucky?"

"Can't I check in on my daughter?"

"Sure," I say, "although not much has changed since the last time we talked."

"We never really got to finish our conversation," she says. "It's that time of year, you know."

Of course, I know. Every winter for the past ten years, she hasn't let me forget. Mom had big plans for me, and I wasted them when I decided to drop out.

"I don't want to talk about it," I tell her. "I've moved on."

"Have you though?" she says. "Becca, really. What are you doing with your life? Waiting tables. Trying to become a writer."

"Yes, the second part is what I'm doing with my life," I say. "The first part just pays the bills."

I think of the extra fifty bucks I just spent on my car. That's at least two or three more tables I'll have to kiss up to. It's not an ideal living, but it's my only option at this point. Everything else I've tried I've either hated or has been ruined for me by the black hearts.

"I'm your mother," she says. "It's my job to have the hard conversations with you. Thirty has come and gone, and I think it's time you do something with your life. You could try working with another school system."

"No, Mom."

My mind goes back to my assistant position at the school. I remember being crouched down in the toilet stall, crying into my hands like I was a hormonal teenager. I wasn't meant to work there, and returning will only increase the likelihood of me losing my mind.

"Maybe you could go back to school then," she says. "How many credits would it take you to finish your degree? A year's worth of classes at most."

"And then what will I do?" I ask her. "A creative writing degree won't guarantee me a book deal. I can keep doing what I'm doing now and get there faster."

"What if you never get there? It's a hard business, Becca. If you don't become a writer, will you just be a waitress the rest of your life? At some point you're going to have to pick a path and commit to it."

She makes it sound like I'm self-sabotaging, when that's not the case. I'd like to find a career that makes me happy. I was happy about the idea of studying massage therapy, until the black hearts came along and ruined that opportunity for me. And now they're back. Two hearts in a week, I think with a shudder.

"While I have you on the phone," I say to my mother, "has anything strange been happening at the house?"

"Strange? What do you mean?"

"It's been so long since I visited," I say, and yet I can still remember seeing that heart carved into the tree trunk in my backyard, the black paint staining the bark. Maybe there have been other signs recently I've missed, other messages I haven't found.

"Yes," my mother says, her stern tone bringing me back to the present. "It has been a long time."

"I've been getting these random notes. I was only wondering if anything showed up at the house."

"What kind of notes?" she asks, her voice filled with skepticism.

"It's hard to explain," I tell her, careful not to divulge too much information. My mother already thinks I'm a failure; I don't need her thinking I'm crazy, too.

"You know what?" She pauses, and I catch myself holding my breath. Maybe I'm right, and weird messages have been arriving at my childhood home, too. My mother exhales. "I think you're trying to change the subject, just like you always do when I corner you about your future."

"Mom—"

"No, Becca. You listen to me. No one is sending you strange notes. No one is sabotaging your future, except for you!"

The sound of screeching tires grabs my attention. A car horn blares, then another. The world outside my window sounds as frustrated as I feel during this conversation.

"I'm sorry I'm such a disappointment to you, Mom," I say.

"Not a disappointment, darling," she says, and her voice sounds weaker, like she's giving up. "Just wasted potential."

I quickly come up with an excuse to get off the phone and hop in the shower. As the water splashes against my skin, I try to wash away my mother's words, the sense of the failure that reeks off me like a bad smell.

Hopping into a clean pair of sweats, I pull my hair into a high bun and slip on some ChapStick. I have an afternoon shift at the restaurant, but a few errands that need to be run before then, now that my car is working again.

I rush downstairs, hurrying to not be late for another shift, when I'm astounded by the crowds standing on the street.

There are several police cars blocking the road, and my car too. Looks like I won't be going anywhere soon. Groups of people have gathered. I notice the man who dropped off my car is still there, speaking to one of the officers. His gruff demeanor is gone, replaced with skin white as a sheet.

"Becca!"

A few steps away, I see Crystal. She waves me over.

"What are you doing here? I thought you'd be at work."

"I walked across the street for some coffee before my first client meeting," she says. "Now this happened, and I'm stuck."

"What happened?" I ask, looking at the crowds.

"Someone was hit by a car."

"Hit?"

"Yes. This woman was crossing the street and a car just plowed into her. There were a lot of people standing around who saw the whole thing."

"My goodness, is she okay?"

"I think she's going to be," she says. She points ahead, and I see a woman sitting in the back of an ambulance. She's sitting upright, holding an ice pack to her head while an EMT looks at her legs. The woman is bruised up, but at least she's alive.

"I can't believe you didn't hear the commotion," Crystal says.

Thinking back, I remember the sounds of screeching tires and honking horns. I was so frustrated with the conversation with Mom I didn't think to look out the window. Everything else must have happened when I was in the shower.

"What about the driver?" I ask.

"That's the worst part," Crystal says. "They just took off. I'm guessing that's why there are so many police. They're probably trying to gather as many statements as possible. Hopefully they'll catch the bastard."

"A hit-and-run," I say, half to myself. Just like in Victoria's story from the last Mystery Maidens meeting.

"The holidays bring out the crazy in people," Crystal says. "You might be onto something, staying home all the time."

"It's definitely safer." As the words leave my lips, a flash of the black hearts enters my mind, and I wonder if that's true.

"At this rate, I think I'll be better walking a few blocks and getting an Uber," she says, walking away from the crowd. "Don't wait up for me."

I wave goodbye, thinking of how quickly Crystal abandoned her plan for safety. She might talk about the holidays bringing the crazy out in people, but she doesn't really believe it. She's never lived her life in fear, even when most people in her position would have. She's not like me, constantly looking over her shoulder for the next threat.

As I turn to walk inside, something catches my eye. A black heart sticker is plastered onto the railing outside my building. I run my hands over the paper, making sure it's real, not just some figment of my imagination. The metal railing is cold beneath my fingers, the sticker wrapped tightly around it.

The crowds are still staring ahead at the maelstrom of police cars and emergency responders, while I have my own crisis right in front of me. Another black heart. It must mean something. I know it wasn't here this morning; I would have seen it when I came downstairs to pay the car repairman. This means someone must have left it after I went back in, right around the time that pedestrian was struck by a passing vehicle.

I look over my shoulder, searching for a familiar face, but find nothing. Countless faces, all of them ignoring me, and yet one of them must be here because of me. One of them must have left this message.

Three hearts in the past two weeks.

Two of them found at scenes that were ripped directly from the Mystery Maidens' stories.

Something is happening, and it appears the target for everything is me.

THIRTEEN

Throughout my shift, my mind keeps returning to the similarities between the Mystery Maidens stories and the events of the past week. One of the biggest writing rules is that coincidences happen in life, not in fiction. However, the timing of these two incidents—my slashed tires and the hit-and-run on my street this morning, followed by the presence of more black hearts—makes me wonder if there isn't something larger at play. The hearts have been out of my life for more than a year. Why start reappearing now? Nothing in my life has changed.

"Becca!" Nikki shouts, her screeching voice snapping me back to reality. "Your order is up."

Several plates of food sit beneath heat lamps on the food line. The blazing ceramic stings my fingertips as I move them onto a large tray.

And why did both things happen to me? *My* tires slashed. A hit-and-run on *my* street.

"Don't forget your side dishes," Nikki says, standing uncomfortably close. In the kitchen, it's all jutting elbows and dancing around co-workers, but feeling the heat of Nikki's breath on my neck makes me want to scream.

"Getting them," I say, adding ramekins of Parmesan cheese and marinara sauce to the overloaded platter.

If someone is trying to mess with me, acting out the events from our stories, it would have to be one of the other Mystery Maidens, wouldn't it? They're the only ones with access to our stories, the only ones who could draw such a close connection between reality and fiction. But why would one of them want to target me? The black hearts have been appearing for the past decade. Could one of the group members have been sending them all this time?

"Becca," Nikki says. "You just got seated again at—"

"Chill, Nikki!" I shout, hefting the tray over my shoulder. "Let me get out of this godforsaken kitchen. Please."

I'm irritated, not just by Nikki's micromanaging, but by this bizarre riddle that's stuck in my mind. Coincidences are rare in real life, too. It's difficult for me to wrap my mind around the fact that two crimes just happened to take place within days of having read about them in stories.

I wipe the thoughts from my mind, and I'm all smiles by the time I arrive at my table. I pass out the heavy pasta bowls—"Be careful, it's hot!" I warn—and check that my customers are satisfied. They should be my last party of the night. It's near closing time, and what I want more than anything is to go home and rest.

As I'm turning to head back to the kitchen, I spot Nikki watching me from across the room. Just then, I remember her barking order that I'd been sat another table. My annoyance subsides when I see it's only Chaz, sitting at one of the high tops by the bar.

"I was about to be annoyed someone came in right before closing," I say, once I make my way over. "Then I saw it was you."

"Not here to make your job harder," he says. "Just want to kill time and get a meal."

He orders his usual again. I drift to the back of the restaurant to ring it up in the computer. As I'm tapping into the screen, an idea enters my head.

Another complaint in crime fiction is that the protagonist doesn't act like a reasonable person in their situation would. They don't call for help. They don't involve the police. They run back inside the house.

I look back at Chaz, a police officer. A person who could possibly help with the black hearts situation has been delivered straight to me. I've not had the best relationship with cops in the past, but Chaz knows me on a personal level, as much as anyone knows me, that is. Maybe I should tell him about what's been happening.

My party table exits right around the time Chaz's food order is ready. By now, the restaurant is near empty, only a few customers scattered around the room finishing their meals. I carry Chaz's dinner over and sit across from him.

"Can you talk and eat at the same time?" I ask.

"Multitasking is my superpower," he says, taking another swig of beer. "Something bothering you, or just bored?"

"Both." I look around the lonely restaurant. Nikki is busy in the back, inspecting each table to make sure the condiments are stocked, and the floors are swept. The hostess at the front has just switched the sign from Open to Closed. "There is something that's been bugging me. A mystery of sorts."

"Are you needing help with one of your stories?"

"It's not something I'm writing," I say. "Someone is messing with me, and I wanted to get your thoughts."

He's already aware that someone slashed my tires. His original theory was that some neighborhood kids were to blame. I'd thought as much, too, until I found the black heart. And now something else happened outside my apartment this morning. Both events were pulled from Mystery Maidens stories. I'm beginning to wonder if that is intended, and that's exactly what I tell him.

"It's an interesting theory," he says, when I finish. "But I'm not convinced someone is out to get you."

"You don't believe me," I say, dejected.

"I'm not saying I don't believe you," he says. "But we need proof. Not speculation."

"This is all I have. Someone deliberately slashed my tires, like in the story. This morning, someone was run over in a hit-and-run. Just like the other story from group."

"Were those the only two stories your group read lately?"

"No," I say hesitantly. There was *Rosebud*. Some other random stories. The first and second parts of *The Mistake*. "Still, don't you think it's weird?"

"I do. In a déjà vu type of way."

"Déjà vu, like it's not real."

"I'm not saying that. Haven't you ever come across a new word in a book or on television, and next thing you know, this word you never knew existed seems to be everywhere?"

"Sure, but—"

"Maybe these two incidents stood out in your mind for whatever reason. It makes it easier for the other stuff to catch your attention. If you hadn't just read about a vandalized car or a hit-and-run with your writing group, would you still think you're being targeted? Or would you chuck it up to bad luck?"

"I... I don't know." The events of the past week aren't enough. He needs more. "Actually, this isn't the first time something like this has happened. For years now, I've been getting these strange messages. Little notes left for me at work and where I live, and I know they're from the same person because they always come with a black heart."

"A heart. Like a charm?"

"No. It's a drawing, usually on the outside of whatever note they've left." I pause. "I found a black heart beside my tire, and on a railing near the hit-and-run."

"So, you're telling me someone has been sending you messages for years, and you're just now going to the police?"

"No, I went once before," I say, cringing at the memory. "They didn't do anything about it then either. But this is different. Before, it was only messages. Now, they're leaving them at the scenes of crimes. I just thought maybe you could look into it."

"Problem is, where would I even start? You have a hunch. An inkling. That might get the ball rolling in one of your little crime books, but in a real investigation, we need more than that."

"My *little* crime books."

"Sorry. I didn't mean it like that. You have this job too long, you turn cynical. Let me give you an example. A few years back, this woman said her ex-boyfriend was stalking her. Showing up at work. Leaving messages at her apartment. She couldn't ever prove it, but all these weird things kept happening to her and she was sure they were all linked back to him."

"And?"

"We couldn't do anything about it. There was never any proof."

"What about a restraining order?"

"She took one out. She didn't see him anymore, but that didn't stop the letters from coming. She could never *prove* it was him."

"What happened?"

"Lucky for her, she got a new job and relocated. I told her to reach out if her problems persisted, but they never did. I guess she was no longer an interesting target from the other side of the country. It all worked out."

"Yeah." All she had to do was uproot her entire life to get the guy to stop. "What about the women where it doesn't work out? They feel threatened and targeted, but no crime is ever committed. Sometimes a person's first crime is assault or worse."

"That's a gray area in the law. Sometimes we can see the bad guys from a mile away, but we still have to wait for them to do something to get involved."

Something has happened, I think. Two separate crimes. I just have no way of proving they're linked to me.

"Remain vigilant," Chaz continues. "Maybe you're right and someone is trying to mess with you. Or maybe it's just a weird coincidence. You really think one of your writing buddies is out to get you?"

In reality, I can't picture any of them coming after me, but there's no one else with access to our stories. Maybe Marley. She's the newest member, and I've felt defensive around her since the first time I saw her.

"The black hearts have been part of my life for so long, and now they're connected to the stories from group," I say. "That must be significant."

"These black hearts. How long have you been getting them?"

"Ten years."

Admitting the timeline out loud seems to disprove Marley as the stalking suspect. She would have been a child when I received the first black heart. Still, I can't shake the feeling that there's something off about her, and I didn't start making connections until after she joined the group.

"And they couldn't be from an ex-boyfriend or something? Some friend you wronged?"

My cheeks flush with shame, and I stare into my lap. It's true that I have no clue who is sending the black hearts, but there's an obvious reason why they're being sent, and I can't tell Chaz that. I can't tell anyone. I have to keep it locked away with my treasure trove of secrets.

His radio blurts, and Chaz looks away. "I gotta take this. I don't feel like I helped a lot."

"It's okay. You're just being honest." That familiar feeling of defeat returns. Just like last time, there wasn't enough information for me to be believed.

"Becca!"

Across the restaurant, Nikki is waving to get my attention, a clipboard in her hand, no doubt ready to dish out the evening's side work.

"Looks like duty calls for me, too," I say.

"You should still come by the station and report that someone vandalized your car. If we are able to find out who did it, at least we'll have a paper trail."

"Sure."

Begrudgingly, I walk in the direction of Nikki, ready to complete my laundry list of tasks before ending tonight's shift. Chaz has given me a lot to think about, but one thing is clear:

I'm in this by myself.

FOURTEEN

I'm running. My chest feels like it's about to burst, each intake of freezing air piercing my insides, but I must keep moving forward. To give up now would be to die.

Something is following me. In my periphery, dark shadows creep, and I'm too focused to face them, but I can feel the approaching danger. An urgent voice tells me to keep going.

Next thing I know, I'm flat on the ground. Did I fall? Was I pushed? My palms feel wet soil, thick and clumpy, making it difficult for me to find my bearings.

Someone is standing over me. One of the shadows, a phantom, ready to pounce—

I wake up with a start, gasping for breath, much like I did after my night terror. Slowly, I familiarize myself with my surroundings. My cotton bed sheets, my lumpy pillows, the hard rectangle of my cell phone beside my head. It's nearing six o'clock in the morning, much earlier than I usually get up, but I'm home. I'm safe.

Still, my chest feels like there's a drum inside it, the adrenaline only starting to fade. This is my second night terror in recent weeks; before this, it was almost a decade. Reluctantly,

I think back to the conversations with my mother. She's worried about me this time of year, and I hate to admit she might be right. Perhaps the past has a firmer grip than I'd like to admit, and trying to fight it just makes the grasp that much stronger, a python coiling tight around what's trying to break free.

Or maybe this is all in my head, and my dreams are my subconscious' way of telling me to slow down.

I roll over, staring at the bare wall across from me. It mirrors the blank canvas in my mind. Ten years ago, my mistakes caused something terrible to happen. I dropped out of college, sending my future down a different path, and after all this time, I'm still not sure where I'm headed. As much as I want to admit I'm fine, it isn't true, and maybe those insecurities have manifested in paranoia, about the present and about those around me.

My conversation with Chaz last night is still fresh. *We need proof, not speculation.* Did I really think one of my writing group members was out to get me? That one of them had been behind the black hearts all along? All because of two incidents that were similar to the stories from our group? I must have sounded like a complete maniac, and now, in the quiet and dark of early morning, I'm starting to wonder if I am.

Just as in my most recent night terror, maybe the person I'm running from is myself, my own worst enemy for the past decade and more.

Fully awake, I pick up my phone and begin scrolling. No new emails, which means *Night Beat* is still a lost cause, but at least I didn't receive another rejection. My mind isn't awake enough to even consider writing, so I scroll through social media, waiting out that awkward intermission between getting up and starting the day or rolling back over and returning to sleep.

A couple of posts down is when I see it, an article from a

local newspaper that's been shared several dozen times, despite the early morning hour:

BREAKING OVERNIGHT: WU STUDENT KILLED

Whitaker PD confirms a female body was discovered last night in a drainage ditch close to campus. Emergency services were dispatched, and the victim was pronounced dead at the scene. A name has not been released, but officers did confirm the female victim was a WU student. A cause of death has not been released, but foul play is suspected. They are waiting to notify the next of kin before releasing further details.

I read and re-read the short article. A female student murdered. Her body left in a drainage ditch. Just like in my story.

Desperate for more information, I type targeted phrases into the search bar. Sure, the police might be waiting for confirmation, but no one else is ever that patient. There must be information out there about a woman murdered, a student missing, at least.

It doesn't take long for me to find it. Post after post with sparse information, mainly pictures and short captions.

RIP Jessica

Prayers for your friends and family

My best friend, never forgotten

It's the same person in each photo. A plain-faced brunette with bangs that rest just above dark eyes. She's smiling, carefree. A woman in her early twenties who could never have predicted her life would end so soon. The media and police haven't announced it yet, but this must be the WU student that was murdered.

Below the last photo, a recent comment grabs my attention. A black heart.

It's not just one, but several, each left in a separate post by the same user. They rain down the comments section, leaving a trail for me to follow.

I immediately click on the user's profile, but the account is private. Empty, really, with no friends or recent posts. A random mourner leaving a flurry of black hearts on a post about a murdered woman. What are the odds? Other people have left hearts and similar emojis to express their condolences, but I can't shake the feeling that these symbols were meant for me.

Another story from the group re-enacted in real life. Another black heart left for me to find.

I fall back on my bed, staring wide-eyed at the dark ceiling. The doubts from earlier go away, and a new reality takes shape in my mind. This is more than another coincidence, and now it seems whoever is copying our stories—this time *my* story—is escalating. From vandalism to assault to murder.

FIFTEEN

The glass door to McCallie's Pub is etched in frost; it looks like dozens of snowflakes are glued to the surface. There hasn't been any snow but judging from the gray skies above and the cooling temperatures, winter will be making an early appearance.

Still, I'd rather stand out here, shaking, than enter.

I almost skipped out on tonight's meeting entirely. Since reading the news alert about the murdered WU student, I've done little more than hide in bed, thinking. More details have been released, including an official identification. Jessica Wilder is her name, only twenty years old. She'd last been seen leaving a bar close to campus, and it's believed she was killed while walking back to her dorm, her body left in a ditch—just like in *The Mistake*.

The similarities between the story I wrote and her death frighten me, and given the other strange incidents of the past week, I'm convinced there's no coincidence. In the past, I've only received the black hearts at random intervals, never connected to any other element of my life. Now, there have been three hearts appear after incidents that mirror the groups' stories. Someone is acting out the crimes we wrote about, trying harder than ever to get to me, and it's working. My emotions are all over the place, my nerves rattled. And the guilt. It weighs heavy on my chest, at times, making it difficult to breathe. Because this time, the black hearts stalker isn't only targeting me, but harming other people, too.

"Becca?" Marley is standing behind me, uncomfortably close. Layers of scarves are wrapped around her neck, and she's wearing a wool coat the color of amethyst. "I thought that was you. What are you doing standing in the cold?"

Seeing her sends another chill rattling through me. I wrap my arms around myself and stare at the glass door, still trying to work up the nerve to enter. "I had a phone call," I lie. "I was just about to go in."

"Good," she says, walking ahead. Her heavy perfume—floral and citrus, at odds with this somber winter evening—marks a trail between where I stand and McCallie's entrance. "I thought I'd be late. Now, we can arrive together."

A voice inside warns: *You shouldn't go in there at all*. It's more than random coincidences now. Someone is committing crimes, and the black hearts at the scenes leave a trail of bread-crumbs back to me. I should be going to the police. Then I remember the way Chaz looked at me when I first shared my suspicions. He didn't believe me, so why would anyone else? I'll have to prove I'm right before sharing my theory with anyone, and hopefully before the trail of black hearts results in the secrets from the past resurfacing.

I allow Marley to lead the way, the journey to the back of the pub feeling slower than usual. Most nights, I'm eager to meet with the girls, to share my writing from the week. Tonight, I haven't prepared anything, and I don't plan on pretending otherwise. In fact, the only reason I'm here is to gauge the others' reactions. If one of them is the black hearts stalker, and worse, if one of them killed Jessica Wilder, I must figure out which one it is.

As we walk through the crowded pub, I study Marley, her long curly hair cascading down her back, small braids intermixed with the waves. The way she glides through, leading with confidence and an air of mystery. The most obvious suspect for re-enacting our stories would be her. None of the crimes took place until after she joined the Mystery Maidens, and there's something about her that's irritated me since our first meeting. An intuition that warns me there's more beneath the surface. It would be easier if she were the culprit, much more convenient than admitting one of my friends could be a potential murderer.

Still I can't decide how Marley could be connected to the black hearts. She wouldn't have started sending them as a child, unless there's some other connection I don't know about. Perhaps she uncovered the truth about my past and my drama with the hearts. It's not like I haven't tried telling people about my stalker before. Could she have found out about them from someone else and decided to include them in her twisted re-enactments? Or maybe she's working with someone older, someone who would understand the significance of the hearts and what they mean.

For that reason, I'm committed to looking at each of the others closely, too. I must find answers before going to the police again, and before anyone else gets hurt, before my murderous stalker turns their violence toward me.

"There you are!" Victoria says once we reach the back booth. She and Danielle are sitting beside each other, their laptops already out, two glasses of wine nearby. "We thought everyone was going to ditch us."

"It took me forever to find an Uber," Marley says. "Becca, what's your excuse?"

"I haven't felt the best today," I answer honestly. "Afraid I'm coming down with a cold."

I study their reactions. If one of the women here committed a murder, would they suspect someone catching onto them this fast? Would they think there is another reason for my sudden illness? If they're leaving a black heart at every scene, they must want me to know.

"It's that time of year," Danielle says. "We are running late, though. Should we get started?"

"Where's April?" I ask. I can't be the only person to recognize our group isn't complete.

"She's sick, too," Victoria says. "Her whole crew is. She messaged earlier to say she was skipping out."

That's strange. Rarely do any of us miss a meeting, especially April. This is the one event each week that's about her and not her family; she wouldn't give that time up lightly. But if she is reeling from having committed a murder, maybe that's why she isn't here?

"You need to go first?" Danielle asks me. "If you start to feel worse, you could head out."

"Nothing new from me this week," I say, trying and failing to get more comfortable in my seat. I feel their eyes on me, like little spotlights highlighting my insecurities. "Still waiting to hear back about *Night Beat* and haven't felt inspired to write anything new."

"I liked the story from last week," Marley says, shimmying off her coat. "About the girl who was murdered, right? And the boy who killed her."

I stare at Marley, before moving my gaze, studying both Victoria and Danielle just as closely. Have any of them seen the news? Have they put together the similarities between the story I shared last week and the student who was found on campus? Victoria works there. Surely, she's heard about it.

Then again, the news is so recent, it hasn't yet made its rounds around the local news circuit. There is limited information available online, but nothing about Jessica Wilder's murder in the morning's paper. I already checked. If one of them is the murderer, they must know what happened, but their reactions give nothing away. They all stare back at me, blank-faced, ready for a response.

"Not sure where I want to go with that one," I say. "I need to start something new, I'm just not sure what."

"I'm with Becca," Marley say. "I've been slammed with school and didn't get around to writing anything. I'm just here for the moral support."

Maybe it's not school that's been keeping Marley busy, but slashing tires and running people over. Murdering a fellow student. Why was Marley waiting for an Uber anyway? Most students have a car. Is it possible hers was damaged during the hit-and-run? Every statement sparks suspicion in my mind.

"Looks like it'll be a short night after all," Danielle says. "I'll go first. I've been working on a story inspired by one of my cases."

She pulls out her laptop and begins reading. I listen closely, paying attention for any plot devices that could later morph into some type of crime. Thankfully, no murders take place. It's mainly about a drug ring being ratted out by an informant, a tense story under normal circumstances, but meaningless given my mindset tonight. Victoria's story is just as uneventful. The main character is suffering from mental illness, but doesn't commit any notable crimes. When she finishes reading, I relax in my seat for what feels like the first time all night. At least I won't expect any other crimes in the following days.

"Well, I guess that's it for this week," Victoria says. "If there's nothing else to share, I'm going to head home. I have a stack of student papers to grade."

"Is one of them mine?" Marley asks cheekily.

"I believe it could be." Victoria stands, putting on her coat. "Same time on Monday?"

"Sorry about not having anything this week," I say. "Once I'm feeling better, I'll come up with something."

"No worries. Taking a break is part of the creative process," she says. "Maybe one of our stories will give you some inspiration."

Inspiration. To write a story or commit a crime? It doesn't matter what's been said, I unpack every statement as though it's hiding something.

"See you next time," Marley says. She waves, her fingers dancing in the air, grating on my nerves.

"Are you okay?" Danielle says, still sitting in the booth across from me.

"Yeah. Just feeling a little sick."

"I meant about Marley," she says, her voice low. "You're staring at her like you want to rip out one of those bohemian braids."

"Is it that obvious?"

"Probably not to the others. Definitely not to Marley." She leans back in the booth. "I'm good at reading people. It comes with the job. I can't help noticing she seems to get on your nerves."

"She does," I admit, watching as Victoria and Marley make their way through the crowded pub to the exit. "Is it just me, or is there something off about her?"

"She's a bit shiny and new," she says. "I think that energy can become draining when you're old and boring like us."

"I wouldn't say either one of us is old."

"Compared to her we are. Do you remember what it was like to be that careless and fun? Feels like a lifetime ago for me," she says, leaning back, a look of nostalgia on her face. "But she is talented. I suppose that's why Victoria allowed her to join the group."

There's no denying that Marley is a gifted writer, and although I won't admit it to Danielle, that's probably the main reason I dislike her. She's the epitome of everything I want to be, everything I once was. That, and she's the most likely culprit behind the copycat crimes. Is it possible my story unlocked something inside of her? Made her start lashing out at others?

When the waitress walks past our table, Danielle flags her down and orders another drink.

"Not in a hurry to get home?" I ask.

"To my lonely apartment? Nah, I'll stay out for one more drink. Maybe I'll go to sleep faster."

"No boyfriend or girlfriend?" I continue, realizing immediately that's the most personal question I've ever asked Danielle.

She laughs, raising her glass. "Not at the moment. With the schedule I have, I'm not sure it will ever happen."

"You're quite the catch," I tell her. "Beautiful. Smart. And a gifted writer."

I think about the first time I met Danielle. If it weren't for her, I never would have joined Mystery Maidens, and funnily enough, what put us in contact was the black hearts.

I reached out to Danielle's firm after I'd been fired from the MedSpa, hoping I could sue them for lost wages. My anger was intense because I knew I'd done nothing wrong and the black hearts were to blame, but because the sender remained a mystery, it seemed more logical for me to direct my fury at my former employer.

The moment I stepped into Danielle's waiting room, I was intimidated. Shiny new floors and clean, posh furniture. Being around lawyers made me as nervous as being around cops, but I felt I had to do something to get my job back, and I hoped threatening a lawsuit might do the trick.

I became even more unsettled when I stepped into her office and saw her. I'd been expecting an older woman, someone around my mom's age with a Marcia Clark-like confidence. Instead, I saw someone my own age. Beautiful, smart, accomplished. She greeted me with complete professionalism and kindness, yet as I retold my version of what happened at the MedSpa, I felt my voice weakening, like the very ground beneath me was shifting. I never did get the courage to tell her about the black hearts; I'd hoped there'd be a way to get my job back without bringing them up.

"Is there anything we can do?" I asked, hoping for once I'd get a win, a break from the constant cycle of disappointment.

Danielle leaned forward, her delicate wrists accented with simple, expensive jewelry. "The fact there aren't cameras helps us," she said. "They can't prove you stole the cash, just like you can't prove you didn't. However, the fact you were there less than sixty days works against us."

"How?"

"If they were citing theft as the reason they fired you, we could challenge them on that front. Typically, if someone is let go in the first sixty days, an employer doesn't have to have a reason. They could simply say you weren't the right fit."

"But that's not true." I felt my cheeks reddening, my desperation scratching at my throat. "They fired me because they think I stole tips, and I didn't."

"I believe you," she said, calmly. "But if I were in your shoes, I'd walk away. It would be easier and save you time and money in the long run."

"That was the first job I've had in years I actually enjoyed," I said under my breath, feeling a familiar hopelessness.

"Have you started working anywhere else?"

I exhaled, leaning against the velvet backrest. "I'm waiting tables at a place downtown. Mario's Pizzeria."

"That's a good restaurant," she said, for the first time failing to sound genuine. "I've always heard servers make more than hourly workers anyway."

"It's good for the time being." I cleared my throat, desperate to sound less like a loser. "My real passion is writing. I'm working on my first book, actually."

A broad smile spread across her face, and she leaned back,

resting a silver pen against her lips. "Really? What kind of writing?"

"Mysteries and thrillers, mostly," I said. "They've always been my favorite to read."

"Very interesting, indeed." She leaned forward, elbows on her desk. "This isn't why you came to see me today, but I might be able to help you after all. Let me tell you about the Mystery Maidens."

The rest was history. That chance meeting introduced me to the group, which led me to where I am now. Although we've all been meeting for more than a year, we only know superficial amounts about each other's lives. I wonder what quiet moments of desperation exist in all our lives, if the desperation became too much to handle for someone, pushed one of us over the edge.

"I think I like the way my life is," Danielle says, bringing my thoughts away from our first introduction and back to the present. "I don't answer to anyone else. If I want to work late or write or stay for an extra drink, I can. Not everyone is in that position."

"How about family?" I ask.

"I completed my undergrad back home before I moved here for school. Like you," she says, taking a sip of her drink. "I always thought I'd move back after I graduated law school, but one thing led to another. I suppose this is my home now, for better or worse."

I don't plan on telling her I never finished my degree. It's a fact I've managed to keep quiet for over a year; I assume most of them believe I graduated and am only working as a waitress to support my starving artist lifestyle.

Like Danielle, I never planned on staying here either. Sometimes I wonder why I did.

"My mom and I have always been at odds," I say. "I guess I figure the more distance between us the better."

"Sometimes distance is a good thing," she says. "Although, I've been away from my hometown for so long most of my friends have moved on with their lives. Moved on from me. It took me a while to realize I don't really fit into other people's circles, which is why I focused on creating my own."

"I know the feeling," I say, although I've yet to find a place where I really belong, outside of the fictional worlds I create. For a moment, I'm taken aback by the similarities in our situations. Both Whitaker transplants, both here for several years without finding our footing, and both trying to turn our hobby into something substantial, although at least she has a career to fall back on.

Could Danielle be the person behind these murders? As she's just admitted, she has time for little else outside writing and work. Even if she managed to fit messing with me and murdering a co-ed into her schedule, what would her motive be?

"Are you dating anyone?" she asks me.

I laugh, harshly. "No. Come to think of it, I've only had one relationship, and he cheated on me. Kinda sad when you think about it."

"Men are dogs," she says, taking another sip of her drink.

"Well, he didn't do it alone," I say. "What's that make the woman involved?"

"A bitch."

We nearly choke on our own laughter. I knock over my almost empty glass, quickly grabbing a napkin to wipe up the mess.

"It's funny, isn't it? We spend all this time together and know so little about each other."

"I always thought that was one of the positives of the group," she says. "We're able to look at each other's work more objectively the less we know."

On the flip side, I think, it makes it harder to gauge which, if any, of the group members might be a killer.

"It's nice making new friends, though," she says. "Lessens the sting of knowing everyone else moved on without me."

"It is nice," I say.

"The only one who really tells us anything about their life outside of writing is April," she says. "Moms are natural over-sharers."

I laugh at the truth of the comment. "Strange she missed tonight," I say, watching Danielle for a reaction.

"Struggles of being a mom," she says, finishing off the rest of her wine. "I guess."

After my conversation with Danielle, reminiscing on the way we first met, how she introduced me to the others, I can't see her risking her privileged, albeit lonely life, to mess with me, which means I'll have to turn my focus to the other group members.

April didn't show up for tonight's meeting—the first meeting after Jessica Wilder was killed—and I want to find out why.

SIXTEEN

April's house is located in one of the many subdivisions outside downtown. I've been there only once, when she insisted she would host last year's Christmas meeting. She ushered us into her grand kitchen, all slow-release cabinets and stone countertops, where she'd set up a candy cane martini bar alongside various appetizers.

Thinking back to that time, I remember feeling out of place. My social gatherings are limited to the Mystery Maiden meetings. On the rare occasions I do visit someone's place, it's usually an apartment or a condo. The rest of us are centrally located to downtown, really—Danielle has an apartment within walking distance to her law office, and Victoria's condo is close to WU. My two-bedroom looks like something a broke college kid would beg to rent.

April's house is a real, mature home. Instead of a white picket fence, a large black privacy fence surrounds the perimeter of her backyard, blooming rosebushes decorating the front. I remember walking around her living room and dining room, candy cane martini in hand, admiring all the little details. The crisp white molding along the ceiling. The heavy frames which held abstract artwork. The colorful vases she'd purchased on her honeymoon in Venice. It wasn't just the material things that stood out to me. In the corner of each room were large wicker baskets filled with children's toys. Family portraits were scattered around the house, a loving presentation, by no means boastful.

I left that Christmas party believing April lived a charmed life. Happily married. Two beautiful children. And she still managed to carve out time for her writing. She's exactly the type of woman my own mother would love to have as a daughter.

Those were all superficial observations. Tonight, I'm visiting her house to try and gauge whether she could be the person who is taunting me. It's strange that she skipped tonight. In the year I've been part of the group, she's not missed a single meeting. Even when her kids are sick, which seems to always be the case in the fall and winter, she arranges for her husband to watch them. Writing is a priority for her. Maybe the only reason she missed tonight's meeting is because she has a guilty conscience.

I walk up the immaculate brick pathway snaking through her front lawn. The porch is alight with lanterns and adorned with fall décor. The doorbell rings loudly, and it's only seconds before I get a response.

"Hello?"

The voice is clearly April's, but I don't see her. I look behind me trying to make sure.

"Come closer to the door," she says. "I can't see your face."

I move nearer, trying to peer through the pockets of ornate glass, but it's impossible to see anyone through the warped pane.

"Um, it's Becca," I say, still trying to figure out who I'm speaking to. "From Mystery Maidens."

"What a surprise," she says, and it's hard to tell through the speaker if she's taken aback or annoyed. "Just a second."

"Where are you?" I ask, still looking around.

"Upstairs. I'm watching you on my door cam," she says. "It's hard to spot unless you bend down."

That's when I see it. A small white rectangle beside the door hinge. Now that I've noticed it, the modern technology looks out of place alongside the traditional décor. I bend down closer, catching my tiny reflection in the lens.

The door swings open. April stands in the doorway wearing an oversized lounge set, an ensemble that screams casual comfort. Her hair is pulled away from her face, covered with a patterned silk scarf.

"Becca, what brings you out all this way?"

"I don't want to bother you," I say, raising the small brown package in my hands. "Victoria said your gang was sick, so I thought I'd bring over some minestrone from Mario's. It always makes me feel better when I'm under the weather."

The idea to bring soup was a last-minute one, but I needed some excuse to visit. Even though a married mother of two isn't high on my suspect list, I must investigate every possibility, and this is my opportunity to corner her alone. If she is the person behind everything, she'd get too suspicious if I showed up on her doorstep empty-handed.

"That's so sweet of you," she says, looking behind her. "I'd invite you in but—"

"Do you think I could use your bathroom?" I ask quickly. "It's about a twenty-minute drive back to my place."

Her smile is tense, and I notice she grips the door tighter.

"Sure," she says, stepping back. "You really didn't have to come all this way."

"It's fine. I didn't have anything better to do."

I step into the house, the warm air in the foyer surrounding me like a hug. A vanilla candle scents the air, and, just like last time, everything looks immaculate, although she clearly hasn't brought out the decorations yet.

"I'll take that," she says, reaching for the box.

"Yeah," I say. "I'll just be a second. Don't want to bother you when you're sick."

I walk straight ahead and duck into the hallway bathroom. It looks the exact same as last time I was here, only the Christmas hand towels have been replaced with auburn ones with embroidered leaves around the hem. Maybe it's the tight quarters of the room, but I begin to wonder what I was hoping to accomplish by coming here. She says her family is sick; how am I supposed to prove otherwise? I remind myself that whoever is doing this must have me in their sights. Even a quick conversation could be enough to see if I notice a change in her behavior toward me.

When I exit the bathroom, the first thing I notice is how quiet the house is. April's kids stayed with relatives during last year's holiday party, but I imagine on an average evening they're quite noisy, feet pattering, squeals ringing. They must be ill if they're not making a peep.

I make my way back to the kitchen through the dining room, looking around for anything I remember during my last visit. Some of the family portraits are still on the walls, but I swear there were more last time. There are things missing, too, I think. The vases. The artwork. Even the basket filled with toys is gone.

"This was really nice of you," April says. She's sitting at the breakfast bar in the kitchen. The soup I brought has been reheated and transferred into a ceramic bowl. "I'm starving. Haven't eaten all day."

"You must be really sick to miss a meeting," I say, watching her closely. "You've never done that before."

She clears her throat. "Yeah, I hated to miss, but I just

wasn't feeling up to it. I haven't worked on anything new, anyway."

"I figure you're still in celebration mode," I say. "An offer of representation is a big deal."

She smiles weakly and nods her head. "Yeah. I'm gearing up to get back in the editing phase. It could be a while before I work on anything new."

I look around the kitchen, noticing that it is also noticeably bare. It no longer gives off the homey vibe I remember from last year. Instead, it almost looks like a showroom, something a realtor would stage before taking pictures. In fact, it looks like everything has been cut back. Maybe April's moving and hasn't told us.

I study her. She eats the soup ravenously, but beyond that, her complexion is as radiant as ever. I haven't heard a cough or a sneeze since I arrived. She doesn't appear sick at all, except for a slight smudge of darkness around the eyes.

And the quiet. I could swear we are the only two people in the house. Where is her husband? The children?

"What is it?" April has both her hands on the table, staring at me quizzically. I never have had a good poker face.

"Nothing," I say. "Just admiring the place. You have a beautiful home."

"Thanks." She picks up the spoon again, the clinking of the utensil against the bowl filling the silence.

"The kids must really be sick," I say. "I've not heard a sound the whole time I've been here."

"The kids..." Her voice trails off, her gaze fixated on something in the other room. I look behind me and see she's staring at one of the family portraits on the far wall. Her eyes are glossy with tears.

"April," I say. "Is everything okay?"

She clears her throat again and stares into her lap. "It's nothing. Really."

"It seems like something is bothering you."

As the statement leaves my lips, I realize I'm not asking as an amateur detective, but as a friend. There's something off with April's behavior, but she's not acting like someone who has been targeting me. Her pain seems more personal.

"The kids aren't here," she says, her voice flat. "They're staying at their father's tonight."

"Their father's?"

"Chase and I are getting a divorce." She exhales, as though she physically couldn't contain the statement inside a second longer. When she looks at me, the tears start trailing down her cheeks. "We've been separated for a few months."

"April," I say. "I had no idea."

"No one does. I mean, besides our immediate family. It's not something I'm ready to share with the world."

"I'm sorry I came by," I say, hot anxiety climbing the back of my neck. This conversation feels too personal, too intimate. I'd come here for answers, but this isn't the mystery I was trying to solve.

"No, you were just being nice. Besides, I need to come to terms with what's happening. It's just hard."

That explains why half their belongings have disappeared. They're in the process of sorting assets, and clearly the kids are living somewhere else half the time. If I hadn't seen the place with my own eyes, I never would have believed it. April is constantly sharing stories about the kids and Chase. I'm certain she's posted photos online, masquerading as though everything is just fine. She even said Chase sent her flowers to celebrate her writing news, that they were supposed to go out at the weekend.

"Do you want to talk about it?"

"It's all too cliché, really. Chase is leaving me for another woman." She looks at me again, the hurt in her eyes replaced with a flash of anger. "Right now, I'm just grieving the loss of what we had. Every day I wake up, and I can't believe this is my life. We're talking about selling the house. Chase has his own apartment. I'm having to split time with the kids." Her words come out so quickly then run into one another, and she has to take a deep breath to pause herself. "All this change is overwhelming."

"I can't even imagine." I chuckle, leaning on humor to lessen the tension. "Although, this does explain why the husband keeps dying in all your stories."

Thankfully, she laughs. "I guess what we're feeling inside bleeds out onto the page, right?" She sighs, staring up at the family portrait again. "Anyway, I was having a pretty low day. As much as I wanted to come to group, I just couldn't."

I sit beside her, placing my hands over hers. "You don't have to explain yourself. It's good for you to take some time to process."

"I thought I had a perfect life. We were so happy, until we weren't, and I'm afraid that what we're going through now will mess up the kids for the rest of their lives."

"Lots of families find ways to navigate a divorce. You are a brilliant mother, April," I say, sincerely. "Whatever you decide to do, I know you're putting them first."

"I'm trying," she says. "It's just still hard to admit it's come to this."

I don't know what else to say. The only adult relationship I had was with Jasper, and even though he cheated, too, we didn't have the history April has with Chase. The foundation. It seems blasphemous to offer advice to someone who is going through this heavy a heartache. I settle on, "I'm here if you need me."

"I appreciate that," she says, smiling. "I know I can lean on all of you. I just haven't wanted to admit we're getting divorced out loud yet because then it becomes real."

"At least you have the agent news to celebrate," I say, trying to add some positivity to the conversation.

She smiles genuinely. "I know! I'm still excited about that. I swear, it came at a time when I really needed it. It's true about one door closing, another opening. Maybe my career taking off is what I need to get me out of this funk."

"It could be," I say. "You really deserve it."

"Thank you." She nods toward her bowl. "And thank you for the soup. You must have a sixth sense or something. I've been too down to cook a meal, and here you come with exactly what I need."

"I was just trying to be nice."

A pang of guilt jars my insides. I wasn't trying to be nice at all. I was merely investigating, suspicious of April's involvement. It never occurred to me she was dealing with something so upsetting.

"While you're here," she says, standing and walking over to the fridge, "want to share a bottle of wine?"

"Sure."

For the next hour, we sit at the breakfast bar sipping Sauvignon Blanc. We don't talk about divorce or kids or writing. It's all mindless stuff. What television shows we're watching and new movies we want to see. It seems like a nice way to ease the tension, and by the time I'm ready to leave, I'm confident April is in a much better mood than when I arrived.

"We should do this again," she says as I'm putting on my coat. "Outside of the Mystery Maidens. When we're together, all we talk about is writing. It would be nice to get to know the other parts of each other's lives, too."

"I agree," I say, realizing her sentiment echoes the one Danielle made earlier tonight. Maybe I'm at the point in my life where I should finally start letting people in, but then I think of the black hearts, I remember what I came here to find out, and the thought flies away.

"About Chase," she says, hesitantly. "Don't mention it to the others."

"I promise I won't."

"I'll tell them, eventually. Right now, it just feels so embarrassing. Did I tell you he cheated on me with a girl I knew from college?"

"You're kidding," I say, shaking my head. "One of your friends?"

"In all fairness, we're not friends now. We used to party together, ages ago. Still, who would have thought the girl I downed tequila shots with would break up my family?"

April tries to sound funny, like the situation is ironic, but I sense the hurt behind her words. My own stomach turns just imagining. "People change, that's for sure. Never know what to expect."

"Tell me about it." She pours the last of the wine into her glass and leans back. "The worst part of it is I have to see her face every time I go on the highway."

"What?"

"You know that realtor sign on I-40? That's the girl." She drinks half the glass in one gulp. "The biggest slut at WU turned Whitaker's celebrity realtor."

I turn quickly so April can't see the reaction on my face. The realtor on that billboard is Crystal, my roommate. She's the woman who broke up April's marriage? A wave of dizziness puts me off balance as I realize more areas of my life are intersecting.

"That is awful," I say, voice shaking. "How did you find out it was her?"

"Let's just say I found messages between them," she says. "Worse than the smut I read in my spare time."

I smile weakly before returning to my car, my head swimming with new information. Crystal and April are connected through Chase, and both have ties to me. Worse than that, they've known each other since college. I knew April had attended WU, but I've never put together she was there at the same time as me. If she was acquaintances with Crystal, she would know about what happened ten years ago.

The idea that April has a connection to me I didn't know about is unsettling. Could she have been watching me this entire time? In April's quest to learn more about her husband's mistress, could she have uncovered something about my past? I try to recall our interactions over the past year, but the mystery only becomes more tangled in my mind.

I crank the ignition, ready to head home. Yet, as I drive in the direction of downtown, I can't help wondering about how easy it was for April to hide her ordeal from the rest of the group. If you were to ask any of the other members, they'd assume she is happily married, the calm and collected Supermom of your Instagram feed's dreams, just like I did.

She's been struggling for months but was able to hide it.

How easy would it be for her to hide something else?

SEVENTEEN

I hurry home, hoping for a chance to confront Crystal before she goes out for the night. To my surprise, she's waiting on me in the kitchen when I arrive.

"Get dressed," she says, tossing something at me as soon as I walk in the door. "We're going out."

The mesh fabric is soft and luxurious against my hands. It's obviously a dress from her closet—nothing I own is that delicate or stylish. I look at her, confused. "Why?"

"There's something I want to talk to you about," she says, her skin glowing. "And I think it's best to talk about business in the right location." She looks around the room, disappointed. "New surroundings."

"Crystal," I say her name sternly. "What's going on?"

"I have an idea I want to run by you—"

"Then tell me now." My voice is raised. I'm getting impatient. "What is it?"

"My agency just posted a new position for an agent assistant, and I think it would be a great opportunity."

"For me?"

"Yes, for you. Wouldn't it be cool if we got to work together?"

My head is spinning with what I need to confront her about and this random job proposal she's dropped in my lap. Why would she even consider me?

"I don't know anything about real estate."

"It's okay. You'd just be my assistant, at first. I could show you the ropes, help you study. You could have your own license within the year, and then we'd be working on the same level."

I scoff. Even when Crystal is trying to be nice, she has a way of making everything a competition. Her job proposal is ridiculous, and it's getting in the way of what we should be talking about. The affair with April's husband.

"Look, there's something I want to talk to you about—"

"No, no, no. You're not doing this." She marches closer to me, making it difficult for me to move around her. "I'm not letting you change the subject."

"I have absolutely no desire to work in real estate."

"Why not?" she asks, hands on her hips. "What do you want to do with your life?"

"You sound like my mother." I mean it as a joke, but then I notice the way she averts her eyes. She takes a step back. "Crystal, have you been talking to my mom?"

"She has always been so kind to me, ever since college. She reaches out on Facebook from time to time."

"Oh my gosh." My cheeks flush with heat as I slap my arms against my sides. "What did she say to you?"

"She's worried. She doesn't know what you're doing, and every time she tries to talk to you about it, you brush her off. Just like you're doing now."

"It doesn't matter what I'm doing with my life! It's *my* life. Not hers. Or yours."

"She thought real estate was something you might enjoy."

"Mom doesn't care about me enjoying anything. She just

wants me to have a real job she can tell her friends about when they meet up for their weekly card game. Being a writer and a waitress isn't sparkly enough for her."

"It's not just that," Crystal says plainly. "She says you don't tell her anything about your life. She didn't even know I was living with you."

"Well, that's been a recent change," I say, and one I'm starting to regret. Crystal may be one of my oldest friends, but I preferred her like everyone else, at a distance. The idea that she's watching everything I do and don't do, and reporting back to my mother, makes me cringe.

"My relationship with my mother is shaky," I say. "You know that. I don't need you getting involved."

She raises her hands in the air like a surrender. "I won't get involved anymore. I did think the assistant job was a good idea. There's a lot of potential there, and in this market—"

"You were complaining about the market a few days ago."

"It's tumultuous, but what field isn't? You mean to tell me you have more stability with writing?"

I grind my teeth. Knowing Crystal, she didn't mean for it to come out as a jab, but it did anyway. Always a competition between me and her. She's recovered and flourishing and will never let me forget it.

"You always do this," she continues. "Look for any excuse to walk away from something once it gets hard. How many jobs have you left in the past few years? This is an opportunity for you to grow and thrive."

Crystal makes it sound like I'm the world's biggest slacker, but she doesn't know that some of those jobs were ruined for me by the black hearts. I never told her because I couldn't stand the possibility of another person not believing me.

"I appreciate you taking such an interest in my personal life," I begin, "but I really think you should take this time to focus on yourself."

"What's that supposed to mean?"

I pause, bracing for her reaction. "Are you sleeping with a married man?"

She places her hands on her hips and raises her chin. "I just called off my engagement. Why would you even think that?"

"His wife told me about it." I pause again. "Does the name Chase ring a bell?"

Her eyes are large. "He's not my boyfriend."

"Are you sleeping with him?"

"It's casual, yes." She turns away from me now, putting distance between us as she wanders toward the living room.

"He's married with two kids, Crystal," I say, following her.

"Not according to him. He says they've been separated for weeks."

"Even if that's true, don't you think it's a messy situation to enter?"

"Now *you're* giving life advice."

"I'm not trying to. Trust me, I didn't go looking for this information." I raise my hands in an attempt to show her I'm not being judgmental. Rather, I'm concerned, like she claimed to be. "It just fell into my lap, and I knew I had to ask you about it."

"How do you just stumble onto information like that?"

"His wife is in my writing group. Her name is April." I pause again, watching to see if the name rings a bell. "She says she knew you from college."

"I vaguely remember her." Her arms are now folded across her chest. "I mean, we weren't close, or else you would know her."

"That's what I thought." Then again, Crystal always ran in wider social circles, even then. Could she have been closer to April than I realized? Could April know more about the past than she is letting on?

"We were acquaintances, at best," she continues to defend

herself. "It's not like I'm betraying a friend, or anything. And I'm not some homewrecker, either. Chase told me they were separated."

"I think they are. Now. The timeline might be a little fuzzy on his end," I say. "April seems to think you're one of the reasons they're breaking up."

"It's always the other woman's fault, is that it? Look, Chase is a casual thing. I could cut it off in no time. Lord knows, I have a line of guys waiting on their chance with me. The problems in your life, however, are a lot harder to fix."

"Thanks for the reminder." I resent the cruelty of her comment because it's true. "If it's so easy for you to end things with Chase, then prove it."

Normally, I admire Crystal's confidence, her ability to take on life fearless and head-first, but her reaction to sleeping with a married man bothers me. She's making excuses, when we both know she's too smart to fall for his lies and half-truths. After witnessing what I went through with Jasper, I thought she'd be more sympathetic. In fact, my breakup seemed to rekindle our friendship, made her a bigger part of my life again. I've tried extending that same olive branch in the wake of her broken engagement with Thomas, and look where that's gotten me.

"Fine. I will," she says, uncrossing her arms. "But please, don't let this argument overshadow what I was trying to say before. It's time you start living your life again. Enough time has passed."

"Has it? Remind me, how long did it take you to move on after what happened?"

In a conversation filled with accusations and digs, this is the one that proves most brutal. Crystal and I never talk about what happened. Not really. We dance around the topic, afraid to get too close. Now, Crystal looks at me, the pain from the past decade etched across her beautiful face.

"Moving on isn't the worst thing in the world. You should

try it. It might make you happy for a change." She moves back toward the kitchen, grabbing her purse off the kitchen table and slinging it over her shoulder. "I'm not a villain for living my life. Don't make me out to be one."

"Crystal, I wasn't trying to—"

"I'm going out. Maybe we can make plans for another night." She opens the door. "At least think about the job?"

"I will," I lie.

There's already too much for me to think about. Jessica Wilder's murder. The possibility that one of the Mystery Maidens is the culprit. The black hearts. My life is in shambles, and I'm lost on how to fix it.

EIGHTEEN

I picked up another afternoon shift at the pizzeria. As always, having the extra cash won't hurt, but there's another reason I wanted to work today.

Due to the proximity to campus, Victoria is known to stop by on Fridays for lunch. She's the only original member of the Mystery Maidens I haven't yet investigated.

Investigated probably isn't the right term, but that feels like what I'm doing. Talking to each of them in an isolated setting, trying to determine whether they could be the person that killed Jessica Wilder. Both Danielle and April have stressors outside of the group—the former's admitted loneliness and the latter's impending divorce—but I'm not convinced it's enough to make either of them go on a crime spree, especially one that's so clearly targeted at me.

My aim with talking to Victoria today is twofold: get an idea of whether she could be behind the crimes, which is doubtful, and find out more about Marley. After all, Victoria knows the most about her because Marley is a student. Victoria is the one who introduced her to our group, and because the crimes took place after her arrival, it's most likely she's the one who has been copying our stories. She could be working alongside the black hearts stalker or have found out about them some other way and started using them herself. In all the years I've played victim to this stalker, this feels like the closest I've ever come to finding out the truth, and that realization pushes me forward.

As expected, Victoria enters the restaurant right after the lunch rush dies down, which is around the time her afternoon class wraps up. When she sees me standing behind the hostess stand, she smiles, and I act equally surprised, as though I hadn't been hoping this exact meeting would occur.

"I didn't think you'd be working," she says, standing in front of me.

"I can always use the extra cash with the holidays coming up," I say, nodding to a booth at the back of the restaurant. "My shift's almost over. Maybe I can join you for lunch?"

"I'd love that," she says, genuinely, following me through the emptying restaurant.

I quickly take her order, adding on an extra entrée for me to eat. Mario never cares if we eat a meal during our shift, although he usually prefers we eat in the back. However, I need this time alone with Victoria to feel her out.

"How's work?" I say, sitting across from her at the table.

"Busy, busy," she says. "At least the semester will wrap up soon, which should give me some time to focus on my own writing."

"When's the next book come out?" I ask.

"Sometime after the first of the year," she says. "I have an editorial calendar I try to follow, but I'm not sure I'll meet my goal. That's the beauty of self-publishing. If I need to rework the system, I can."

"What you've been sharing in group has been great. I'm sure you'll meet your deadline."

"Thanks." Victoria's eyes survey the thinning crowd in the restaurant, before focusing on me. "I'm happy I ran into you, though. I've been wanting to talk to you," she says, "away from the group."

"Oh, yeah?" I'd thought I was the one with an ulterior motive. "About what?"

"The story you've been working on lately," she says. "*The Mistake.*"

My posture straightens. It's the first time any of us have raised our writing in a one-on-one conversation. Is it possible she's made a connection between the stories we share and the things that have been happening in my real life?

"The Layla story?" I ask, trying to keep my face from betraying my emotions.

"Not the most recent ones," she says, her eyes getting big as she hurls a compliment. "Those have been excellent, don't get me wrong. Your writing has been great, really gripping, but I keep going back to that first part. The one that centered around an attack, where you introduced the Layla character at the end. It felt so..." She pauses to find the right word, and my mind fills in the gap. *Terrifying. Claustrophobic*—

"Personal," she says. The word lands like an anchor in the water, pulling me down, down, down.

"It made me wonder if you were writing it from experience."

This wasn't the confrontation I was expecting. My eyes are beginning to water. I clear my throat before I speak. "All writing is rooted in experience, right?"

"Sure. I just..." It's obvious Victoria has rehearsed this, and yet she still fails to find the right words. "You know, if you work on a campus long enough, you get familiar with the culture. Lots of students have come to me over the years." She pauses. "If you were assaulted when you were a student—"

"I wasn't." I stop her before she can finish the sentence.

She nods slowly, her smile tight, waiting for me to continue.

"I almost was. Just like in the story," I say, "and that was enough."

"Yes, it is." She places her hand over mine and squeezes. "We all have close calls."

My mind traipses through time, away from this winter of my adulthood, back to the summer of my youth, when all my surroundings felt shiny and new and full of promise.

You're lucky if you have just a handful of days like that in your life, days where it feels like the entire world is at your fingertips. It's the kind of effervescence Marley exudes now, the type of power I once possessed.

But with that promise comes naivety, and I can still remember the moment it all came crashing down, when I was made aware that the world is never as beautiful and promising as it might present itself to be.

I'd made a last-minute decision to accompany some classmates to a fraternity party. It was out of character because, typically, I only went out with my closest friends. However, one was visiting with a friend out of town, and the other had a date, so instead of staying alone in the apartment, I tagged along.

The girls I went with were nice, but I barely knew them. Good for conversations and laughs and drinks, but as the night wore on, we'd gone our separate ways. I spent most of the evening leaned against the wall of the fraternity house, wishing I'd never come at all.

Until *he* started talking to me. He offered me a drink, then another, all while entertaining me with light conversation. That's all it was. Idle chatter and party talk. Nothing flirtatious or romantic, and yet, that's the point of the night when my memory starts to get fuzzy, hazy, like my vision was pulled underwater and I couldn't see through the waves and ripples.

What happened next came in flashes, sensory interruptions that brought me out of that haze and back to the present.

We were in a different room, and it was dark. Music continued to blare, but it was far away, beneath me, or so it felt. I was on something soft, a bed or sofa. My breathing was short and heavy. And I could feel *his* hands on me.

In the next second, my brain would fizzle out again, remembering nothing.

Then, like a ride I couldn't abandon, I'd be back. Dark room, soft bed. *His* hands on my body. I felt him tugging at my clothes, and I couldn't understand what was happening, how we'd even gotten here. Hadn't we been in the basement, surrounded by Christmas lights and people, moments ago?

A single word escaped my lips in a whisper. "No."

Then I was out again, back in that state of nothingness.

When I returned to the present, the room was no longer so dark.

A bright light shone inward from the hallway. And I was no longer alone with him. There were other people in the room. Shouting.

"What the hell are you doing?"

"Get out of here, creep."

"Are you okay?"

I could do little more than nod my head. Everything felt heavy. It was hard to move.

And then there was water going down my throat, washing life into my body. It came back just as quickly, sickening bile rushing out of my mouth and landing in a commode. How had I even made it to a bathroom?

"You're going to be okay. He didn't do anything to you," a voice said. Now that my senses were coming back, I recognized her as one of the girls from my class. "Thank God someone came in."

"I only had two drinks," I said, my stomach reeling at the

thought. My body braced for another round of regurgitation. "I don't know why I'm so sick."

"Someone must have slipped you something," she said. "It happened to me once, and I was a mess. Just like you."

I had the sudden desire to leave, but when I tried to stand, my legs were like gelatin, wobbly and useless. It took two people —I'm not sure who the other person was—to hold me up. Time has eroded my memories of the rest of the night, but, somehow, I eventually made it home, to the safety and comfort of my bed.

The next morning, when my roommates returned home, I didn't say anything to them about it. And I've tried to stop thinking about that night for the past ten years.

Until I started writing *The Mistake*.

"I'm not sure why I decided to write about it now," I admit to Victoria, shutting my eyes to hold back the tears. "I've been struggling with writer's block lately, and out of nowhere, it all came back to me."

"Trauma has a way of doing that," she says. "It can lie dormant in the body for years, then return with a vengeance."

"It's why I don't want to continue writing it," I admit. It's true, although the other reasons I want to drop the story, I can't tell her. "You think the others picked up on it, too?"

"Probably not," she says. "Like I said, I think I'm more attuned to those things after years of being on campus. I wanted to check on you. I know the only thing worse than experiencing an assault is feeling like you have no one to talk it over with."

"I appreciate you coming to me," I say. "Please, can we keep this between us?"

"Of course. I'd never tell a soul," she says. "Besides, I have plenty of drama in my own life that needs sorting."

"Really?" I say, eager for the opportunity to change the

subject. "It seems to me like you always have everything together."

"I don't know." She exhales shakily. "My mind's been all over the place lately. Between my classes and everything else, it's getting hard to focus."

"I understand," I say, looking around the restaurant. I wonder, why exactly has Victoria's head been all over the place? That doesn't sound like her. She's usually the most regimented of our bunch. "Anything been going on?"

"Just life," she says, but I notice her face closes like a book. She fiddles with the straw inside her glass, refuses to meet my eyes. "My love life, rather."

As with the others, Victoria doesn't talk much about her personal life, but in mentioning it, she's gifted me with a string I can pull.

"Are you dating someone new?" I ask.

"Was," she says, sourly. "It didn't work out."

"What happened?"

"Things were going great. At least, I thought they were. We'd been seeing each other for a couple months, and I thought, with the holidays approaching, it might become official. That was, until I found out he was married."

"You're kidding."

"That's the problem with meeting guys online, I guess. They put out there whatever image of themselves they think is desirable, whether it's true or not."

"How did you find out?"

She exhales, as though she's unsure she wants to share, but continues talking regardless. "His wife contacted me, as humiliating as that is."

My cheeks burn at the thought of it. "What did she say?"

"I guess she had her suspicions and decided to go through his phone. She found his online dating profile, which led to me and all the messages we'd exchanged. Let's just say, she wasn't very kind in letting me know my boyfriend was already taken."

"It's not your fault," I tell her, placing my hand over hers. "If he lied about being married, how could you know?"

"I still feel so guilty. And used. Here I was thinking our relationship might go somewhere, and all the while, I was his dirty little secret."

"He's the scumbag, not you."

"Becca, food is up!" Nikki calls from the back.

"Give me just a second," I tell her, wishing I didn't have to leave the table at such an emotional moment.

I certainly empathize with Victoria. Like with April, I don't feel equipped to give the best relationship advice because I have such little experience of my own. However, I can imagine the feelings of betrayal and shame she must have felt when she realized her new boyfriend had been lying to her. It's the type of reaction I'd expected to see when I confronted Crystal, instead of the callous indifference she displayed.

Could this love triangle be enough to send Victoria over the edge? This is more emotional turmoil than she has ever admitted to dealing with before. A breakup always provides ample motive when it comes to crime fiction, but in reality? Even with a broken heart, I'm not sure Victoria is capable of harming others.

When I return to the table with our food, I can tell Victoria's been crying. She dabs at the corners of her eyes with the paper napkin.

"I'm such a mess," she says. "You're looking forward to a break from work, and all I've done is talk about my problems."

"That's what friends do," I tell her. "You don't have to apologize for letting me know what's going on with you."

"Maybe we should share more often. Talk about more than just writing," she says. "I think that's why the breakup is hitting me so hard. I've kept everything in instead of expressing how I really feel."

"Pour it into your books," I tell her.

"There's an idea," she says, laughing. "My next victim can be a cheating scoundrel."

"Whatever works," I joke back, then, with a shudder, I remember that, for at least one person in our group, "next victim" might not be a fictional remark at all. My heartbeat accelerates when I recognize how much is at stake.

"Thanks for letting me vent," she says. "And please, don't mention it to the others. I don't want them judging me."

"Your secret is safe with me," I say. "I take it they didn't know about your boyfriend?"

"I'd mentioned him in passing," she says. "But they don't know about the breakup, and I'd like to keep the details quiet. Of course, Marley doesn't know anything about it. I've made an exception by letting her join the Mystery Maidens, but she's still my student, and I have to keep that boundary clear."

I'm so excited she brought up Marley, I have to control my expression.

"She's really talented, isn't she?" I say, thinking about the first, and only, story she shared with the group. *Rosebud.* "Are your other students as talented?"

"Gosh, no. I mean, they all have potential. It takes some longer than others to get where they need to be, and I trust many of them will develop into talented writers, if they stick with it. Every now and then, you get a student with raw talent. That's how Marley is, and it's why I asked her to join us."

I try to ignore the pang of jealousy I feel inside. I wonder, which category does Victoria believe I belong in? Am I still developing my potential, or am I one of the few that's naturally gifted? Shaking the questions off, I try to re-center the conversation onto Marley.

"Have you had her in class before?"

"No, which is surprising. She's not even a writing major, if you can believe it," she says. "I think she's one of those students that doesn't realize her true gifts until later, but I'm hoping she'll reconsider. It would be such a talent to waste."

Maybe Marley's gift isn't just writing but taking the stories of others and putting them into practice. After my separate conversations with each of the women, I'm even more convinced Marley, the one I know the least about, is the one behind this.

"I'm surprised you haven't met before," she continues. "Seeing as she lives so close."

"Really?"

Victoria points out the window. "Her apartment is just a block away from here. You know that cute little row of buildings across from The Coffee Shop?"

"I had no idea," I say. "That is close."

Too close. If Marley is behind the most recent string of black hearts, it would be easy for her to watch my every move.

"Much nicer than the places we had to live in when we were in college, right?"

My old college apartment appears in my mind. I try to avoid it at all costs, but Victoria knows where it is. I told her about it once, and she informed me it's currently under renovation. Being torn down and built into something shiny and new.

If it were up to me, they'd never rebuild.

"I need to get back to campus for my office hours," she says, pushing her plate away. Her sandwich is only half eaten, and I assume her lack of appetite is linked to the recent heartache. "I've taken up enough of your time."

"Please. You've given me an excuse not to work," I say. "It's been nice talking."

"It has."

She doesn't have to remind me to keep our conversation private. In fact, all the women have confided in me this week, which makes me feel valued, and only slightly guilty for snooping into each of their lives.

Victoria leaves a hefty tip before she leaves, even though I tell her she doesn't have to. I hurry through my side work and duck out of the restaurant before Nikki can corner me. I'll be punished for anything I haven't completed later. Right now, I have somewhere more important to be.

I hurry down the block and find an outdoor table at The Coffee Shop. Sure enough, there's a trendy row of apartments right across the street. I can almost guess which one belongs to Marley. Tie-dye tapestries and incense pots litter one of the balconies. I'd bet this afternoon's wages that's hers.

She's not home, and there's no telling when she will be.

That's fine. I have nothing but time to kill.

NINETEEN

I remained at The Coffee Shop for over an hour, until the afternoon sun dipped so far behind the trees that the entire street turned gray, chilly air ushered in along with the shadows. I'd been hoping I might catch Marley arriving home after one of her classes, that I'd get the chance to spy on her in her natural environment, see how she acts when she thinks no one is watching.

Having had no luck, I returned home, to the warmth of my apartment, and decided to do some spying on the internet.

In a world where every detail of a person's life is documented and recorded online, Marley Theroux seems to have appeared out of nowhere.

She has social media. Of course, she does. If she were impossible to find online, I'd be even more concerned, but what I am able to track down doesn't reveal much.

Both her Facebook and her Instagram are less than two years old. No Twitter. She has a TikTok, but appears inactive, no posts of her dancing to trending songs or galloping around campus. In fact, the other platforms are equally as bland. She usually shares political memes (a total lefty) and inspirational quotes (about using the past to better the future). There are only a few selfies, and they're so close-up it's hard to tell where she's taken them.

It feels hypocritical to deem this behavior suspicious; I'm not active on social media either. But Marley is nearly a decade younger than me. Some of my peers, like Crystal and April, are active online, but her generation is even more so. Her limited presence makes me wonder, is she trying to hide something? I know the main reason I stay offline is to distance myself from the past.

I try typing her name into Google, searching her the old-fashioned way, but nothing comes up. According to Victoria, this is only Marley's second year on campus. She hasn't been there long enough to leave a paper trail, at least not one that's easy to find.

I lean back on the sofa, stretching my neck and staring at the ceiling. It feels like I'm Alice lost in the tunnel. Maybe it would be easier to climb out now before I continue falling. That's what Chaz had suggested in our conversation. *We need proof, not speculation.* If proof that Marley is up to something is this hard to find, it could mean there are no secrets at all.

Still, I can't shake the similarities between the stories and what's happened in the past few days. Slashed tires. A hit-and-run accident. Jessica Wilder's murder, which copied the plot of *The Mistake.* All those incidents have a connection to me through the Mystery Maidens, and the only new addition to my small circle of acquaintances is Marley. What would make her want to go to such lengths to ruin my life, push her to the point of harming others along the way?

Besides, I did my best to spy on the others, and came up with very little. April was hiding something, but it's about her personal life. I have no reason to think she's deceiving me about anything else. Same goes for Victoria and Danielle. They both seemed completely oblivious to my suspicions, and I've known these women for over a year.

Crystal exits her bedroom and makes a beeline for the front door. We've barely seen each other since our argument, and neither of us is good at breaking the ice.

"I'm heading out for dinner," she says. "Would you like to join?"

"I'm busy writing," I say, looking down at my stained pajamas. "Thanks for the invite, though."

She pauses with her hand on the doorknob. "I broke things off with Chase. You were right. There are plenty of men out there, and I don't need to get wrapped up in his family drama."

"Good." This news pleases me, but part of me wonders if Crystal is only telling me what I want to hear.

"Did you say anything to his wife?"

"There's no point. Telling her you're my roommate would only make things awkward for us."

Crystal nods. "Have you thought anymore about the real estate job?"

I look back at my computer. "I appreciate you thinking of me, but it's not the right fit. I want to see how things go with *Night Beat* before I look into starting something new."

When I glance at her face, she appears disappointed. We still haven't addressed the most important part of the argument —what happened ten years ago and how we've reacted in the aftermath. Following our pattern, we won't anytime soon. "If you change your mind about coming out, let me know."

The door slams shut, and I'm momentarily overwhelmed by the silence in the apartment. Isn't it pathetic that I spend every weekend like this? Repeating the same ritual of work, write, sleep, repeat, and it's getting me nowhere.

Tonight, however, instead of writing my own fictional stories, I'm focused on something else entirely. I have a mystery to solve, and Marley Theroux is at the center of it.

Problem is, I still have little information. Nothing from Victoria. Nothing online. I can't glean anything about the type of person Marley is—her favorite spots, her interests. She doesn't even post about writing.

Most aspiring writers believe their craft is a fundamental part of their being. I've always felt that way. You'd think she'd at least mention it on her social media profiles, but there's nothing.

Perhaps what bothers me most about Marley, and what I'm reluctant to admit, is that she's talented. Before I started making the connection between stories and crimes, I was blown away by her initial short story. *Rosebud*. It's better than anything I could have written at her age. Hell, it might be better than anything I've written now.

I type '*Rosebud* by Marley Theroux' into the search bar, but nothing comes up. I was hoping maybe she'd shared an excerpt online before, posted it on a forgotten Reddit account or Tumblr. Just like everything else, my search comes up blank. Marley Theroux, the writer or the person, barely seems to exist.

A little further down the search results, I see something that catches my eye. It's about *Rosebud*. As I look closer, I see it's the first line to Marley's story. Perhaps she posted it after all but used a pen-name to hide her identity.

I click the link, my eyes scanning the page. *Rosebud* is there in its entirety, but the author's name is different. Annabelle Jones. Is that the pen-name Marley uses online?

I rejig my search, this time typing in '*Rosebud* by Annabelle Jones' to see if anything new pops up. The screen fills with different results, each one linking to the same short story. Apparently, it's been published in numerous anthologies, and there are even accompanying study questions for teachers to use in their secondary classrooms.

On the most recent page, I click on the author's name. I'm taken to a short biography, and, more shocking than that, a picture. Annabelle Jones is an acclaimed writer in her fifties.

She's published numerous short story collections and novellas.
I've never heard of her, but she's more successful than I could
ever dream. Still, Annabelle's career achievements aren't what
stings. It's the fact Marley clearly pulled her acclaimed short
story from the internet. She plagiarized the whole thing to
weasel her way into our writing group.

Marley Theroux is a fraud.

TWENTY

I've been a member of the Mystery Maidens for more than a year, and this is the only time I've ever been the first to arrive at a meeting. Ever since finding out Marley plagiarized the *Rosebud* story, I've not been able to stop thinking about confronting her.

Now that I know she's not a writer, it's clear she has ulterior motives for joining the group. I must do more than simply call her a liar, though. If I want the police to take me seriously, I need to highlight the connection between our group's stories and Marley's actions, and I think I've figured out a way to catch her in the act.

"This is new," Danielle says, resting her bag on the table. "I got all excited because I thought I'd be the first one here."

"No work today," I say, dancing my fingers across my closed laptop, finding it hard to control my anticipation. "Nowhere else to be."

My heart is fluttering. Tonight's meeting isn't just about exposing Marley and proving myself right; it's about taking back control of my own story. For years, the black hearts stalker has maintained leverage over me, ruining my relationships and opportunities. And I've let them, acted like some weak-minded character in whatever narrative they created. Now I'm the one deciding what happens next. After tonight, no one will think I'm crazy or paranoid.

Danielle leans back in the booth, crossing both arms over her chest. "Working on anything new?"

"Yes, actually," I say with pride. "I have a new story I can't wait to share."

"A new story?" Victoria says, walking up behind me. She unwraps the thick scarf around her neck. "That's exciting."

I don't plan on sharing my latest addition to *The Mistake*. My purpose for this evening's meeting is to share a story where I can control the aftermath.

"An idea came to me," I say, pulling out my laptop. "I'm thinking this could be the start of a new book."

"How exciting!" Victoria says, eyeing the menu for this evening's specials.

"Maybe it'll inspire me," Danielle adds. "I don't have anything new this week."

We continue our small talk while we order drinks and appetizers. Eventually April arrives, apologizing for being late, and then finally, Marley. It's all I can do to not start reading my hastily written story right away, but I wait; I don't want to appear too eager. So, I listen as Victoria shares an excerpt from her latest book. It's an interesting scene about a police interrogation, but no notable crimes take place. The tension inside my body unwinds, knowing there won't be any other crimes I have to worry about preventing.

"Danielle?" Victoria says, after she finishes. "Anything you want to share?"

"Just an observer tonight," she says. "Becca said she's been working on something new."

"That's right," Victoria says. "Go ahead, Becca. Tell us all about this new story?"

I must calm myself as I begin reading. "I got this idea the other night when I was walking home from work and crossed by Banyon's Bridge."

Banyon's Bridge is in the center of downtown Whitaker. It hovers above the roaring river that snakes its way through the business district. The bridge receives a lot of foot traffic, especially on nights and weekends, because there are many local restaurants and pubs in the area. Really, in all of Whitaker, there's only a few lively spots. Right outside WU, where we currently are, the other half of downtown where Mario's Pizzeria is located, and the strip of establishments near Banyon's Bridge.

"Cute," Victoria says. "I love a story inspired by a local setting."

I begin reading the story I crafted only a few hours ago. It's about a man being pushed over Banyon's Bridge by a sadistic passerby. It was hastily thrown together, and, stealing a page out of Marley's book, I even took some of the plot points from stories online. I have no interest in writing a compelling story. Instead, what I'm doing is setting a trap, hoping whoever is behind this, the most likely culprit being Marley, will arrive at Banyon's Bridge later tonight to take the story into her own hands.

I made sure to make the setting winter and specified that the murder took place on a Monday night at midnight. If someone is trying to use the stories in our group as an inspiration for murder, I've given them the perfect setup. I will no longer be at the mercy of the black hearts or Marley's re-enactments. For once, I'm one step ahead, and that gives me a sense of authority I haven't felt in a long time.

When I finish reading, the rest of the group applauds, as they always do.

"Looks like you were able to shake off your brain fog from last week," Danielle says.

"That was excellent," April agrees.

"I just needed to reflect."

"I told you taking a break is part of the writing process," Victoria says. "And you've come back with a really chilling story."

I angle to face Marley, waiting for her reaction. "What about you? Did you come up with anything new this week?"

"Not this week," she says, plainly. "Still struggling."

"Two weeks in a row?"

"I guess *Rosebud* really took it out of me," she says, her smile falling flat. Just as quickly, her eyes light up again. "Good thing I have the rest of you to inspire me with all your talent. So, who's next?"

"I'll go," April says. "Like Becca, I needed a couple of days to recharge."

She begins reading her story (about another lackluster husband, surprise surprise), and the rest of the group listens. As the minutes pass, I find it harder to follow what she's saying. I'm too busy eyeing the members of the group, especially Marley, replaying my own writing about Banyon's Bridge.

The story is out there. Now it's time for me to put the second part of the plan into action.

TWENTY-ONE

I rush home, knowing that leaves me little time to drop off my belongings and head to Banyon's Bridge. If by chance Marley is keeping tabs on me, I want her to think I've gone home for the night, my usual routine after a meeting.

Once inside my apartment, I open my computer screen, reading through the details of *Murder at the Bridge*. The location is clear, as is the timing. If I can make it to the bridge before midnight, I'll be able to see if Marley—or anyone else from the group—arrives just as in the story. They'll be caught red-handed, unable to deny they're there by mere coincidence. My presence is crucial for another reason: I can't allow an innocent person to get hurt. Whoever shows up, I won't give them the opportunity to bring another story to life.

The Mistake is the next tab over, but I try not to think about it. There's only one story that demands my focus tonight, and it's the one that will help me catch whoever has been making our stories real.

I rush into my bedroom, changing into clothes that are warmer and discreet. Thermal black leggings, a black hoodie and boots. When I look into my bedroom mirror, I see a winter-

ized bank robber staring back at me. Ridiculous, but it's important I don't draw attention to myself. The last thing I need is
Marley noticing me before I see her; she could leave without me
ever knowing she was there.

I slick my hair into a low ponytail and sift through my closet
for a dark hat. Rushing out of my room, I pause when I see
Crystal standing in the living room, a bewildered look on her
face.

"What the hell is this?" she says, her face uncharacteristi-
cally gaunt.

She's pointing at my laptop, the screen fully alight.

"My computer."

"This story," she says, pointing more vehemently. "Did you
write this?"

I move closer to the table, bending down to read the screen.
The Mistake is pulled up.

"Yes," I say, snapping the screen shut.

"It's disgusting," Crystal says, repulsed. "A girl being
murdered on her way home from the bar? All the things you
wrote about the guy that did it!"

"Mystery Maidens is a group for scary stories," I say.
"That's all it is."

"It's not!" she screams back. "I knew you were a crime
writer, but this? It's incredibly dark, Becca."

"What were you doing looking through my computer
anyway?" I spit, trying to match her anger.

"I wasn't," she says, exhaling. "The screen was already
pulled up. I just started reading."

"Well, it wasn't meant for anyone to read."

"You just said you wrote it for your writing group."

"Not *for* them." I'm getting so frustrated, it's difficult to put
sentences together. "I never planned on sharing it with anybody
else."

I sling my computer bag around my shoulder and march for the door.

"Where are you going?"

"I have somewhere I have to be."

"It's almost midnight," she says, skeptically.

"Can't I have plans for a change?"

"Becca, I want to talk about this," she says, her voice serious. "You're my friend and my roommate. That story is disturbing."

"I'm not going to explain my creative process to you," I say, storming into the hall.

Before I slam the door, I hear Crystal calling me. "Becca!"

I don't have time to argue with her. I must get to Banyon's Bridge and deal with Marley.

TWENTY-TWO

I exit the car, cold air biting my cheeks. I burrow into myself, hands in pockets, chin buried into my scarf, as I make the short walk to Banyon's Bridge. This time of night, there aren't many people out. Marley should be easy to spot, but I want to keep my own presence a secret.

A small metal bench rests by the entrance of the bridge. I sit, the cold metal slats making my legs itch. Phone in hand, I try to appear busy, occupied. I want to blend in with the other passing pedestrians. It's ten until midnight. Last call should have been twenty minutes ago, which means most people are crossing the bridge, heading to their cars parked on the busier side of the square.

Water babbles, although it's impossible to see. The overhead lamps barely illuminate the railing and wooden planks below. A couple hurry across the bridge, and I get a whiff of cologne and whiskey as they pass.

Five until midnight.

Now, there's only one person left on the bridge. An elderly man wearing a heavy, but tattered, trench coat. He's likely one of the few homeless people known to frequent the area. There's a shelter a few blocks from here, but I know from experience working at the restaurant, most people will stay out, even in the cold, hoping to get some food or money at the end of the night.

There's a trash can located at the center of the bridge. The man makes his way to it and starts rummaging, confirming my theory that he's homeless. From a story standpoint, I acknowledge he'd be the perfect victim. There's no one around. It could be days before someone reports the man missing, if they ever do. If Marley, or anyone, is looking for a nameless victim, he would be it. In this moment, it hits me: this isn't fiction. Maybe it's the unforgiving cold or the heartbreaking image of a man sorting through garbage on a November night that makes me realize. This is real. I've set this entire situation up to catch a killer in the act, not fully comprehending I'd be placing another innocent person in harm's way. I can't have another person's blood on my hands. Jessica Wilder's death is already too much.

My instincts tell me to warn the man, but what exactly would I say? *I wrote a story and now I'm afraid one of the members of my writing group will come here to kill you.* It's ridiculous, and yet my heartbeat races at the idea I've put this man, and myself, in danger.

In the distance, church bells from the local cathedral ring, the beautiful melody injecting some life into the cold, barren darkness.

It's midnight.

The man, still the only person on the bridge, doesn't raise his eyes from the trash can.

Just then, I hear footsteps. I look behind me, back to where my car is parked, but I see no one. The old cobblestone streets make the sound deceptive, and it's difficult for me to tell where they're coming from.

On the other side of the bridge, a person comes into view, a featureless, dark shadow moving in my direction. My heart starts beating faster as I watch. The person mounts the bridge, moving closer to the unsuspecting man.

I stare at them. Is it a man? A woman? Marley. Whoever it is, they walk with intention, head low, hands deep inside the pockets of his or her dark coat. When I first wrote the story, it was nothing more than bait, a way to lure Marley out of hiding. Now, I wonder how easy it would be for fiction to shift over into reality. How easy would it be for Marley to attack this poor man and toss his body into the waters below? Maybe my presence will steer her away? Or maybe she won't care at all.

The person is only a few steps away from the homeless man, his arm swallowed by the trash can as he digs inside. I stand quickly, my body urging me to intervene. Sweat builds between my skin and clothes, my lungs ache as I take in a sharp inhale of frigid air. I run over to the bridge, hoping I can do something, anything to stop what will happen next.

The person stops just behind the homeless man. If he or she sees me, there is no reaction. All their attention is on the man on the bridge, the next victim.

I break into a run, am about to call out, when I see the shadowy figure place a hand on the homeless man's shoulder.

He turns.

The person reaches into one of their pockets and pulls something out. It gleams against the overhead light illuminating the bridge. It's a handful of coins. Not much, but enough to buy something from the vending machines across the way.

In an instant, everything slows. My pulse, my breathing, my thoughts. I lean over, steadying my hands on my knees, like a person who has just finished running a marathon. Relief develops into exhaustion as I realize I wasn't just about to witness a murder. There is no crime. No Marley. Only a person walking home in the cold, offering money to a beggar in need.

I'm still bent over, taking deep breaths, when the stranger walks past me.

"Everything okay?" the person asks. Only steps away now, so I'm able to make out their face. It's an older woman, mid-fifties. A stranger.

I'm too stunned to answer, so I only nod. She passes me, and I look ahead at the homeless man, who is gathering his things and moving across the bridge.

Standing upright, I take in my surroundings. Another typical, sleepy weekday night. Bars are closed, which leaves no one on the streets, or the bridge, but me. I check the time. Five after midnight. My plan—an utterly foolish and absurd plan, I realize now—didn't work. Marley isn't going to be lured out of hiding so easily. Or perhaps, as Chaz insisted, there's no crime to uncover at all, only a series of coincidences. If that's the case, maybe I am going a bit mad, determined to see only what I want to see.

I walk over to the area where the homeless man was standing, peering over the edge to look at the waters below. I hear the roaring of the river and am immediately thankful I was wrong. There will be no bloodshed here tonight.

I raise my head, and that's when I see it.

Attached to the lamppost is an envelope, speckled with drops of river water and condensation. A black heart is drawn on the front.

Icy fear shoots through me as I reach out to grab the envelope, my eyes darting from one end of the bridge to the other, searching. Still, there's no one here. Only me and this message left behind.

I tear open the envelope.

The first sheet of paper is handwritten, a single line on the page: *Becca, you're better than this.*

The second sheet of paper isn't a message, but an old newspaper article. A copy of one, at least:

CIVIL SUIT DROPPED AGAINST TWO CO-EDS

A civil suit was dropped this week against the two college students accused of endangering their friend. The suit was brought on by Charles and Lena Williams, parents of the murdered Whitaker University student, Layla Williams.

Last winter, Williams' case horrified locals when her body was found in a drainage ditch on campus, not far from the local bar where she was last seen. After a swift investigation, Michael Massey was arrested and charged with her murder. Massey has a court date later this spring.

The Williams made headlines again when they decided to go after Layla's roommates in court, Becca Walsh and Crystal Meyers.

"We have to hold people accountable," Lena Williams told reporters at the time. "Michael Massey might have taken my daughter's life, but he never would have had the opportunity if she'd not been abandoned by her friends."

The decision of the Williams family to bring charges against the girls was controversial, with many in the community rallying behind the grieving parents, while others defended the young girls. When asked to comment on the dropped case, the Williams family declined.

Dallas Layman, who represented the girls in the civil suit, told reporters, "We ask for consideration and kindness for the Williams family during this difficult time. The man who murdered Layla is behind bars, and it's important we remember that. He is the only person to blame for this tragedy."

By the time I finish reading the article, my hands are shaking. I'm suddenly so disoriented and woozy, there's the very real possibility I could faint and topple into the icy waters below.

TWENTY-THREE

I met Layla and Crystal on the same day. We were gathered for freshman orientation in the lobby of the dorm building we'd soon call home. None of us roomed together back then; we'd each been assigned to bunk up with other random girls. Yet, the three of us somehow locked eyes, found ourselves giggling in unison at the RA's archaic rules and corny jokes.

"I'm Layla," she said, her fingers dancing as she waved. She had a true bohemian whimsy about her, from the rows upon rows of friendship bracelets on her wrists to the small braids tangled throughout her long brown hair. When she smiled, the room around her grew brighter, inviting everyone in.

That's the cliché, isn't? That every murder victim somehow lit up a room. But with Layla, it was true. I can picture that first meeting all these years later, and I still feel warm inside.

The three of us clicked immediately, and soon became inseparable. We were located on the same floor, thankfully, and spent that first year exploring everything together. The Dos and Don'ts of campus parties. The best coffee shops to visit in between classes. We had a running list of professors to avoid and which ones to impress. Not once did I feel that pang of loneliness my other high school friends used to talk about, the homesickness that plagued them in those first few months away. And it was all because of Crystal and Layla.

That and *Friends*. Whenever we started to feel low, it was our tradition to binge-watch the show together. It all reminded us of home and our families in different ways. Layla was the Phoebe of our group, free-spirited and kind-hearted. Crystal, of course, was the Rachel. Chic and adorable, with just a hint of selfishness. That made me the Monica. Dedicated, determined, reliable.

Layla and I were both Whitaker implants, which bonded us further. Crystal was born and raised here, but for us, our every experience was new, different from the sleepy towns where we grew up. Rarely did we talk about our childhoods; we found it more meaningful to build new lives and identities for ourselves on campus. For some reason, I always thought Layla had a bad home life. She'd come back from weekend visits shaken, but she'd never want to talk about what happened. Sometimes seeing people from the past can be uncomfortable—I certainly felt that way every time I visited my mother—which made my friendships on campus even more important.

With each passing year, our bond grew. By the time we'd entered our junior year, the three of us decided to rent a house together on Magnolia Avenue, the perfect location between campus and the lively downtown. Layla and I were never big drinkers, were more often witnesses to Crystal's over-the-top antics. Over time, I think that's how Layla and I became even closer; while Crystal was busy being the center of attention, we clung to each other.

Over a decade has passed since the night she died, and yet it still haunts me, looms over me, my forever shadow in the dark.

Things were never meant to unravel the way they did. It was supposed to be a typical Thursday night. Ordinary. Crystal, Layla and I were at Twisted Timmy's Lounge for their infa-

mous ladies' night. We were supposed to drink and dance and
shoot pool. We were supposed to stumble home and submit to
sleep. At worst, we might snooze through our alarms and be late
for class.

But nothing about that night ended up being ordinary, nor
has any other part of my life been ever since.

The three of us sat at the bar enjoying discounted bottled
beer and a platter of greasy cheese curds. It was nearing the end
of the fall semester, and what we needed more than anything
was to blow off some steam, as we had so many nights before.

A young man took the corner seat at the bar, the one beside
Layla. I don't think any of us noticed him at first; we were so lost
in our own conversation. Then, he laughed at something one of
us—probably   Crystal—said.   Slowly,   he   entered   the
conversation.

"I'm Mike," he said, his eyes smiling. He held out his hand
to shake Layla's, and I could feel the energy between them like
static electricity in the air. Something else, too. Like I'd met him
before, but neither his name or face rang any immediate alarms.

Layla never paid boys much attention, had far bigger interests, but something about Michael, something about *him*,
captured her attention that night. Anyone nearby could tell.

"Want to hit the dance floor?" Crystal asked, her eyes
speaking a secret language. She knew I was nowhere near drunk
enough to enjoy dancing, but she clearly wanted to give the two
some privacy.

"He's cute, right?" I said to Crystal, cutting my eyes back to
the couple at the bar.

"Totally," Crystal said, looking over my shoulder. "Good for
her."

In between songs, I'd glance back at Layla. She looked so
incredibly happy. Blushing cheeks. Hair tossing with each full-
bellied laugh. Mike appeared gentle, the way he'd lean into her
without getting too close. Layla was never shy about telling guys

when they were making her uncomfortable. That night, she appeared more relaxed than I'd seen her in months.

As the night carried on, I thought about them less and less. Crystal ordered more drinks, eventually started downing my shots when I confessed to reaching my limit. Soon, my concern became her. She was getting sloppy, losing her balance and bumping into strangers.

It became clear we needed to call it a night. As I made the march back to the bar, it suddenly hit me where I'd met Mike before.

It was *him*, from the frat party. The one who'd put something in my drink. The one who'd tried to assault me, before other people walked in the room and stopped it. At least, I *thought* it was him. Even then, the night came back in flashes and spurts, so I couldn't be sure. My emotions still felt raw, fear over what could have happened, relief that nothing did. That experience had scarred me in a way I hadn't fully processed. Even Crystal and Layla didn't know what almost happened to me, so I questioned whether it was the same Mike from the party, or my own mind playing tricks on me.

"Water, please," I shouted to the bartender when I reached the bar, looking over at where I'd left Layla.

I locked eyes with her then. Mike had stepped away for a moment. "We're going to have to get out of here," I said. "Crystal is getting out of hand."

"You two go ahead," she said.

My eyes landed on the empty seat beside her, where Mike had been sitting. It was uncharacteristic for Layla to stay behind without us, and the paranoia inside of me shrieked louder. *Tell her.* "Are you sure you're okay?"

"I'm having a great time." She smiled. "Mike's a doll."

From behind me, Crystal's voice screeched out, "Two more shots!"

I shook my head, motioning for the bartender to ignore her. I looked back at Layla, a beating in my head starting to pulsate.

"Look, I don't know how to say this, but that guy gives me the creeps," I said, plainly. "I think you should come home with us."

Layla laughed. "What are you going on about? We're only talking."

"I know but..." My words trailed away, overcome with thoughts of that night at the frat house. What almost happened. There wasn't enough time to tell Layla about it now, and was I even sure it was the same guy? I'd been drugged. What were the odds—

"You better get her home," Layla said. I followed her stare across the room and saw Crystal trying to dance, however, she was falling all over herself instead. Just then, Mike emerged from the bathroom. My pulse quickened.

"Look, Mike is dangerous. I know it." My voice was urgent. "Please, just come home with us."

"Don't be ridiculous." Layla shook her head, like I'd just told a joke she didn't quite understand. "Can't you just let me have fun this once? It's always about Crystal or you."

"Or me?"

"Yes! I follow you two anywhere you want to go." Her voice was different than I'd ever heard before. Defiant and bitter. "For once, I'd just like the night to be about me and what I want."

This unspoken resentment between us was something she'd never shared before, but I pushed it out of my mind. She needed to listen to me. "Layla, I'm only trying to protect you."

"I don't need your protection!" She lowered her voice as Mike returned, sat beside her. He didn't so much as give me a second glance. "I'll be fine, Becca. You don't need to worry."

Just then, the bartender slammed a glass of water in front of me. I took it, looking over my shoulder at a hunched over Crystal. Turning, I stared at Mike one more time. Trying to be sure.

He seemed harmless, normal... just like the guy from the frat house. But were they the same? Surely, he would have remembered me, and yet Mike gave me no attention whatsoever. Crystal let out another drunken yelp, and, in that moment, I decided I was wrong. I was letting my traumatized memories intermix with the chaos of the night. My close call at the frat house didn't mean everyone else was in danger. If Layla wanted to continue the night, it wasn't my responsibility to stop her.

"I'll text you." Before walking away, I said, "Be careful. Please."

"I will." She waved, her fingers dancing like they did on the first day we met, giving me one last glimpse of the black heart tattoo on her wrist.

It took another ten minutes to get Crystal on her feet and out the door. Before we started the short walk back to our apartment, I looked back, peering through the open patio to the inside of the bar. Mike was beside Layla, the two of them laughing.

Crystal started puking the moment we arrived at the apartment, and I spent what felt like hours nursing her hangover. I didn't mind staying awake, however. I wanted to make sure Layla arrived home okay. Once I got Crystal to bed, I texted Layla, as promised, to tell her we'd arrived safely, then I chugged some water myself and waited. When I finally drifted off to sleep, it must have been after three o'clock.

When I woke up that next morning, my first thought was Layla. I hadn't meant to fall asleep, and I never heard her come in. Mike's face flashed through my mind, and I felt my stomach start to turn. What if I'd been wrong and I'd left her alone with my attacker? That's when I noticed Layla's closed bedroom door. I was almost positive it had been open the night before, so I assumed she'd arrived home safely, and my nerves settled.

My romantic poetry class was a bore, as was the mythological literature that followed. Normally, I felt at least a twinge of inspiration from the material we were studying, but that day, probably because of the hangover, my brain operated in a fog. It wasn't until I stopped at a nearby restaurant for lunch that something finally shook me out of my haze.

"Did you hear a body was found on campus last night?"

The question wasn't directed to me, was spoken in conversation between students I'd never even met. At first, I wondered if they were even talking about our campus; the possibility of someone dying seemed outrageous. Could it be a medical emergency? Had someone overdosed?

"They're saying it's murder," said the second student.

That word fully captured my attention, a strange queasiness hijacking my stomach. *Murder.* It was bizarre and salacious and shamefully entertaining.

I typed out a message to Crystal and Layla, but only the former replied.

You. Are. Kidding. Me, she responded. I could hear the words coming out of Crystal's mouth, imagined her thumbs moving rapidly against her keyboard, scouring social media for more information.

As I walked in the direction of my third class—creative prose, my favorite—I heard other people whispering about it, too. It was a girl, they said. Found in a ditch. One person said she was strangled. Another said she was hit over the head. A landscaper had found her early that morning. Someone's roommate's boyfriend caught a glimpse of the body.

My class was nearly over before I registered that Layla had never texted me back. She wasn't as big on gossip as Crystal, but a murder on campus warranted even the tamest of people to show some interest. I remembered she had a test that morning, but wasn't that class finished already? By now, she should be headed back to the apartment. Surely, she'd seen my text, had heard the rumors.

A strange shudder racked my body—was I even sure Layla

had returned home? Sure, her bedroom door was closed, but that could have happened during last night's drunken confusion. This morning, I'd never laid eyes on her, and she wasn't responding to my messages. She could have stayed over at Mike's, I thought. Still, why hadn't she replied to my texts? By the time class ended, I had sorted through a half-dozen what-ifs, and just as quickly shot each possibility down.

I was almost at the apartment when I finally received a text. From Crystal, not Layla.

Come home now. It's important.

Somehow, I already knew. I willed myself not to scroll social media, not to type her name, as though avoiding the news would keep it from coming true. My horrible suspicions were confirmed when I walked inside the apartment and saw Crystal's tear-stained face.

Apparently, Layla and Mike had stayed at Twisted Timmy's until near closing. A fight had broken out at the bar, and they disappeared sometime during the scuffle. A few pedestrians came forward and said they remembered seeing the couple walking in the direction of on-campus housing.

What happened next remained a mystery, but it was Layla's body that was found in that drainage ditch beside campus, her vibrant life cut short. No one had seen what happened, no nearby security cameras captured the altercation. Crystal and I gave our statements to the police, described Mike to the best of our ability. It didn't take long for officers to track him down, and when they told us about his history—two dropped sexual assault allegations—I think we all knew what happened.

I knew, because it had almost happened to me. It was the same Mike from the fraternity party, and if I'd trusted my instincts, he never would have been left alone with Layla.

"At least he didn't get the best of her," Crystal said, some days later, our first time speaking to each other after the news broke.

"He murdered her!"

"He didn't *assault* her because she fought back," she said, as though death were some sort of consolation prize. "That's probably why he killed her."

We were all relieved to hear there was no sexual assault, and the police agreed with the theory that because Layla had fought back, Mike's violence escalated, resulting in her death. At first, he proclaimed his innocence, but once the other two women came forward again with their allegations, his legal team urged him to take a deal. Michael Massey was sentenced to over forty years in prison, sparing Layla's parents the heartbreaking details that would have come out in a trial.

Layla's murderer had received punishment, but that didn't ease the guilt Crystal and I felt. We had been with her that night, had been with her almost every night since we were freshmen. If it hadn't been for us leaving her behind, Mike would never have had the opportunity to attack her.

I'm having a great time.

My last conversation with Layla haunted me, as did every detail of that night.

Crystal and I weren't the only ones struggling with blame—Layla's parents believed we were just as culpable in their daughter's death. They explained to every news reporter that would listen that friends abandoning friends was just as unethical as what Mike had tried to do, even criminal. They filed the civil suit against us soon after. Even though the suit was dropped—legally, we hadn't done anything wrong, only returned home after a night of drinking—I felt the heavy weight of my guilt, as did Crystal, although we dealt with it in different ways.

Crystal busied herself with socials and activities and clubs, trying to involve herself with the campus community and somehow erase her reputation as the girl who'd left her friend behind. She cultivated a new image for herself, one even shinier and more spectacular than the one before.

I pulled away entirely. I dropped out of college, stopped thinking about my future altogether. Writing was still important to me, but it took on a different role in my life. It was no longer an activity that I enjoyed but something I needed to do, a way to separate my mind from the past and the present.

To separate myself from Layla, and the role I played in her death.

Each day became a task of pulling myself further and further away from that night, diving into a world of make-believe, into a mundane present.

Until the other night when, fueled by lack of sleep and a vicious night terror, I revisited Layla's story.

And then I shared it with the world.

TWENTY-FOUR

All I want is to get away from Banyon's Bridge. My chest wheezes with each harsh inhale, my boots tapping against the gray cobblestones. I'm alone, seemingly, but I can't shake the feeling that I've been duped. Whoever left the envelope with the black heart on it is one step ahead of me, could still be here, watching my stunned reaction.

Layla isn't something I talk about. Ever. Not even with Crystal, the one person in my life who experienced the brutal ordeal alongside me.

The most notorious true crime stories have an aura of mystery surrounding the cases. The straightforward murders—girl meets boy in a bar, he attacks her and is swiftly arrested—are easily forgotten. The name Layla Williams still lingers in some true crime circles, but not widely, because of its quick resolution. This article was left strategically, and whoever left it not only knows my past, but is threatening me with it.

Thankfully, my connection to the crime seems to have been forgotten, except, most notably, by whoever has been sending me black hearts for the past ten years. The implication behind the symbol is clear. My stalker blames me for Layla's death, tries reminding me of it at every major turn in my life, as though I could ever forget. They've thrown a series of slurs at me in the past decade—*Fraud, Abandoner, Cheat.* And what hurts the most is that the black hearts stalker is right. Layla's death was always my fault.

I slam the car door shut and crank the engine, holding my frigid fingers in front of the heating unit, waiting for warm air. I believe I know who left the message behind on the bridge, the same person I was following in the first place, the culprit I've been hoping to catch in my carefully laid trap.

Marley.

I realize now what's bothered me about her since our first meeting. She reminds me of Layla. Their flowy maxi skirts and layered accessories. The way both their hair is a tangled mess of curls and bohemian braids. Even the small tattoos—a black sparrow and a black heart. When I first saw Marley, standing beside my table at McCallie's Pub, it was like seeing a ghost, a long-lost friend I'd expected to never see again. Marley didn't belong, just like Layla has never belonged in the avoidable tragedy that took her life.

Could it be yet another coincidence? Two college students, a decade apart, with similar styles. If Marley left the article and the black heart at the bridge, it means she knows about my past. Her intentions might be darker. Maybe she's purposely dressing herself like my deceased best friend, another way for her to get under my skin.

Once my fingers are warm, I wrap them around the steering wheel and reverse onto the street. It's foolish to confront a could-be killer at all, let alone after midnight. Yet, anger overrides my logic as I drive in the direction of Marley's apartment.

There's ample street parking across from her building. I remain inside the car, peering out the window at the old-world apartment complex. Ivy climbs the dark redbrick, a wrought-iron fire escape connected to each floor. That's where I see her.

Marley is alone in the dark, lounging in a cushioned seat at the corner of the fire escape. The dangling fairy lights wrapped around the railing illuminate her silhouette.

It's awfully late and too cold to be sitting outside alone. She's in college, I remind myself. Midnight is when things typically get going around that age. Yet Marley isn't at some kegger or pub, she's sitting alone in the darkness. Why? Perhaps she just recently returned home from Banyon's Bridge.

In the passenger seat, the photograph of Layla stares up at me. The article used the same one that all the papers did, an old senior portrait. There were more recent ones, but I suspect publications chose this specific picture for a reason. Her clear blue eyes speak to her youthful innocence, her wide smile reminds people, like me right now, how cruelly she was taken from the world.

I replay that last night we had together, her last night on earth, over and over again. What I said to her during that conversation haunts me, but I'm more bothered by what I didn't say. If only I'd been more assertive when I told her about what Mike did to me, or what he tried to do, maybe she wouldn't have stayed behind. I'd been so afraid to admit what happened, even to myself, that I let my uncertainty overthrow what was right, and Layla paid for my mistake with her life.

Long-buried regret rumbles in my chest as I open the car door and meet the cold night air. The article clenched in my fist, I cross the street, standing directly below Marley's balcony, the tie-dye tapestries ruffling in the cold night breeze.

"I know you're up there," I shout, an angry Romeo calling out to a twisted Juliet. Several seconds pass before Marley approaches the railing. Shadows obscure her features, but it's clearly her peering down into the near-empty street.

"Becca?" Marley is wearing dark loungewear, her hair atop her head in a messy bun. A lit cigarette is pinched between her fingers.

"Are we going to talk about this?" I raise the article and shake my fist at her. My voice is louder this time, fully conveying my anger. The potential someone might hear me doesn't register. In fact, I welcome witnesses. Strength in numbers and all.

Marley raises the cigarette to her lips and inhales. "What is that? I have no idea what you're talking about."

"I know it was you," I say, my anger overriding that small, sane voice inside that insists I'm in over my head. "I know everything was you. I wrote that story to draw you out to Banyon's Bridge, but you figured me out."

Marley puts the cigarette out on the iron railing, small sparks sprinkling down. "Becca, I have no idea what you're talking about. If you want to come inside—"

"Do you really think I'm that stupid?" I scoff. "I'm not entering the apartment of a murderer."

That last word comes out in a thud, echoing down the quiet streets. Marley's grip on the railing tightens.

"Fine. I'll come to you. There's a diner down the block. I can meet you there in ten minutes," she pauses, "and we'll talk."

I stare up, saying nothing. I thought it would be harder to get her to cooperate. I anticipated more back and forth, more yelling. Denial. Maybe Marley is more strategic than I gave her credit for. If she is a narcissistic murderer, the last thing she needs is her neighbors to overhear the accusation. And the diner provides more cover and safety for me, even at this desolate time of night.

Tightening my coat around me, I hurry down the block. I assume she's talking about the Red Buzzer; it's the only all-night establishment around here. I need to get there before her and give myself plenty of time to think about what I want to say. My anger craved a confrontation, but now I need to be smart. This might be my only chance to prove my suspicions, and I can't mess it up.

Surprisingly, the diner is packed. I suppose that's to be expected since it's so close to a college campus. There's a free booth by the far window. I snag it, my fingers shaking as I flatten the envelope and article on the table. The waitress arrives and I order a coffee, just as I see Marley, a heavy coat over her comfortable clothes, enter the building.

"Want to tell me what's going on?" She sits across from me, her hands in her pockets. There's a look of annoyance on her face, or maybe it's amusement and she's gaining some kind of sick pleasure from watching me squirm.

"You know what's going on," I say with confidence.

"I can assure you that I don't." She smiles when the waitress returns to our table and orders a coffee. Her voice is laid-back and easy, like she doesn't have a care in the world. Once the waitress walks away, she leans against the backrest and crosses her arms over her chest. Those light-gray eyes narrow. "Care to tell me why you were screaming outside of my apartment in the middle of the night?"

I hold up the article. She leans closer, her eyes scanning it. She shakes her head.

"What is that?"

"It's the message you left for me at the bridge," I say, growing more irritated by the second.

"What bridge?" She raises her hands at this, flapping them in the air. "Becca, I'm completely lost here."

"Banyon's Bridge. The one in my story," I say with conviction. The waitress returns to deliver Marley's coffee, and I realize how loud my voice is getting, how irrational I must appear. I clear my throat and begin again. "The story I shared tonight was about a man that was murdered on a bridge, remember?"

"Vaguely."

I ignore the dig. "I wrote it because I know what you've been doing."

"And what is that exactly?" She raises the mug to her lips, waiting.

"You've been copying the stories we write about in group. First it was the car with the slashed tires. And then the hit-and-run on my street." I pause, lowering my tone an octave more, fully aware of how paranoid I sound. "And then there was the woman murdered outside the pub."

Marley's beautiful gray eyes go wide. She carefully puts her coffee mug on the table, laces her fingers together and leans forward.

"I'm sorry. Are you accusing me of murder?"

"I am," I say, determined. Here, in this setting, with the article about Layla beside me, it no longer seems ridiculous. I look at Marley, and I see someone willing to go to extreme lengths, if for no other reason than her own entertainment. Leaving the article was her way of toying with me, my punishment for catching onto her games, but by calling her out, I'm making it clear the match isn't over yet.

"I'm listening," she says, never shifting her eyes away from me.

"I started noticing the connection last week. I wrote the story about a man being murdered at the bridge because I wanted to lure you there and confront you before anything happened. I wanted to catch you."

Marley raises her eyebrows. "You were willing to put an innocent man at risk to prove you were right? That's interesting."

"Yeah, well it didn't work, did it?" I raise the article again. "Somehow, you figured out what I was doing and left this behind to punish me."

She casts her eyes over it, reading, a quizzical look on her face.

"Oh my," she says. "You're the Becca in this article, aren't you?"

My teeth grind against each other. "You know that I am."

Marley raises her hand in the air, calling over the waitress for a fourth time.

"I think I'd like to order the stuffed French toast with a side of grits," she tells her. "Looks like we're going to be here a while. Want anything, Becca?"

I remain silent. She must be more psychotic than I thought. I've just accused her of murder, and she's rewarding herself with food.

"I've already gone to the police, you know." I must keep control of the conversation, make Marley understand her little mind games aren't affecting me.

"You did?" She feigns surprise. "Let me guess, they laughed you off."

I lock my jaw, fighting not to show a reaction.

"It doesn't matter," I say. "I know you're behind this. Even if people don't believe me now, it won't be hard to find proof. Everyone makes mistakes."

"That they do." She takes a packet of sugar and adds it to her coffee. "Quick question, why have you settled on me?"

"Excuse me?"

"Well, your theory is that someone in the Mystery Maidens is using our stories as inspiration to go out and commit crimes," she says. "Why me?"

"I've been a member of the group for over a year, and nothing like this has ever happened before. Not until two weeks ago, after you joined."

"I see. That certainly makes sense."

The playful quality of her voice angers me. She's getting too much enjoyment from this confrontation.

"You're not even a real writer," I say. "I know that *Rosebud* was plagiarized."

Marley snorts. "My, my. You have done your research."

"I've just accused you of murder and you're acting like this is some kind of game," I say. "Don't you have anything to say for yourself?"

Marley exhales, leaning harder onto the table, the skin of her elbows flattening against the Formica surface.

"I hate to tell you this, Becca, but you have the wrong person." She pauses. "The good news, however, is that I believe everything you're saying."

My head drops, trying to unravel the riddle she's just presented to me. "What?"

"I believe you that there's a murderer in the Mystery Maidens," she says. "But it isn't me."

"What do you mean, it isn't you?"

"Everything you've been saying makes sense. All your research lines up. Granted, I didn't know about the slashed tires and the hit-and-run. Those events seem to be targeted at you. But when it comes to the girl that was murdered last week, I believe you."

I squint my eyes closed, bright circles dancing across my eyelids. I'm so exhausted and distracted, I'm having trouble following what Marley's saying. Out of all the reactions I predicted, this wasn't one of them.

"You believe me?"

"Yes. Someone in the writing group is committing murders, it just isn't me," she says. "And now, I suspect it isn't you."

I'm still struggling to follow when the waitress returns with Marley's food. The smells hijack my senses, add to my wavering sense of displacement.

Marley begins cutting into her meal with a fork. "Let me get a couple bites in, and I'll explain," she says. "I'd reconsider ordering if I were you. Like I said, we could be here a while."

TWENTY-FIVE

A dollop of whipped cream sits on Marley's upper lip. She takes several more bites of the sugary meal before speaking.

"I'll give it to you, I'm impressed," she says. "I mean, given how crazy everything you just said sounds, I can't believe there's two of us that believe it."

"What are you talking about?"

"That one of the women in your group is a murderer."

"I don't think it's one of the women in the group," I say, pointedly. "I think it's you."

"That's where you're wrong." She points her finger at me. "I can see why you think that, though. In your narrative, all these weird happenings didn't begin until I'd joined. It makes sense you'd be suspicious of the newest member, but your timeline is off."

"What timeline?"

"The girl who was murdered last week in an eerily similar way as the girl in the story you shared," she says. "That wasn't the first murder."

I blink rapidly, struggling to follow along.

"You're saying there's been another one?"

"Two, by my count," she says. "Which makes the woman found in the ditch the third victim."

"You joined the group two weeks ago," I say. "I didn't notice any murders similar to the ones in our stories until then."

"That's because they happened more than a year ago." Marley picks her phone out of her coat pocket and taps on the screen. She lays the device flat on the table, and points. "Right here. A Whitaker University student was found bludgeoned. He was killed in almost the exact same way as a story that, I believe, Danielle wrote. *Flower Man* is the name of it, I think."

She swipes a few times, pulling up a second article. "Here's the second murder. Another man died unexpectedly. This time, the death was just like a story April wrote, but I forget the name. All her stories sound the same to me after a while."

I glance at the article, searching for details and facts.

"I don't understand. Why do you think these murders are connected to the stories from group?"

Marley leans back, crossing her arms again. "I know about the stories because Victoria shared them with our creative writing class. I couldn't help noticing the similarities between them and the actual deaths on campus."

"Anyone could have died that way," I say. "There's no connection to the group."

"I'm guessing that's exactly what the police said to you when you told them about your Layla story."

My cheeks flush. I never got a chance to speak with Chaz after Jessica Wilder's death. He had already treated me like I was foolish before that. "No, that death was targeted. I'm convinced."

"And I'm convinced about these other two. See, you're right. I'm not a writer. I'm only taking that stupid creative writing class because I need a few more English electives for my major. And you caught me on that *Rosebud* story, too."

"Okay." By the restaurant's entrance, two drunken college students stumble, knocking into the table closest to them. The scene distracts me, and I shake my head, trying to refocus on what Marley has to say. "I don't understand. Why pull a fake story off the internet and join our group in the first place?"

"The stories I mentioned that were related to the first two deaths? Victoria used them in our creative writing class. She often pulls random stories and brings them in for us to critique. Trust me, everything you're feeling right now, questioning whether or not you're crazy for thinking there could be a connection—that's how I felt, too. I mean, what were the odds that two stories almost exactly mirrored the deaths of two locals?

"At first, I thought my teacher was a raging psychopath. That these were stories she'd written about crimes she'd committed." She pauses, letting the idea sink in. "See? Crazy, right? Then Victoria admitted she'd pulled those stories, and several others, from her own writing group."

I'm in shock, not only about what Marley is saying, but over the fact Victoria would use our group's stories in her writing class. It feels like a violation, knowing how hard we've worked on our craft to share with a select few. I was convinced the murderer had to be in our group because we were the only ones with access. The list of potential suspects just got much longer.

"Anyway," Marley continues. "That's when I knew even if she wasn't involved, it was definitely someone in the Mystery Maidens."

When she says the group name, there's a sing-song quality to her voice, like she's talking about Superman or the Boogeyman. As closely as I'm watching her, Marley is studying me, trying to gauge whether I follow her train of thought.

"So, you joined the Mystery Maidens because you thought one of us was a killer?"

"Exactly." She leans against the backrest, satisfied. "I

wanted to learn a little bit more about you, and since I'm a shitty writer myself, I had to pull a story off the internet to get in. I had to make Victoria think I had some talent if I wanted an invitation."

"And she hasn't figured out that all your stories are copies?"

"I know, right? I figured she'd flunk me for submitting a fake story in class. I guess between being a college professor, mystery author and potential serial killer, she doesn't have much time for weeding out cheating students."

"You can't actually think Victoria is a killer."

"You thought *I* was," she says, pointedly. "Again, I don't know if it's Victoria. I think it could be any of you. Although, I'm less suspicious of you now, considering you put this whole thing together. You'd have to be a special type of twisted to put this much effort into finding a killer if it was you the whole time."

"It's not me." I look down at the table, the bizarre nature of our conversation becoming overwhelming. "But I don't see it being any of them, either. I was convinced it was you because everything happened right after you joined the group."

"I get it. It's much more unsettling to admit that someone you're close to could be a killer. In most cases, that's how it ends up."

The drunk people at the front of the restaurant are getting louder. I wish I could leave, but there's still more information I need to get, and I still don't know if I can trust Marley, not enough to venture out in the night streets with her.

"I get you made a connection, but how?"

"I already admitted I'm not a writer. Hell, I don't even read unless it's required for school. Literature just doesn't do it for me. It's the true stories I find the most interesting. I'm a true crime junkie. Podcasts, YouTube channels, Reddit threads. Anytime there's a local crime, I read all about it. It wasn't hard for me to compare the similarities between the deaths and the short stories. And it didn't take long for me to figure out this is a story that could sell."

"So, you're a journalist?"

"Psych major. I've always wanted to understand the human mind, the good parts and the bad. But I'm not going to walk away from a potential goldmine. I'm pulling all my research together to create my own podcast."

"You're hoping to make money off all this?"

"Don't make it sound so greedy," she says. "You mean to tell me it doesn't sound fascinating? The idea of a serial killer targeting students, mirroring their crimes after fictional stories. Listeners will eat it up."

There's definitely more to Marley than is visible on the surface. I got that right all along. She lied about herself and her credentials to infiltrate the group, but not because she was a murderer, rather because she wants to capitalize off the world's fascination with crime.

I watch her carefully. Marley gives off paradoxical vibes, making it hard to completely trust her. An open book with a few pages ripped out. I want to believe she's telling the truth, but I can't shake the instinct there's more she isn't telling me. I need to keep at least some information to myself, because having Marley know that someone has been tailing me for the past decade gives her more power than I can trust her with.

"The first murder, the one where the guy was bludgeoned. It happened two years ago."

"I know." She averts her eyes, fiddling with a loose thread on her jacket sleeve. "Certain cases stick with you. The murder was almost identical to what happened in the story, even down to where the body was found. My theory is whoever killed those men found their inspiration in the stories that were shared, which makes the killer a member of your group."

I just stare at her, my mind not willing yet to make that connection if the murderer is not Marley.

"You said you noticed a link between the stories and the crimes after I joined," Marley says. "What was the first thing you noticed?"

I backtrack, telling Marley everything, beginning with the slashed tires and the hit-and-run, and ending with the eerie similarities between the Layla story and the most recent death. She listens intently, dropping her eyes to the news article on the table between us.

"This Layla girl. It's not a story you made up. What happened to her was real."

For so long, I've used my writing to cope with my trauma, but now the lines between fiction and real life are blurring. The idea of Layla's case being pulled into Marley's web turns my stomach, but there's not much I can do to back out now. I readily told her about everything. Except the black hearts. Shame, hot and twisted, riles inside, like a serpent fighting to get out. I should have known better than to use Layla's tragedy in a story. She deserved more than that.

"We were best friends. College roommates," I explain. "What happened to her was a decade ago. I've been struggling to come up with new story ideas, ever since I finished writing *Night Beat*. I only wrote about what happened because I couldn't stop thinking about it."

Marley reaches her arm across the table, resting her hand on mine. I pull away.

"A lot of writers do that, you know. Use personal trauma. It can be cathartic really," she says, her voice gentle and soothing. "You don't have to feel guilty for that."

"Whoever left this article at the bridge is judging me for it," I say. "This is their way of letting me know they're on to me just like I'm on to them."

"That's what intrigues me. What happened tonight proves we're both right. Someone in the group is using stories as an inspiration to commit crimes, and we need to work together to find out which one it is."

"And how are we going to do that?"

Marley leans forward again. "We need to go back to the police."

"I already tried that."

"I'll go with you this time. We'll bring them all our research. They can't laugh the both of us away, not when we're able to highlight every connection between these deaths and the stories that inspired them."

"There isn't enough to prove either one of our theories," I say.

"Come by my place. I can show you all the information I've gathered so far. It would be nice to get some input from someone who knows these women better." Her excitement deflates when she sees my uneasy expression. She starts over. "Or you can wait here, and I'll bring my files to you, if that makes you more comfortable. Don't worry, I'm not offended that you don't trust me."

"It's not that—"

"It's smart," she cuts me off. "I wouldn't trust anyone either, until we figure out who is behind this."

"I'm not going back to the police," I say, clenching and unclenching my fists under the table. "Not after what happened tonight at the bridge."

Her jaw clenches. "What do you mean?"

"Say that we're right. Someone killed all three of these people and used the stories from our group as inspiration. Clearly, they also know about what happened to Layla and they're using it against me. I've spent years distancing myself from what happened back then. I'm not going to go to the police and admit that all this started when I wrote a story about my old roommate's murder."

"They won't see it that way."

"Won't they?" I say. "Forget the first two murders. Look at all the strange things that have happened the past couple weeks. And now a message being left for me at the bridge. Whoever is doing this is focusing in on me."

"Maybe that's because they figured out you were onto them," she says. "That's the beauty of having me involved now. They probably haven't realized that two of us are working together."

"We should keep looking into this ourselves," I say. "Telling the police about my past will only make them suspicious of one person in the group: me. They'll think I'm involved because this new murder mirrors what happened to my roommate years ago."

Marley opens her mouth but stops. She must understand there's some truth behind my fears. The last thing we need is to give off the impression I'm a woman come unhinged by grief.

"What if another person dies?" she says, watching me closely for a reaction. "We can't let that happen."

"It won't. We'll keep an eye on the other three. Track them if we must," I say. "I'm not against going to the police at some point, but I'd like to gather more information on our own first. Give them the name of a suspect so they don't assume it's me."

"All you're doing is wasting time," she says, her stare fixed on the table in front of us. "It's been years since the first two murders, which are still unsolved. The police aren't going to get involved unless we bring all this to their attention."

"You're looking into all of this because it's a good story," I say. "For me, it's personal. I have to be sure."

Marley's demeanor changes quickly. Her light-hearted expression is gone, replaced with something angry and bitter. She grips the paper napkin on the table, wadding the paper with her fist. It's obvious she isn't used to hearing the word No.

"Let's meet at Mario's tomorrow," I say, trying to salvage the conversation. "My shift doesn't start until four o'clock. I'll come in early, and we can go over everything then."

"It's a date." She raises her hand, signaling to the waitress we're ready for the check. She still seems angry, but at least she's willing to meet with me again.

"It's better for us to work out what we're going to say," I tell her. "And it's too late for either one of us to think clearly. We'll go to the police when we're ready."

Marley reads over the bill, takes out a twenty, and tucks it beneath the corner of her dirty plate. When she sees I've barely moved, she says, "You coming?"

"I'm going to stay for one more coffee," I say. "It's a lot of information to take in. I need some more caffeine before I drive home."

"Well, be careful," she warns. "Not that I'm trying to scare you, but if someone left a message for you to find, they're threatening you."

"Yeah, I will be."

As Marley leaves, the waitress returns to the table, refilling my mug and collecting the dirty plates. I keep my eyes on Marley, watching as she crosses the street in the direction of her apartment. Eventually, it's too dark for me to see her silhouette.

I look down in my lap. The conversation we had was exhausting. It feels like we were in the diner for hours.

It was only forty-eight minutes and seventeen seconds. I know because the recording app I had playing continues to run. My phone is slippery in my hands from the tight grip I had on the device throughout our meeting.

It may have been foolish to meet Marley alone like this, but I would at least ensure whatever we talked about would be recorded. I'd been hoping to get a confession on tape. Instead, she claimed that whoever killed Jessica Wilder has been active far longer than I realized. I was convinced the copycat killer was targeting me over something related to Layla, but what if it's something much larger? How am I supposed to protect myself when I don't know who to trust? Danger looms nearby, like a cold chill settling in.

TWENTY-SIX

The backroom of Mario's Pizzeria remains closed until dinner. Most days, that's where servers will go to eat a quick meal during their shift or roll silverware when business is slow. Today, it's where I've asked Marley to meet me.

For over an hour, we've been alone, discussing the likelihood that one of the other members of our writing group could be a killer, and as bizarre as the theory sounds every time I say it aloud, the possibility is slowly beginning to materialize.

Mainly, because I can now attach names and faces to the previous crimes Marley told me about.

To my left, is a pile containing all the information about the first murder.

Brandon Davis, a WU freshman. He's the one that was bludgeoned in an alley outside of a bar. Friends had seen him leave the establishment alone. Somewhere along the ten-minute walk back to his apartment, he'd stumbled into an alley and was hit over the head almost a dozen times with a blunt object. His body was discovered by a city trash worker the following morning.

"Here's the story that goes along with that one," Marley says, handing it over.

Flower Man by Danielle. It's a story I've never read before, one that was shared before I joined the Mystery Maidens.

I scan the story again, pulling for details that carry it over the threshold into nonfiction.

The live band's music mellowed as the man left the bar... the darkened alley carved between the laundromat and the takeout shops became his final resting place... the wooden slab shot into the sky before making brutal contact with his head... blood splattered on his shirt...

There are obvious similarities between the story and the crime, but my confidence still wavers.

"I'm seeing a short story about a man that was attacked and a news report about a man that was murdered," I say. "It's not like it's the most original idea or the first violent crime to ever happen. How do you know there's a link?"

Marley shuffles through the stack of papers, pulling out a photograph. It's a shot from the crime scene, a man laying inert on the pavement, dark splotches on his vibrant shirt, a mangled mess where his head used to be.

"Wow, Marley, that's enough," I say, shielding my eyes. "Where did you even get that?"

"Some of the photos were leaked online." She looks down, pointing. "Really study it. Look at the businesses closest by—"

"China One Takeout and Ninth Street Laundromat," I finish her sentence, pushing the crime scene photo away. "I get what you're saying. It's just like what's in the story, but there's no proof there's a connection."

"I could say the same things about *The Mistake* and the murder of Jessica Wilder," she says, pointedly. "You're convinced they're connected, aren't you?"

The implication is clear. I'm treating her no different than Chaz did when I first brought him my suspicions. If I expect to be believed, I need to at least hear through the rest of Marley's theory.

"Okay. What makes you so convinced the second murder was connected?"

We move our attention to the stack of papers directly in front of me. The second murder took place almost six months after the first. Similar location and victimology. Looking at their photos, the two men even look the same. The main difference is that the second man, Rudy Raines, died from strangulation.

The story Marley believes inspired this murder is titled *Lost Cause* and was written by April. It's about a philandering husband who is encountered by his jilted lover and murdered. She lures him into a park late at night, where she wraps a belt around his throat and strangles him.

Marley sifts through papers again.

"Please, if you're sharing anymore gruesome photos, don't," I protest.

"I left the most gruesome ones back at the apartment. Things would have been a lot easier if you'd agreed to meet me there." Finally, she finds what she's looking for. It's another photo from the crime scene, but this time it's only of the victim's hand. "Do you see that?"

"It's a hand," I say. "I'm more worried about your access to such disturbing images."

She ignores me. "Look at his ring finger. Do you see that white band? That's where his wedding ring *should* be, but he wasn't wearing it."

"Maybe he was divorced. Or separated."

"Nope. Wife and two kids, according to the obituary. After some more digging online, I discovered Rudy had the reputation of being a cheat. Just like the character in the story."

"What about the murder weapon?" I ask, becoming more uneasy.

"Nothing was found at the scene. Based on the indentations around his neck, cops thought it could have been a belt."

"Just like the story."

My eyes bounce between the various piles, trying to make sense of everything. There's undoubtedly a connection between each crime and its corresponding story, but there's no smoking gun, no remarkable coincidence that convinces me these crimes were inspired by anything at all.

Unlike Marley, I'm well-read when it comes to the crime genre. If I were to scroll through any random writer's catalogue, I'd likely find a story where someone was bludgeoned or strangled with a belt, killed in an alley or dumped near a playground. You read enough of the same material, all the elements blur together. It's near impossible to come up with anything original these days; why should murder be any different?

"You still have that look on your face," Marley says, displeased. "If you don't believe me about the first two murders, what makes you so convinced the most recent one is connected to the group?"

"For starters, everything that's happened to me started in the last two weeks. The murders you are talking about happened two years ago."

"Not too long after the Mystery Maidens group started. And I know, the stories we're looking at were written by different members. You, Danielle and April."

"Are you suggesting it has to be Victoria?"

"Maybe. But that seems too simple," she says. "All of them would have read the stories. It doesn't matter who wrote them. My theory is one of the members decided to act out the murders they read about."

It's the same theory I've proposed about Jessica Wilder's murder, and the other copycat crimes that took place before, but all those incidents have a clear connection back to me and the black hearts. If what Marley is suggesting is true, someone was acting out stories before I even joined the group. "Why would they do this?"

"What pushes anyone to commit a crime? Especially random ones. Something psychological beneath the surface."

I recall my conversations this week with the Maidens. They each have stressors in their lives. April's divorce. Victoria's married lover. Danielle's loneliness. But is any of it enough to push them over the edge, make them start committing murders? Maybe we're looking at this puzzle all wrong. My black hearts stalker and the recent crime spree could be separate crimes, different culprits. If you add Marley's theory into the mix, it could be another sequence entirely. Yet, why are the two suddenly interconnected?

"The first victims were also men," I say, popping my knuckles. "Why kill a woman this time?"

"Because that was the victim in *your* story!" Marley says this as though it's clear and I'm being stupid.

"I get what you're saying, I do," I say, feeling the need to calm her before my co-workers come wandering around asking questions. "I'm convinced the Layla story inspired a murder because of the timing. Less than a week after I shared it, a girl was killed in the same manner."

I tap my knuckles against the third stack, urging Marley to look. She scans the details of my story, cross-referencing them with the information provided in the news article.

"There are more similarities between the Layla story and this murder," she admits.

"They're nearly identical."

A surge of guilt rattles through me, stronger than I've ever felt before. For years, I've blamed myself for Layla's death. Clearly, the black hearts stalker agrees. If I'd been more forceful with Layla, told her the truth about why I felt she was in danger, she wouldn't have died. Now, because I chose to revisit her story through my writing, Jessica Wilder's blood is on my hands, too. At every opportunity to make things right, I've floundered, leaving nothing but heartache and tragedy in my wake.

"Maybe so." She puts the paper flat on the table. "But that's not why you're more passionate about this crime than the others. It's because you already knew the Layla crime was based on your friend's murder. You have a personal connection to this story, so a new body being found brings it all back."

"If I had a reaction every time a woman was found murdered, I'd have been in a nuthouse by now," I say, my jaw clenched. "Unfortunately, a woman being taken advantage of on her way home isn't an original concept."

"The point is you care about your friend. The details of her murder stuck with you. They inspired you to write the story. And the idea that someone took those details and used them to commit a new crime infuriates you."

Marley has put a lot of research into her theory, but I've lived these experiences firsthand. The wounds from the police and the civil suit are still fresh, even after all these years. Everyone talking and taking sides. Blaming me. Clearly, the black hearts stalker still faults me, and I'm not going up against them without more proof.

"We should meet with the Mystery Maidens again," I say. "Before going to the police."

"Fine." Slowly, she begins collecting the papers she brought with her. "It's just unnerving, isn't it? Continuing to meet with a group of women when you're convinced one of them is a killer."

"We've narrowed it down at least," I say. "Only three left to suss out."

"Does that mean you no longer consider me a suspect?"

Before I answer, I consider the question. Marley would be wasting a lot of time swapping information with me if she is the killer. I'm not sure what her angle would be, or why she'd toy with me in such a personal way. Regardless, now that we're closer, it will be easier for me to keep tabs on her. There's a feeling in my gut that tells me I still don't know the full story.

Likewise, she still doesn't have the full truth from me. I haven't told her about the black hearts, that the person behind all of this might have been messing with me for the past decade.

"My shift is about to start," I say, swerving a response. "The next meeting isn't until Thursday. We'll touch base before, figure out how we want to play this around the others."

"Sounds good." She doesn't appear disappointed that I didn't say I trusted her. Odds are, she still has reservations about me, too. "Hey, can I eat back here? I'm absolutely starving."

"You look tired, too," I say, watching as she leans into the booth.

"Yeah, well it was hard to sleep last night after everything we talked about," she says, rubbing the back of her neck.

I can certainly relate. My lack of sleep over the past two weeks has taken its toll.

"I'll grab you a menu."

"No need," she says, securing all her evidence inside her purse. "I'll take potato skins or buffalo wings. Whatever's cheapest. This seems like the type of place that would offer both."

I'm not sure what's more irritating, the fact Marley can eat whatever she wants and remain a size two, or her dismissive attitude to everything and everyone around her. College kids. It's enough to make you want to knock them over the head with something.

With a shudder, I recall the brutal deaths we were just talking about and walk back to the main dining room.

TWENTY-SEVEN

It's been a long night.

Some people, my own mother included, assume that because someone is writing down orders and carrying out steaming entrées with extra sides of ranch dressing, that service workers deserve less respect than people with *real* jobs.

In reality, I've worked harder as a waitress than I have any other job in my life. You stack responsibilities in your head, making sure the needs of each and every customer are met. You learn how to read people, distinguish between the tables that want every need catered to and the ones who only want to be left alone. And after a full night of running around, fighting what feels like a losing battle, you're tasked with mandatory upkeep. Tonight, that meant I was set to scrubbing the bathroom toilets and sinks.

My body aches with exhaustion, my clothes tinged with the unwelcome smells of frying grease and bleach. At least a hectic work shift meant I didn't have time to think about the other issues in my life. I don't think about Layla or the Maidens or the possibility of a killer on the loose until I've walked several blocks away from the restaurant. In an instant, I remember, and from that moment on, I spy every roaming shadow and passing pedestrian with skepticism and fear.

When I walk inside my apartment and click the lock behind me, I lean against the closed door and exhale a sigh of relief. I'm home. I'm safe. Images of myself sleeping in until noon comfort me.

"You're home late," Crystal says.

I open my eyes and see her sitting at the dining-room table. A steaming teacup sits to her right, and she's facing the entrance of the apartment, as though she's been waiting on me.

Shit, I think. Because of our conflicting schedules, we're often like ships passing in the night. It's easy to forget I even have a roommate, mainly because for so many years, I haven't. We haven't come face to face since I caught her snooping through my computer, right before I left for Banyon's Bridge.

"It was a busy night," I say, hoping she'll take pity on me and let me go to bed.

"We need to talk," she says. No such luck.

I slump into the chair across from her and lean back, waiting.

"Are you wanting to apologize for invading my privacy?" I ask.

Crystal lowers her head, hits me with an unbothered look. Easy pettiness flows between us, the way it only can after years upon years of knowing another person.

"Do you think I should apologize?"

"Well, I've been kind enough to let you stay here." My tone is pompous, nothing like how I normally speak. "You know I'm protective of my writing."

"And now I see why," she says. "You're writing a story about Layla of all people. How could you do that?"

"I'm not writing a story about Layla—"

"You used her name!" Crystal shouts. "All those details.

The bar and the walk home and *him*." She shakes her head, disgusted. "Why would you do something like that?"

I exhale, trying to think of a way to explain myself. In the ten years since our friend's death, I can count on one hand the times Crystal and I have talked about her. We've both found it easier to not bring it up. Bring *her* up. I'm just as ashamed of myself, but I can't let her know that. After years of knowing Crystal, it's never a good idea to let her think she has the upper hand in a conversation, even when she does.

"I've been struggling with writer's block," I say. "For weeks, I haven't been able to write about anything. The other night I had a nightmare about Layla. I couldn't get her off my mind. So, I wrote a story about what happened. I never had any intention of publishing it. It was just my mind's way of getting those thoughts out of my head."

Crystal nods, as though understanding what I've said, but her simmering anger remains. "It was upsetting having to relive those details, especially knowing you wrote them."

"You didn't have to do anything," I say. "You're the one who chose to go through my computer."

"I wasn't snooping, okay? The screen was on, and the story was pulled up. I was curious. You always talk about what you're writing, but I've never really had a look. The last thing I was expecting was to read a story about Layla."

"It's never happened before." I say the next part with finality. "And it will never happen again."

"Did your friends from your writing group read that story?"

"They did."

Crystal clenches her jaw and looks away. "Layla deserves more than to be entertainment for some murder-obsessed freaks."

"It's not entertainment for any of us. I already told you; it was my own way of working out what I was feeling. None of them know that story was based on a real event."

But at least one of them does. Two, if you're counting Marley. The person who is toying with me and left that newspaper article at Banyon's Bridge knows the truth of what happened ten years ago.

"The anniversary is coming up, you know," Crystal says. She's looking down at the table trying not to cry. "I've been thinking about her more and more lately."

"I have too," I admit, recalling the recent string of phone calls from my mother. She wants to remind me of what happened, when all I want to do is forget. "Writing that story was like therapy more than anything. I'd never use what happened to Layla for personal gain."

Crystal nods, slowly. I sense she believes me now. Even though we don't talk about that night, I believe the details live in her head just as vividly as they do mine. I believe she carries the same blame that I do. If she hadn't been so drunk, we would never have left her in the first place. Although, what I did was worse. I knew Mike was dangerous, but I left her behind anyway.

I move to the kitchen, grabbing a glass from the cabinet and filling it with tap water. I lean against the counter, drinking furiously, overtaken with a sudden need to rehydrate and cleanse myself from the inside out. In the corner of the kitchen sits a bouquet of flowers in a vase. A seasonal selection. Reds and greens and small white clouds of baby's breath.

"You bought flowers?"

"No, someone sent them," Crystal says, not even raising her head. "I'm sure they're from Thomas."

"He's still trying to get you back?"

With everything that's been happening, I almost forgot why Crystal is here. Her engagement fell apart, her wedding called off. Night after night, I've watched her go out on the town, envious of her ability to move on from what happened to Layla. I forget not everything has been easy on her.

I move closer to the flowers, touching them, the petals soft like velvet, the floral scent fresh and alive, at odds with everything else inside this apartment. In the center of the arrangement, rests a card. I step back so fast, I almost send the entire bouquet crashing to the ground.

"You don't know for sure?" My voice is high-pitched and painful.

"There wasn't a name." She looks at me now. "Why?"

I return to the bouquet, plucking out the card. There's only one word: *Remember*. Beside it, is a black heart.

"Have you ever seen one of these before?" I ask, holding out the card.

"A florist's note?"

"No. The symbol on it," I say, annoyed. "The black heart."

"I guess. I mean, it's not really that special, is it?"

But it is, at least to me. And could be, to her. For the past decade, I've been receiving these warnings and threats. I've always known they must be tied back to Layla, but I never imagined that Crystal had been receiving them, too.

"Ever since Layla died," I begin, my voice struggling to find strength, "these weird things have been happening. I keep getting these messages, and they always have a black heart on them. Just like Layla's tattoo. They've shown up at my mother's house, where I work, in my ex-boyfriend's car. Even here, at this apartment. I need to know, have you been getting them, too?"

Crystal sits, lifting her chin just enough to let me know she's thinking, retreating far enough to try and find an answer.

"Now that you mention it, I have received messages like that before. I'm trying to remember—"

"How couldn't you know?" I shout, outraged. "Someone might have been stalking you for the past decade, and you've never really thought about it?"

"You're making it out to be more than it is. Like it's some kind of threat."

"It is a threat."

"It's a piece of paper. Someone messing with me. And with you, it seems. But that's all it is. No one is actually doing anything."

"That's not true," I say. "At least not anymore. Last week, someone slashed my tires and left a black heart beside my car. And remember that hit-and-run on our street? One was found there, too."

"Why didn't you say anything?"

"I thought it was only happening to me. But it makes sense. If this is about Layla, of course they'd be after you, too. We were both there that night."

"No one is after me," she says. "Someone might have been sending me messages, but that's all it is. You can't make them into something more."

Her last comment bothers me. Is she suggesting I'm at fault for everything that's happened? I've lost my job, my relationships, all because of the black hearts. Could it be they have ruined my life all these years because I gave them the power?

"Try to think," I say, changing the subject. "Even one instance."

"When I moved into my apartment with Thomas, there was one on our front door. I remember it clearly because the whole place was cleared out and then there was this random piece of paper, but I wadded it up and threw it away. I didn't think anything about it."

Our reactions to the same threat are jarring, really. While I've spent years in isolation, looking over my shoulder for the next black heart, she didn't give the messages a second thought, didn't even stop to consider their significance.

"I've been getting these since right after she died. The weekend I moved back home, in fact. I've been trying to figure out who it is, and this is the closest I've ever been."

"I can tell you who it is."

"Who?"

"Her parents. They're the only ones who held her death against us."

She's right. The article that was left for me at the bridge was an abridged version of the saga that took place with Layla's parents. They blamed us for her death, kept saying they'd trusted us to keep their daughter safe. Her real friends back home would never have left her alone.

"You really think they could be behind this?"

"Of course, they could. They tried to sue us, remember? They wanted to ruin our futures. At the time, I felt sorry for them. They'd lost their only daughter, but they let that grief turn into something menacing. Unhinged."

"I've barely thought about them since the case was dropped." And, honestly, I never considered they'd be capable of stalking me. They were so overwhelmed with grief. I remember hearing they went into early retirement, found it too difficult to leave their home, let alone follow me around town leaving messages. The death of their only daughter ruined them.

"Maybe that's the point." She walks over to me, and lifts the card, reading it. "Remember."

"They never forgave us for what happened," I say, thinking.

If Layla's parents have been sending the black hearts all these years, how would they have access to the stories from the group? And how could they be linked to the murders Marley has uncovered? It suddenly feels like there are too many crimes I'm trying to solve at once. Maybe the same person who has been stalking me for the past decade is not the same person copying crimes from the stories. Maybe one of the members from the group has crossed paths with Layla's parents, and now they're working together. Trying to unravel these endless possibilities makes my head hurt. I worry how much more of this I can take.

"It's just not fair, is it? Layla had so much to offer the world. More than either one of us, if we're being honest," she says, wiping her nose. "Why is it always the good ones that get taken away?"

I wonder if she's aware of Jessica Wilder's murder last week. If she is, she hasn't said anything about it. Maybe she read about it in the papers, and that's why she is so emotional now.

"I'm not sure if you saw, but there was a girl who was killed—"

"I don't want to hear about it." Crystal raises her hand, hardens her voice. "I'm not like you, okay? Writing messed up stories and reading the news doesn't help me cope with my feelings. I try to ignore it. I *want* to ignore it. I need to believe I live in a world of rainbows and butterflies, even if that's bullshit."

I close into myself. It's easy for me to brush off Crystal as materialistic, but maybe she's unlocked the secret to moving past tragedy. Living in the moment prevents her from being consumed by the past, and though I'm reluctant to admit it, she's accomplished much more in the past ten years than I have, even if there have been some missteps, like with Chase. She has a thriving career and social life. Breaking off the engagement with Thomas was a setback, but she seems to be bouncing back effortlessly.

Then there's me, wallowing in my own self-pity.

"Are we going to be able to move past this story?" I ask her. "I didn't write it to hurt you or anyone else."

Her posture softens. "Of course, we will. You're, like, my oldest friend."

"I'm sorry it upset you," I say. "That was never my intention."

An hour later, when I'm in bed, trying to fall asleep, I wonder, what was my intention writing that story? And what chain of events might I have unknowingly put into action? I'm starting to lose track of how many people have been harmed since I first wrote *The Mistake*.

One thing is clear: there are two new names on the Black Hearts Stalker suspect list.

Charles and Lena Williams.

TWENTY-EIGHT

Layla's hometown wasn't something she talked a lot about. That's the beauty of going to college. You get to take the parts of yourself you like with you, the parts that you haven't fully developed yet, and leave all the rest behind.

Of course, she talked about her childhood at times. Funny stories about recess and holiday traditions. Things like that. I knew she had two devoted parents, still married after more than thirty years. She had an older brother who went to college out of state. Rarely did she talk about people she'd dated, but I knew there was a small group of girlfriends she'd had since elementary school. Based on what she said, it sounded as though Layla lived a charmed life.

Still, there was a feeling I always had, beyond what she said. It's the way she would act after an extended visit back home—holiday breaks and long weekends. Whenever she returned, she always seemed upset. As though the person she'd once been clashed with the person she was now. She'd never elaborate; I figured it was the same sort of growing pains most people experience when they go out into the world for the first time.

After she died, and I saw how viciously her parents went

after Crystal and me in the courts, I wondered if maybe there were more complications in their relationship than she ever let on. Grief is a hard thing to understand. I can't imagine being in their shoes, but I always felt that blaming us for Layla's death was the wrong route. We all had our faults that night, but it was only the choices of Michael Massey that led to her death.

At least, that's what I tell myself when my own conscience says I'm to blame.

What I do know and don't know wrestles in my mind as I make the hour-long drive to her hometown. Layla, like me, was an outsider, and yet, it never really felt that way once we'd found one another.

I never went to her house, although she invited us once. Her parents had asked me to join them for Thanksgiving, but I declined. I was on better terms with my own mother back then. She still brought out my insecurities in a way I couldn't explain, but she didn't really start making me feel like a failure until after I'd dropped out of school. I'll always regret not accepting Layla's offer to join her; it would have been nice to have an extra holiday memory with her.

Even though I never made it to her house, her address wasn't hard to find. A simple search online revealed the residence of Charles and Lena Williams, the same place they've lived for almost four decades.

I wonder if driving out here is a mistake, but if Crystal is right, and Layla's parents are the ones who have been sending me threatening messages for the past ten years, it's not really a conversation we can have over the phone. Not that I'm even banking on a conversation. As with all my other investigative techniques thus far, I'm hoping that after talking to them, I'll have a better idea of what's going on.

I park alongside the curb across from their house. It's a two-story brick, a white picket fence circling the entire property. Like my mom's place, there's a large tree in the backyard, and the image of seeing a black heart carved into the bark flashes through my brain.

I close my eyes and inhale through my nose. My mind needs to stay clear if I'm going to find the courage to knock on that front door, to talk with the couple that once threatened to sue me.

I'm about to open the driver's side door, when there's a noise from Layla's house across the street. The front door opens, and a small child comes running out. It's a little boy, maybe three or four years old. He runs full-force to the backyard tree, and jumps onto a swing. I hadn't noticed it there before.

From the open doorway, comes another person. A woman in her early sixties. She's holding a juice cup in one hand, a big smile across her face. Lena Williams. Layla's mother.

For years, the only image I've had of her is the woman I saw in the wake of her daughter's death. Swollen eyes, sunken cheeks. An aura about her that warned she'd never recover from this heartbreak. That was the woman I'd imagined sending the black hearts over the years. Likely, the woman Crystal had imagined, too.

This Lena Williams is different. She walks to the tree with confidence, gently putting the juice cup on the grass beside it. She bends down and whispers something to the child, then begins pushing him on the swing. I'm not sure who looks happier. The toddler flying through the air, or the proud grandmother behind him, her hands softly pushing at his back.

A moment later, Layla's father, Charles Williams, exits the house. Like his wife, he walks with confidence and grace. He smiles the smile of a person who is at peace. When he takes a seat in the Adirondack chair across from the tree, he leans back, letting the sunlight fall on his face.

Whatever ball of anxiety and shame that's been lodged inside my chest loosens, feels like an iced-over heart that's melting. I never thought I'd see this. Layla's parents, happy again.

More than ten years since their daughter has died, and they've somehow found peace. Imagining they are the ones behind everything that's been happening—the black hearts, the copycat crimes—seems so unlikely.

I pull out my phone, checking my messages for any updates. I had to cancel a shift last-minute in order to drive out here, and I can see Nikki has sent out a message to the group chat, reminding all the servers about the proper protocols for giving up a shift. I roll my eyes. I can't expect her to understand why I needed to take off, let alone the satisfaction I now feel after seeing Layla's parents in the flesh.

I'm about to put the car into drive when someone taps against the window.

I look up, startled, and see Lena Williams standing outside.

That ball of anxiety returns, rising so far into my throat, I fear I might choke. She's staring right at me, with a look of defiance on her face. Over her shoulder, I can see Charles. He's standing now, pushing the child on the swing. My first reaction is to leave, but seeing the way Lena is glaring at me, I know that's not an option.

I roll down my window.

"Hi, Mrs. Williams," I say, with all the unease of a young schoolgirl.

"What are you doing here?" Her tone is curt.

"I..." My mind flails to come up with an answer. Where do I even begin? "I really don't know."

"You came all the way out here from Whitaker," she says. "There must be a reason."

Maybe I was too quick to take her off the suspect list. If she knows I still live in Whitaker, maybe she's keeping tabs on me after all.

"The anniversary is coming up," I say. "She's been on my mind a lot. You all have."

Lena looks over her shoulder, back at the house and her

family playing in the backyard. When she turns back to me, something in her eyes seems to have shifted.

"It's good to see you again, Becca. I think about you often. And Crystal."

Of all the thoughts that must go through the Williams' minds, Crystal and I should be low on that list. We weren't the friends her daughter needed on the last night of her life.

"I'm sorry for what happened," I say. "I think about it all the time."

"I know that," she says, looking down. "I never should have blamed you."

"The lawsuit—"

"The lawsuit was a horrible idea. We were so angry back then, we were looking for everyone and anyone to blame." She looks at me, tears in her eyes. "I know the case was dropped, but I wish we'd never even started it. It was an awful way to treat you in the aftermath of what happened."

My mouth opens and closes, unsure of what to say. I hadn't been expecting an apology from Layla's parents. I don't deserve one.

"I replay that night all the time, even now. I wish we had stayed with her. We never should have left her alone."

A real friend would have done more, wouldn't have let petty feelings and indecision get in the way of Layla's safety. It was a lapse in loyalty and judgement from which I'll never recover. Even now, it's painful being this close to Lena Williams, knowing I've stolen so much from her.

"I forgot what it's like, being young and carefree. It often takes an event like what happened to Layla to remind you how dangerous the world really is. You weren't thinking anything awful would happen when you left her there that night. I understand that now."

I think of my last conversation with Layla, how I didn't have the nerve to tell her about my full experience with Mike, how he might be dangerous.

"A better friend would have stayed," I say.

"Growing up, Layla was always close to the girls around here. In my mind, I thought she'd go to school here, stay beside them. It was scary to send my daughter off into the world, watch her build new friendships and leave the ones here behind. But that's what I wanted her to do. Spread her wings, and she did."

"She's one of the best people I've ever known," I say. "I'd give anything to have her here with us."

"I would too." She turns back to the house and looks at her smiling grandson. "But there are other parts of life to celebrate. Since being a grandparent, I've understood that more. My son still lives in the area, so I'm able to be a big part of his life. Layla's death nearly broke our family, but we've found a way to rebuild."

"I'm happy for you," I say.

"I'll never forget what happened. I still work with WU to ensure safety on campus. I started a charity and it's ran by one of the professors there."

"Really?" I ask. "Who is it?"

"Victoria Johnson. She's done a lot to help build awareness on campus," she says.

My stomach clenches. Victoria works alongside Layla's parents. That must mean she knows more about her death than I ever realized. Could she know I was her roommate back then? That I was the one to leave her behind?

"I'm happy I got to apologize to you in person," Lena says. "It was long overdue."

"You don't owe me anything," I say. "I'm just happy you and your family have found peace."

It's true, I realize, as I make the long and lonely drive back to Whitaker, even more questions about Victoria and her intentions forming in my mind.

TWENTY-NINE

I'm officially not the only person making connections. As of this morning, the *Whitaker Tribune* has too. There was a front-page article comparing the recent murder of Jessica Wilder to a similar decade's old case: the murder of Layla Williams.

The article covered few details about Layla's death, and luckily didn't mention Crystal, me, or the dropped civil suit against us. At least I'm not being dragged back into the public eye. It wasn't sensationalized either, suggesting that because the crimes were similar there must be a serial killer on the loose. Michael Massey's arrest and conviction were made clear; however, the reporter highlighted that safety for women on campus is still a major issue. It was a call for action more than anything, along with a plea that anyone with information about Jessica Wilder's murder contact the police.

Now that her face is splattered across headlines, it's no longer possible to avoid Wilder's murder with the Mystery Maidens; it's all anyone in Whitaker has been talking about, and I've been gearing up all day for it to be addressed at tonight's meeting.

My stomach is a bundle of knots as I wait for the other

Maidens to arrive. I keep replaying the details of my investigation with Marley. Ever since Jessica Wilder's murder, I can't escape the feeling that danger is lurking, and knowing Marley believes two more people have been killed only increases that fear.

Part of me still finds it impossible to think one of the other Maidens could be responsible, but if not them, then who?

"Thirsty Thursday!" April says when she arrives. "Have you already ordered drinks?"

I clear my throat before speaking. "No, I was waiting on the rest."

"Are you okay?" she asks. "You look like you're coming down with something."

My appearance must speak to my inner turmoil. I've had trouble sleeping, and no matter how much I try to act normal, I can't shake the feeling of dread that follows me wherever I go.

"Just tired," I say, quickly putting the focus onto something else. "What about you? How have you been?"

"Better than when you saw me at my house." She lowers her voice. "You didn't say anything to the others—"

"Of course not," I interrupt her.

She smiles genuinely. "Thank you. This is my most positive part of the week, and I want to keep it that way."

"I understand," I say, even though any joy this group brought me disappeared long ago. Now, my sole reason for coming is to try and figure out which of my friends could be a murderer. They've all entrusted me with their secrets in the past week, but I wonder which of them could be hiding something even darker. Is it possible one of them has been tormenting me for years?

Victoria arrives next, followed by Danielle. We exchange greetings and pleasantries, providing bland updates about our weeks. None of them mention the fact that I've met each of them separately recently, which is probably a good thing. I don't need the culprit to know that I am investigating, even though it's clear they know I'm onto them. The note left for me at Banyon's Bridge proves as much.

"Let's get started," Victoria says, pulling out her laptop.

"What about Marley?" I ask.

For the past half hour, I've been checking my phone every five minutes. She should have arrived by now.

"Not coming," Victoria says. "She's busy with exams this week, so I told her to take the night off."

She's not coming at all? After we've spent the past couple of days going over our game plan? For weeks, I've looked at Marley with suspicion. As soon as I let down my guard enough to trust her, she abandons me.

"I'll go first," Danielle says. "I have something really special to share."

"Wait," I say, afraid of losing my chance to confront the group all at once. "I was wanting to talk to you guys first. Since we're all crime writers, I imagine you all follow the news as much as I do. Did you hear about the WU student that was murdered last week?"

This is my plan. Bring up the most recent murder and allow the others to take control of the conversation. I don't want to mention Layla by name. I'd rather see if the other members make connections on their own.

"I read about it this morning," Danielle says, lowering her stare. "It's just awful."

"I saw it, too. Only twenty years old! Her poor parents," April says. She looks at Victoria. "I wondered about you. Did you know her?"

"I didn't," she answers. "But it's been on my mind nonstop."

"What about the other student they talked about in the article?" I ask. Under the table, I clench my fists, waiting for what they all could say. At the same time, my face flushes with heat. "The one that died ten years ago?"

"I remember when she died," Danielle goes on. "It was right around the time I moved to Whitaker to start law school. Not the best way to start a new job or move to a new city."

"You're lucky you weren't a student at the time," April says. "The girl who died was a year ahead of me in school. It terrified me and my friends."

Neither of them seems to have made a connection between *The Mistake* and Layla, so I add, "I remember, too. Right before the holidays. Horrible stuff."

"You know I was in the bar the night it happened," April says. "I kept thinking, what if it had been me?"

My blood runs cold. April was at the bar that night? Could she have seen me and not let on? Or was she there to meet Crystal? I remember something Crystal mentioned during one of our arguments. That anyone could have been at the bar that night, and we wouldn't have known.

"My law firm ended up representing the guy who was charged," Danielle adds.

"Really?" I say, trying to hide my shock. I'd never imagined Danielle would have a connection to Layla's death, too.

"Of course, that was before I joined the firm, but it was one of my mentor's biggest cases. He still talks about it all the time, even though the guy eventually accepted a deal."

"I don't know why we make anything easier on guys like that," Victoria says. "No offense. I know it's your job."

"If I remember, there were other accusations made against him. I think he got less time taking a deal than he would have if he fought multiple charges in court."

"Other accusations?" April asks.

"He'd attacked other women before," Danielle says. "Thankfully, they all survived."

Again, my cheeks redden, and my throat goes dry. Is it just my paranoia, or does Victoria seem to be staring at me? It was only a few days ago that I admitted to her I'd nearly been attacked in college. Would she assume it was by the same person?

"I've met the girl's parents," Victoria says, at last. "They're really involved with safety measures on campus. Nice people, but I can't imagine what it's like to lose someone you love like that."

All three of them had connections to the situation I never knew about. Victoria has worked with Layla's parents, Danielle's firm represented Michael Massey, and April was at Twisted Timmy's on the night it all happened. What are the odds? A few weeks ago, I didn't know about any of these connections. Any of these women could hold me accountable for Layla's death, making them each more dangerous than they appear. I stand abruptly. "I need to go to the bathroom," I say.

I weave in and out of the crowds gathered around the bar, making my way to the narrow space at the back of the pub. It's a one-stall bathroom, and thankfully there isn't a line. I shut and lock the old, splintered door and stare at my reflection in the water-stained mirror.

What am I doing? It's impossible for me to act like everything is fine, carry on and share stories like nothing has happened. I was relying on Marley to be here, if for no other reason than moral support. In her absence, I'm not sure who I can trust.

I splash water onto my face, relishing the instant cooling effects. Maybe Marley is right, and we should go to the police, but I already tried that once—before Jessica Wilder was murdered. Chaz treated me like I was a paranoid fanatic. Presenting the cops with three more crimes will only make me appear more unhinged.

And yet, the very real possibility remains that one of the women out there is a murderer. Even if Marley's theory is wrong and the murders of Brandon Davis and Rudy Raines are a coincidence, I know someone is messing with me. I'll never find out who it is if I don't hold myself together.

I take a deep breath and re-enter the crowded lounge. When I reach the booth, I avoid eye contact with the other women, pulling my computer toward me and scrolling through old files.

"Are you okay?" Danielle asks, and I wonder if she read her story while I was gone, or if she waited on me.

"I'm fine," I say. "Just got a little overheated."

"Are you sure?" Victoria adds. "Your mind seems like it's elsewhere."

"I'm fine. Really. Let's go ahead and start the meeting," I say, struggling to put on my best poker face.

I'm a shitty poker player, and, from the looks of it, an even shittier amateur detective.

THIRTY

I've called Marley three times since last night's meeting, but she won't pick up.

I'm pissed. We were supposed to be investigating the group together. She's the only person who I've shared my crazy theory with who didn't make me feel like I was losing my mind, then she just bails.

I tell myself that Marley is young, unpredictable. Like most college students, she probably got a better offer and didn't think twice about ditching a bunch of older women. But isn't what we're trying to do together bigger than that?

I hop in the shower, promising myself that if Marley doesn't respond to my calls soon, I'm going to show up at her apartment again. She at least owes me an explanation for why she's ditched me.

The air inside the apartment tickles my wet flesh. I wrap a robe around myself, folding my towel like a turban atop my head. I reach for my phone, checking to see if Marley got back to me while I was in the shower.

There's one new notification, but it isn't from Marley. It's an email from one of my top-ranked literary agents.

Dear Becca,

Thank you so much for sending your opening pages. I've just finished reading and absolutely loved...

Giddy with nerves, I drop my phone. I scramble to the living room and log into my email, needing a full screen to make sure I'm seeing what I think I am.

Sure enough, I have a manuscript request from Victoria Lennox at the Lennox Agency. I close my eyes. My heart flutters inside my chest as my mind scrolls through possibilities. Finally, after years and years of struggling, this could be my chance to make something of myself. The iron-clad door between me and the literary industry is opening.

I click on the email.

Dear Becca,

Thank you so much for sending your opening pages. I've just finished reading and absolutely loved them! Your writing is tense and gripping, and I believe readers will be hooked. Please send me the entire manuscript in a Word document.

I'll get back to you within four weeks. Really looking forward to seeing how Layla receives justice!

Kind regards,

Victoria Lennox

I'm so rattled with excitement, it takes a few moments for the entirety of the message to sink in. *Layla?* Why would this literary agent even mention her name? *Night Beat* has nothing to do with Layla.

Confused, I scroll back to the original email. I started

querying agents over a month ago, and Victoria Lennox was on that list, yet the most recent email was sent only yesterday. When I click on it, my stomach drops.

Although the message has been sent from my account, this isn't my original query. In fact, it doesn't mention *Night Beat* at all. The query letter describes a book I've never written... all about a girl who was murdered and her roommate's quest to find the killer.

When I click on the attachment, instead of the first ten pages of *Night Beat*, it's the first chapter of the short story I wrote about Layla.

My breathing gets heavier, my chest rising and falling rapidly. I don't understand. How could someone have used my email address? I scroll through the Sent Messages tab, hoping Victoria Lennox was the only person targeted. The sickening feeling in my stomach grows stronger when I see more than a dozen agents have been contacted, all of them sent a copy of the Layla story.

I slam the computer shut and curse, my shouts echoing through the lonely apartment. For years, I've known someone was messing with me, but this? How did they get access to my private computer? It rarely leaves the apartment, apart from my biweekly meetings with the Maidens. Even then, the computer never leaves my sight. I can't think of a single opportunity where someone would have been able to use it.

I think back to last night's meeting. I was distracted. I remember going to the restroom to cool off when I was feeling overwhelmed, but I couldn't have been away from my computer for more than a few minutes. That wouldn't be enough time for someone to upload my files and send a message from my account, would it? Surely the other women would have seen.

. . .

I stake out a table at The Coffee Shop's outdoor dining area. It's positioned directly across from both Marley's apartment and the university's main crossing point. Since she won't return any of my calls, catching her here is my best option.

My coffee cup is halfway drained when I spot her. She's approaching the sidewalk alongside another classmate, a bohemian dressed student who wears her hair in braids, just like Marley. They're deep in conversation, barely paying attention to me as I cross the street.

"Marley?" I say, my voice innocent. "I thought that was you."

The light in her face dims when she sees me. Her eyes drift back to her classmate. "Catch you later?"

The student offers a smile before she falls in line with the foot traffic, making her way down the sidewalk. Marley's smile vanishes once she leaves.

"Are you stalking me now?"

"You didn't leave me much choice," I say. "You've been ignoring my calls ever since you bailed on the meeting."

She sighs and looks at the ground. "I know."

"What's the point of us meeting up and sharing theories if you're going to leave me alone to do all the investigating?"

"When that article came out in yesterday's paper, it worried me. I don't like how close we're getting to this."

"What about your podcast?"

"Screw the podcast. This isn't a fake story anymore. It's not even a real story about people I don't know. This is my town. My peers. I've been looking into these cases long before you came along." She looks up, holding a stack of books close to her chest like they're armor. "Truth is, I'm regretting getting involved. If we really think there's a killer in our group, we should leave that to the police to sort out. Not us."

"Easy to say when you're not the one being targeted." I pull out my phone and scroll through my recent emails. "Take a look at this."

She holds the phone, raising a hand to block the glare from the sun. Her mouth moves rapidly as she reads. "What is this? An agent is interested in your manuscript. Congratulations."

I snatch the phone away and slide it into my back pocket. "Except it's not for a book I've written. Someone hacked into my email and sent out the Layla story to a dozen different literary agents."

Marley still looks confused. "Why would they do that?"

"For the same reason they slashed my tires and ran over a stranger on my street. One of the women in the group is messing with me, and it's up to us to figure out who it is."

"This is far too personal," she says. "I mean, someone got into your email. You should really go to the police."

"I can't!" I say. "Not yet. We're close to figuring out which Maiden is behind this. I'm just asking for your help."

Begrudgingly, Marley accompanies me over the street to The Coffee Shop. She sits across from me, placing her textbooks on the ground by our feet. It's not like she has some investigative gift, but she's the only person who even half-heartedly believes my theory that something bad is taking place with the group, and I need her reassurance to keep me from going crazy.

"How would someone have access to your email?" she asks. "I'm guessing you've already tried to pin it down."

"I know I went to the bathroom at the last meeting," I say. "I was frustrated you didn't show, and the others could tell there was something wrong with me. Still, I couldn't have been gone for more than five minutes. I don't think that would have been enough time for someone to hack my computer without the others seeing."

"Okay, then they must have accessed the story another way," she says. "Could one of them have gotten into your apartment?"

I consider the question. Things have been in disarray lately, but I could easily chalk that up to having a roommate for the first time in a decade. On the other hand, someone could have been going through my things, and I'd never know because I'd assume it was Crystal moving around.

"I'm not sure," I say. "It's possible. Whoever is doing this is going to extreme lengths."

"Think about your writing specifically. Is there any way someone can access your stories without using your computer?"

It's like a buzzer going off in my head. "The shared drive."

"What?"

"I almost forgot about it." I pull my laptop closer and begin typing furiously. "The Mystery Maidens have a shared folder we use for completed stories. Sometimes we upload our work there so we can critique each other during the week."

"Is the Layla story there?"

It only takes a few clicks for me to find it. "Yes. I upload everything to the drive as a backup, but all the Maidens have access."

"So, if that's the case, all they'd need is your email password and they're good to go."

"That's still hard to figure out."

"Is it?" She tilts her head to the side. "Most people have shit security."

My confidence deflates when I realize she's right. I certainly haven't put much thought into my passwords. For almost all of them it's *Password123*. If someone was driven enough, and I suspect whoever is targeting me is, they could have hacked into my account with ease.

"Okay, so they guess my email password. They download the story from the group's shared drive. Now they can use my account to contact as many agents as they want."

"They could still have broken into your apartment."

"Could have." I stare at the computer screen, thinking.

"This shared drive has been around longer than I've been in the group." I can scroll back and see manuscripts from more than two years ago.

"Including the stories Victoria shared with her class?" she asks. I nod. "Then any of the group members can download whatever they want for inspiration. We can show all this to the police—"

"Marley, no."

"Don't you see how dangerous this is getting? For you, especially. I mean, everything that's happened so far relates back to you." She lowers her voice. "They even murdered someone in the same way your college roommate was killed."

"Exactly. It all relates back to me," I say. "The cops will think I'm guilty."

"You don't know that. Besides, I'll back you up. You might even have an alibi for when the murder was committed."

Problem is, I don't. I spent that night alone at the apartment. Even Crystal wouldn't be able to vouch for me.

"Just give me a little bit longer," I say. "Come to the next meeting. Between the two of us, we can figure out who is doing this."

Marley leans back and looks down into her lap. "I'm not sure I'm up for it."

"What's gotten into you? The other night you were more passionate about this than I was. What's changed?"

"Maybe I realized it's more satisfying reading about the aftermath of a crime than investigating it in real-time."

But that's not it. There's something else there, a hidden agenda that Marley is reluctant to share. Even if I can't trust her fully, she's the closest thing I have to an ally.

"I'll go to the police, okay? I just need a little more time first."

"Just be careful." She nods as she stands. "And in the meantime, leave me out of this."

THIRTY-ONE

I'm not able to make good on my promise to reach out to the police. Before I'm given the chance, they approach me.

When I see Chaz standing by the entrance to Mario's Pizzeria, I assume he's coming in for an early dinner. I barely notice the person standing next to him, an older man in a stiff brown suit, until he displays a dull brass badge.

"Becca, mind if we have a word with you?"

I look between the detective holding the badge and Chaz. "I'm about to start my shift."

"We've already talked with your manager, Nikki," the man says. "She's understanding. Even offered us the back booth so we can have some privacy."

No one has ever described Nikki as understanding. She's probably eaten up with curiosity and glee at the idea of police officers showing up to speak with me. Again, I look at Chaz, but his eyes remain on the ground as we go inside.

We're sitting in the back of the restaurant, the same place I sat with Marley to go over our potential theories. Something about this meeting feels different, the stakes raised. It's intimidating talking to law enforcement, even if you're sure you've done nothing wrong.

Chaz sits across from me in the booth, still staring at his hands. The other officer pulls a chair to the end of the table and sits. "I'm Detective Wooley," he says. "I understand you already know my partner."

"He comes in a couple nights a week," I say, staring at Chaz until he finally raises his head and acknowledges me. "What can I help you with, officers?"

"Chaz said you shared a theory with him," Wooley says, leaning closer. "I'd like to hear it."

My nerves relax. Perhaps, after further consideration, Chaz decided my idea wasn't that far-fetched after all.

"You see, I'm in this writing group," I explain, rambling through the basic dynamics of our group, including Marley, the newest member. Chaz already knows these details, but I explain to Detective Wooley the pattern I noticed between the slashed tires and the hit-and-run, how each crime mirrored one of the stories shared in group.

I don't yet present Marley's theory, that this person might have started murdering more than a year ago. Or that I've made another connection between the story I wrote and the murder of Jessica Wilder last week. I'm afraid if I give them too much information all at once, they'll become overwhelmed and laugh me out of the room.

"So, this group. You meet once, twice a week?" Chaz asks.

"This month we've met twice," I say. "For NaNoWriMo."

"What?" Officer Wooley asks.

"We've upped our number of meetings because we're all trying to write a novel in one month's time."

"So, it's like a contest?" Wooley asks.

"More like a challenge," I say, fearing we're moving off topic. "Anyway, we've already met twice this week."

"Have you noticed any connections between stories shared at the meetings and any recent crimes?"

"No," I answer, honestly. I was so flustered by Marley's absence I hardly paid attention though. "I'm starting to think maybe whoever is behind this knows I'm onto them."

"What makes you think that?" Chaz asks. "Have you received any more of those strange messages? The black hearts?"

"Not exactly."

Now should be when I tell them about the similarities between Jessica Wilder's death and the story I wrote, but I don't want to implicate myself. Before I can add anything else, Detective Wooley says, "Do you spend a lot of time at Banyon's Bridge?"

My insides still, my mind going back to that cold November night I staked out that precise location, waiting for a murder to happen.

"I was there earlier this week, actually."

"Huh," Wooley says, but he doesn't sound very surprised. "For any particular reason?"

"I wrote a story as a way to try and catch the killer in the act." I look down, fully aware of how ridiculous it sounds. "It was about a man being pushed off a bridge."

"Why would you do that?" Chaz asks, more animated than his partner.

"I'd already come to you with my theory, and you didn't take it seriously," I say. "I figured the only way I could convince you was to prove it."

"So, you wrote a story to trigger one of your group members?"

"I thought they might try to re-enact the story," I say, "and I'd be able to catch them."

"Nearby security cameras show you were at the bridge on Monday night."

Cameras? Why would they be looking at cameras? Why would they be looking for me?

"That's right," I say. "I went there hoping to catch one of the other group members, but no one showed."

"Are you aware that someone did die on the bridge that night?"

It's as though all the liquid inside my body has turned cold, hardening, until my entire body is heavy with dread. "What?"

He pulls out a picture. "Do you recognize this man?"

I do, instantly. It's the homeless man I saw rummaging through the trash that night. I got a good look at his face right before I found the article on the lamppost.

"Yes, he was there."

"His name is Darryl Nease," the detective says. "Can you tell us anything else about him?"

"Not really. He was still there when I left."

"Around what time was that?" Chaz asks.

"Midnight."

"That lines up with the video footage we reviewed," Wooley says. "Problem is, this man was pushed to his death close to two a.m."

I shove the picture away, no longer able to stomach looking at a man who, the last time I saw him, was completely fine. "Did you see someone on camera?"

"No, there aren't any cameras on the bridge itself. He'd washed up on the bank of the river. You haven't seen it in the papers because we were waiting to track down a next of kin, which can be hard with the homeless."

"How do you know he was pushed?"

"We don't," Wooley says. "He could have easily fallen or even jumped. But we did find something curious in his jacket pocket."

He pulls out another photo. It seems to be all the items

collected from the victim. Right next to his switchblade and bottle caps is a typed manuscript.

"You're saying the man died with this on him?" I ask, my voice beginning to break.

"Yes," Wooley says, looking down at the picture, reading the title of the manuscript. "At the top, it says *Murder at the Bridge* by Becca Walsh. Is that your story?"

"Yes." I'm breathless.

Wooley nods, his eyes narrowing. "Any idea how it got into the hands of a dead man?"

THIRTY-TWO

On Monday morning, I wake up in my bed, too riddled with exhaustion to get up. As it has all weekend, my mind revisits the conversation with the police on repeat, trying to make sense of what they told me and what it means.

Darryl Nease was pushed from the bridge that night. The very same man I saw rummaging through the trash. When I picture him in my mind now, each detail comes through with complete clarity. His ragged clothes and frostbitten fingertips, the nervous but kind smile he displayed when I approached him.

I recall the anxiety and paranoia I felt when I saw another person on the bridge, how I'd leapt into action, not wanting an innocent person's murder on my conscience.

It was all in vain.

Little did I know, when I was storming off to confront Marley, someone else was at the bridge, waiting. Or maybe they came back several hours later, and poor Darryl just happened to be making his way across again. Either way, he was murdered, and if it weren't for my stupid story trying to lure the killer out of hiding, he'd still be alive. Another person dead on account of my stupid mistakes.

As if that tragedy wasn't enough, now it appears the police view me as a suspect. Video surveillance captured me at the scene, and even though that same recording shows me leaving the bridge shortly after midnight, Wooley and Chaz implied I could have easily come back later, suggested maybe I was only surveying the area so I could pick the precise time and location for the crime.

Neither officer told me if another person was caught on camera. Even if they were, that doesn't leave me much hope. Whoever is behind this has been one step ahead of me this entire time. The message and article were planted for me to find. An excerpt of *Murder at the Bridge* was placed in the victim's coat pocket to further implicate me. I pointed out that if I were the killer I wouldn't have left the story behind, but Chaz and Wooley never once dropped their guarded demeanor.

With a shudder, I imagine what the last few moments of Darryl Nease's life must have been like. Cold. Confused. Was he hopeful that a kind stranger was sparing him a few extra bucks, not realizing that it was really a twisted criminal handing over my story? Who hates me so much that they would kill a defenseless man so cruelly?

As Marley said in our last meeting, this is getting too personal.

She has no idea.

I kill hours watching mindless videos on my phone, every now and then scanning the local news to see if any other mysterious crimes have occurred that mirror any of my stories. Nothing notable. I did receive another manuscript request yesterday, but it was for one of the forged Layla emails. What are the odds that the only story that's brought me a small modicum of success was one never meant to be shared with others?

Knuckles rap against my bedroom door. "Becca, you in there?"

Crystal pokes her head into the room. As usual, her hair and makeup are perfectly styled and she's wearing a stylish jumpsuit. She frowns when she sees me.

"You feeling okay?"

"I think I have the flu," I lie, lacking the energy to tell her anything else.

"Poor thing. Steer clear from me." She takes a step backward. "I just stopped by for lunch. I thought I saw your car parked outside. Just wanted to make sure you're okay."

"Just need some rest." I pick up my phone again and begin scrolling. "I'll join the world eventually."

"Also, there was a note for you in the mailbox. I left it on the counter," she says. "I'm heading out."

She closes the door behind her, afraid I'll contaminate her with my imaginary germs. As soon as I hear the front lock click, I enter the kitchen, looking for the note. The paper is folded over and taped at the ends so no one else can read it. My heart flutters like a caged bird, afraid of seeing yet another black heart. When I unfold it, there's a single handwritten message.

Why are you ignoring me? – M

Marley. Ever since my conversation with the police, I haven't felt up to talking to anyone, even her. I understand why she ditched me at the last meeting now. This is all getting too much. I should have followed her lead and bowed out, but I didn't, and now there's even more death targeted at me.

Marley strikes me as the type of person who doesn't like being ignored, regardless of the fact she ghosted me first. Still, why is she following me now? Because I rejected a few phone calls? There's something about her I still don't fully trust, not that I'm able to trust anything, including my own judgement.

If for no other reason than I hope she'll leave me alone, I call her.

"It's about time," she says when she answers. "You stalk me outside of my apartment and then go totally MIA."

"I needed some space," I say. "I talked to the police on Saturday, and it wasn't a great conversation."

"Yeah. Well, join the club."

I sit up straighter in bed. "What do you mean?"

"The police have talked to all of us."

"*Us?*"

"Yes. The other Maidens, too. I'm surprised you haven't heard from them."

Marley isn't the only person I've ignored. All my calls have gone to voicemail and messages ignored as I've spent the day trying to decide my next move.

"What did the police talk to them about?" I ask.

"I'm guessing they'll tell you all about it at tonight's meeting."

"I'm not going." I fall back onto the pillows, staring up at the yellowed ceiling. "I can't, Marley. Especially now."

"You have to, Becca. Not only is everyone pissed, but this could be our chance to figure out which member of the group is behind this."

"I don't care anymore," I shout into the phone. I take a deep breath, collecting myself. "The police were talking to me like *I* was a suspect. A man was murdered at the bridge because of me."

"Don't you want to find out who did it?"

That poor man's face appears in my mind again, my stomach clenching. There's so much I don't know about what's happening, but I know this: two strangers have died because of me. No, rather, to get to me.

"I do."

"Then man up and come to the meeting. I'll be there with

you this time. I promise," she says. "I think you're going to need the backup."

I'm not surprised I'm the last to arrive, but I wince at the idea they've had plenty of time to discuss the situation without me. Everyone is so deep in conversation, they barely acknowledge me when I join their table.

"So, what do you think the police are getting at? They've talked to all of us," Victoria says, turning to me. "Have you talked to them, too?"

I nod, refusing to make eye contact with any of them.

"Clearly they think there's some connection between our stories and the crimes," Danielle says.

"That's ridiculous," April adds. "I mean, we're a bunch of writers. Not criminal masterminds."

"I think they're just exploring all avenues," Marley says.

"But who brought their attention to us in the first place?" April asks.

It's then I realize that the others don't know I'm the one who first went to the police about the copycat crimes. Of course, that was before events took a deadly turn with Jessica Wilder's murder. The police still haven't made a connection between that crime and the death of my former roommate. They've only questioned the other group members about our stories, so I try to act as shocked as the rest of the women about what's unfolding. Across the table, Marley stares directly at me, silently warning me not to say too much.

"They must have gotten their hands on our writing," I say. "That's the only thing that explains it."

"But how?" April asks. "We're a small group. Some of our stories have been published, but those aren't even the ones they were asking about."

"How would anyone outside of this group have access?" Danielle asks.

"We think we might know," Marley chimes in. "The shared drive."

"Everything I write auto-saves to the drive, and we all have access," I say. "So, even if one of us isn't responsible, it's someone who has access to the drive."

"No one even knows the password to my computer," April says.

"Same here," says Danielle.

"I use the drive on campus," Victoria says. "That's how I share our stories with students."

"What do you mean?" April asks, confused.

"Sometimes I use our stories in my creative writing classes," Victoria says. There's a nervous quavering in her voice, as though she fears she's overstepped. "It's only for learning purposes."

"You never told us that," I say, even though I'd already learned as much from Marley.

"It's important for my students to be exposed to new, fresh stories," Victoria says.

"She only uses them as a learning tool," Marley says, jumping to her teacher's defense. "Promise."

"Didn't you think to ask us first?" Danielle asks, her voice as bitter as the rest of ours.

"I should have asked permission first." Victoria tips her chin, trying to refocus the conversation to the problem at hand. "Regardless, my students don't have direct access to our drive, but it's possible someone could have logged into my computer on campus and seen them."

"Whoever is behind this is doing a lot more than just reading your stories," Marley says. "They're acting them out."

"Let's regroup, go over everything we know," Victoria says. "Treat this like we would one of our crime novels."

"There's been two murders," Danielle says. "A woman died, like Becca's *The Mistake* story. And a man was killed at Bany-on's Bridge."

"Just like another one of Becca's stories," April says, almost under her breath.

The hairs on my arms stand at attention, as though they can feel the stares of everyone around me. It makes sense the police wouldn't mention the other two incidents—my slashed tires and the hit-and-run, which were based on stories written by others. Both of those crimes are minor compared to the recent murders; however, it makes it look like someone is only re-enacting my stories, making me the most suspicious.

"But why?" Marley says, her question cutting the tension between us. "And why now?"

"Two murders in the past couple of weeks," April says.

"That we know of," I add.

Marley, sitting beside Victoria, catches my eye again. She shakes her head. I just now realize that we've not even mentioned her theory, that someone in the group has been actively murdering people since before I was even a member. It's almost like I can read her mind. We can only reveal a little information at a time, as the likelihood that one of the women sitting beside me is the actual murderer is still high.

"I think we all need to stay alert," Victoria says. "Either someone is trying to scare us, or even worse, they're threatening us."

"That's exactly what they're doing," Marley says, and I notice she carefully inspects each woman at the table.

"I don't think we should read any stories tonight," Danielle says. "It's probably safer that way. In fact, maybe we shouldn't meet until this has all been sorted."

"Good idea," April says.

"Before we go, I did have some news I wanted to share," I say. "It might lighten the mood a bit."

"Please," Victoria says. "Go ahead."

"I received a full manuscript request from an agent," I say, carefully. "It seems small compared to everything else that's happening, but I thought you'd all want to know."

Victoria smiles. April's eyes go wide. Danielle places her hands in front of her chest, like she's in prayer. Outwardly, all their reactions are complimentary, but I watch them each closely; one of them must have hacked into my email to send those messages. One of them must know why this manuscript request is nothing to celebrate.

"That is great news," Victoria says. "For *Night Beat*?"

I nod, but remain quiet, still watching each of them.

"Congratulations," Danielle says.

April squeezes my shoulder. "I told you it was only a matter of time."

"Did they give you any idea how long it would take to hear back?" Victoria asks.

"No. More of a waiting game, but it's given me a little bit of hope."

"At least we can end this on a high note," Marley says. "No meetings for the near future, but we can stay in touch?"

"Definitely," Victoria says. "And watch out for each other."

She's the first to leave, followed soon after by April and Danielle. Marley and I remain seated, watching them go.

"That wasn't as bad as I thought it would be," she says. "When they said the police had reached out to all of them, I thought they'd come for blood."

"The cops must not have told them I was the one who talked to them," I say. "Why do you think that is?"

"Maybe they don't want us ganging up on each other," she says.

Or maybe it's because I'm not their only suspect. There could be connections between other group members and the crimes I don't even know about.

"Did you watch their reactions when I told them about the agent request?"

"Yep. That was a smart move," she says, then leans against the backrest of the booth. "Problem is, I think everyone is so genuinely rattled, it's hard to tell if someone is lying."

"Yeah, I couldn't tell either."

"You've known these women a lot longer than I have," she says. "I want you to think. Would any of them have a reason to want to hurt you?"

"They're all my friends," I say. "Or so I thought."

"There's no denying one of them has it in for you," she says. "Your email was hacked. Your tires were slashed. And two recent murders were modeled after your stories. I'm sure you saw the way April was looking at you when that was brought up."

"I did," I say, shuddering. "I felt like they were all suspicious of me."

"Whoever is doing this wants people to be suspicious of you," she says. "This is personal, and this killer is set on making you look as bad as possible."

It's not like I've not considered this over the past couple of weeks, but every time I do, I come up blank. I can't think of any reason why Victoria, April or Danielle would be out to get me. Even when I was suspicious of Marley, I could never settle on a clear motive.

"Your roommate died ten years ago," Marley says. "Could any of them have a connection to that?"

"None of them even knew me then," I say, unthinking. "Let alone Layla."

But as I reconsider everything I've uncovered lately, I'm not sure that's true. It appears all the Maidens had a connection to Layla, however remote. Victoria has worked with the Williams' charity over the years to promote campus safety. Danielle's law firm represented Mike, used his case as a learning point for future clients. April says she knows Crystal from school; could she just as easily have had a connection to Layla?

An idea strikes me, one I hadn't considered before. Even if the Mystery Maidens did have a connection to Layla, I can't see why any of them would resent me for her death.

There's only one person who overlaps my present and past that would.

THIRTY-THREE

Marley has always been right: this is personal.

I realize too late that there's another potential suspect, one who would have much easier access to my life than the group and with an equally strong connection to what happened ten years ago. These bizarre attacks started after I wrote the Layla story, and who would be more connected to that event than Crystal?

Layla, Crystal and I were inseparable. Roommates. The *Friends* of WU. Until Layla was taken from us, and we've blamed ourselves ever since. What if I miscalculated, and Crystal blames me for our friend's death more than I ever realized?

Could Crystal have been the one sending the black hearts? The one I received in my mailbox appeared not long after she moved in. Another black heart preceded my breakup with Jasper, an event that brought Crystal and I closer together. And a black heart was attached to the floral arrangement she brought into our apartment. She could have been strategically leaving them for me all along. Aside from the hearts, Crystal has easier access to my belongings than the other Maidens. She could have hacked into my email and opened the shared drive to access our other manuscripts. I recall her anger when she first read the Layla story. Of course, that's only when I thought she read it. What if she saw the story on my computer earlier and reading it sent her over the edge from stalking to murder?

A soft drizzle dampens my hair and jacket as I march home, but the fiery adrenaline inside protects me against the cold. It's nearing nine o'clock, around the time Crystal usually heads out for the evening, dazzled up in expensive clothes and flashy accessories. At least, that's where I think she's been going. What if her frequent absences are because she's out framing me for crimes? I need to catch her before she leaves, so that I can confront her.

Sure enough, when I arrive home, I find Crystal in the small hallway bathroom, tracing burgundy liner around her lips. She catches my eye in the mirror.

"You're home early," she says.

"Can we talk?"

Glimpsing my reflection, I see a frazzled woman, cheeks red with cold, still bundled up in wet layers, multiple bags hanging off my arms. Crystal notices the distress in my face. She exits the bathroom, taking a seat at the dining-room table. She stretches the hem of her short velvet dress as she sits.

"Did something happen?"

I'm too energized to sit, so I pace the short distance between the table and the kitchen counter. "Something has been happening to me. For weeks, now. You already know that."

"Are you talking about the black hearts again?" Crystal is apprehensive.

"It's more than that, and you know it." I pause, watching her reaction closely. "And it all started after I wrote the Layla story."

As usual, her posture stiffens at the sound of our friend's name. She cocks her head to the side, waiting. "Okay..."

"A few days ago, I found out someone hacked into my email. They sent messages to a dozen different literary agents using my account."

"Why would someone do that?"

"It's another way to mess with me. No one has access to my computer. Except you." I shrug my shoulders, my arms flapping against my sides. "You're the only person who has been around for everything that's happened these past ten years."

She pulls back, like a marionette doll whose string has been yanked. "I'm sorry, are you accusing me of hacking into your email? And doing all that other stuff? The black hearts?"

"We both know you went through my computer once," I say, holding eye contact.

"We've already talked about that, and I apologized. I thought we'd moved on, but clearly you still don't trust me."

"Just answer my question," I say, my voice sharp. "Are you the one who has been sending me the black hearts? Doing everything else?"

She gasps in disbelief. "Wow, Becca. Are we really doing this right now? I told you I've been getting the stupid heart messages, too. You saw the flowers."

Yes, but I can't be sure her explanation is true. Maybe it was just another threat. *Remember*. A message within the walls of my own apartment.

"Answer the question," I say.

"No." Her tone is resolute. "We're best friends. Why would you even think I would do those things?"

"Because of Layla!" I don't mean to shout, but my voice is so loud and raw, it startles us both. "You blame me for what happened to her. For years, you've been torturing me with the black heart messages, and after reading the Layla story, you decided to take things a step further."

"I was upset about the story, and I confronted you about it," she says. "That's what adults do. They don't slash tires and hack into emails. Let alone actually hurt people, like the poor woman on our street. How do you know everything that's been happening isn't a coincidence?"

"It's not! Someone is punishing me, and it all ties into what happened back then." I sling my bags onto the table, rustling through one until I find the article that was left at Banyon's Bridge. "Someone even left this for me."

Hesitantly, she takes the article and reads it, her face hardening. "Why would you think I did that?"

"Someone did, and you're the only one with a connection—"

"We don't even talk about her anymore!" Crystal shouts. "In the past ten years, we've barely brought up that night, and now you've mentioned her twice in the past week. You're writing stories about what happened. It's like you're obsessed."

"That's because someone—"

"No, Becca. No one is out to get you. You're just refusing to move on. You've let Layla's death ruin everything for you, and for what reason? Doing nothing with your life is not going to bring her back."

My teeth grind and my fists clench. "It's not as easy for everyone to move on like nothing happened."

"Is that what you think I've been doing?"

"You certainly don't act like you're in mourning. I mean, look at you now. All dolled up and ready for fun. Sleeping around with other people's husbands. You've got your big smiling face on a billboard on the interstate. Even when your engagement implodes, you land on your feet like nothing happened."

"That's because I'm resilient. When life gets hard, I find a way through because that's the only way. It doesn't mean I'm not hurting about Layla and Thomas and all of it." She's standing now, a splotch of red climbing her neck as her anger builds. "What's the other option? Just totally give up, like you've done?"

"I'm not giving up—"

"Then what *are* you doing? You quit college after she died. You've not been able to hold down a job. You say you want to be a writer, but that isn't going anywhere. If you're not pining for the past, you're consumed by these fake stories in your head. You're living in these worlds that don't exist because that's easier than moving on."

As eager as I am to respond, I know part of what she's saying is true. The argument between myself and Crystal goes much deeper than accusing her of messing with me. Our history has bound us to one another, and yet makes us resentful at the same time. No one will ever understand the guilt we carry from that night and seeing each other is a constant reminder.

"You're the only person in my life now who knew me back then," I say. "Who else could it be?"

"I already told you," she says. "Layla's parents."

"I talked to Layla's parents! Her mom, anyway. She said it wasn't her."

"And you believe her over me?" She laughs cruelly. "This is outrageous."

"We were the only ones there that night—"

"That's not true! There was an entire bar full of people."

"Everything that's happened in the past two weeks has been directed at me, not you," I say. "Besides, if someone else was there that night, they'd surely blame you over me."

Her posture straightens. "What's that supposed to mean?"

"You were the one who was drunk. If you'd been able to take care of yourself, we wouldn't have had to leave in the first place."

It's a weak argument. A cruel one. I know it as soon as the words leave my lips, especially because I still hold so much blame against myself, but I'm wounded at the idea of my friend being my tormentor. All this time I've been investigating people I barely know, it might be the person who knows me best behind it all.

"I can't believe you'd say that to me." The anger in her tone is gone, replaced with sadness. "I've always figured you felt that way, but I can't believe you actually said it. You chose to leave with me. You could have stayed behind."

"I was trying to take care of you."

"You needed to take care of Layla!" The anger returns in full force. "Would you like to know what I've been holding in for the past ten years? My disgust that you knew what Michael was capable of, but you still left her behind."

Of course, it had all come out in the investigation, as soon as Michael Massey was named a suspect. They brought us his name, his picture, wanted to know if we had ever seen him before. I'd told the truth. That I thought he'd tried to attack me once, and that I'd warned Layla about him that night, but she didn't believe me.

"I tried to protect Layla," I say.

"You fought with her and left. If you really thought he was a threat, nothing should have made you leave. Especially not me."

"I told her he was dangerous."

"Did you tell her he attacked you?" We wait in silence, for an answer we both know isn't coming. "You didn't. You didn't tell us about it even when it happened. You should have been more forceful, Becca. Even in the middle of a disagreement, Layla would have believed you if you told her he attacked you."

"I tried. I just couldn't!"

"When it comes to me, you're right about a lot of things. I was reckless and selfish. Just a normal college kid. But at least I had the courage to stand my ground. You didn't, and Layla died because of it."

"You don't mean that," I say under my breath, turning so she can't see my face. I wonder whether these are just vicious insults she's hurling, or if she actually believes what she's saying. I wonder if she's right. If that's what has really been torturing me all these years. My weakness. If I'd been honest about what Michael tried to do to me—the way I was to the police after her death, the way I was last week with Victoria—maybe none of this would have happened. I'd kept the secret, but why? To protect him? To protect some image I had of myself? Whatever the reason, it left Layla defenseless, and she paid the price for all our faults.

Crystal stomps into her room, coming out seconds later with a bag over her shoulder. "I'm crashing at a friend's place for the night. I'll be out of here by next week."

"Crystal, no. I don't—"

"You just accused me of stalking you," she says. "You'd be crazy to still want me here."

I realize, all too late, that I let Marley get into my head. Sure, Crystal's motive might be more personal than the rest, but I also know her better than all the other Maidens. There are elements of their lives that remain unclear. I've had a front row seat to Crystal's life for the past decade, for better or worse. Did I really think she'd be this vindictive? Did I really think she was capable of stalking and murder?

Now that I've thrown these accusations out there, even if I didn't tell her about the worst parts, our relationship will never be the same.

"I still want you here, Crystal," I say.

"Well, I don't want to be here." She stands at the front door. "And if you haven't completely lost your mind, and what you're saying is true, it sounds like it's no longer safe here."

She swings open the front door but takes a step back when she sees two men standing in the hallway. I move closer, seeing Detectives Chaz and Wooley are right outside my door.

"Who the hell are you?" Crystal asks, hateful.

Wooley raises a badge. "We're here to see Becca."

As though our argument wasn't bad enough, the presence of police at my apartment unsettles her even more. She looks back at me, an expression of disbelief on her face.

"I'll let you know when I'll be back to get my things," she says.

The officers step aside, and she walks down the hallway and out of my life.

THIRTY-FOUR

"Did we come at a bad time?" Chaz says, leaning against the doorframe.

"Does it matter?"

I turn on my heels, retreating to the dining-room table. I plop into the hard-wooden chair, waiting for the detectives to follow.

"Is she one of the writers in your group?" Wooley asks, nodding in the direction of where Crystal once stood.

"She's my roommate." I stare at the crumbs on the table's surface, half-whispering to myself, "At least, she was."

"You're having a rough couple of weeks," Chaz says.

"Tell me about it." I sigh, raising my head to meet the detectives' stare. "I know you're not here to check on my wellbeing. So, why are you here?"

"We have a couple of updates we want to run by you," Wooley says, sitting, without invitation, in the seat beside me. "Remind us, what was the first murder you believe had a connection to your little group?"

The heavy amount of skepticism behind the words *murder*

and *little* make me cringe. I slide my hands beneath my crossed legs, trying to keep my temper contained.

"The woman who was killed two weeks ago," I say. "Jessica Wilder."

"She was found by campus, not far off from The Cantina, right?"

"Yes," I say. "And before you ask, I've never been."

Wooley laughs. "Don't worry. We didn't catch you on surveillance this time. We did, however, receive another one of your stories."

Behind him, Chaz reaches into his pocket and pulls out a Ziploc bag with papers inside. They place it in front of me, but I don't need to look to know what the pages are. *The Mistake*. When I do sneak a look, I see a black heart plastered to the front of the manuscript.

"Did you write this?" he asks.

"Where did you get it?" I ask.

"Someone left it at the station. An anonymous tip relating to Jessica Wilder's murder."

I close my eyes, too weak to remain stoic in front of them. I can feel their gaze on me, judging, searching.

"Answer the question, please," Wooley says. "Did you write it?"

"Yes."

"This is our dilemma. We now have two bodies on our hands, the causes of death closely mirroring two different stories written by you."

"I know how it looks," I say. "But I didn't do it."

"Someone who has read your stories did?"

"Yes. That's what I've been trying to tell you." I breathe through my nose, trying to remain calm. "I have no idea why they're framing me."

"Except, with this second story, it doesn't just relate to one murder." Chaz reaches into his pocket again, retrieving another

Ziploc bag. "It's very similar to another death from ten years ago."

I glance down, only for a second, seeing the same Layla article that was left for me at Banyon's Bridge.

"This newspaper clipping was with the story," Wooley adds.

They know about Layla. They know that I wrote the story about an actual murder, and that a copycat killing took place soon after. Between those details and the video surveillance of me at Banyon's Bridge, their insinuations are clear.

"You're a crime writer, right?" Wooley says, that heavy dose of skepticism returning. "If you were us, what would you think?"

"That I'm so lost in grief over my roommate's death from ten years ago, I snapped and started killing people?" I shake my head at the suggestion.

"Sounds like a far-fetched storyline if you ask me," Wooley says.

"It also looks like you have trouble keeping roommates," Chaz adds, flitting his eyes to the front door where Crystal just left.

"I don't know what to say." It's the truth. I can't deny how suspicious everything looks, and I can't find the words to convince them that I'm not involved. "I didn't do this."

"Three murders. All with a connection to you," Wooley says.

"Layla's murderer is behind bars. Michael Massey." His name leaves a bad taste in my mouth, my body shuddering at the memory of him. "You can't accuse me of killing her."

"You were with her the night she died," Chaz says. "I'd still call that a pretty strong connection."

"My friend died, and I wrote a story about her death to cope. I had absolutely nothing to do with Jessica's murder. And I already told you, I wrote the story about Banyon's

Bridge to try and catch the killer. I'm not looking for inspiration to kill."

"Right. It's someone else from your group," Chaz says.

"Why don't you look into it?" I say. "I know you already spoke with them, but you're talking to me like I'm your only suspect. I wrote those stories, but the other women had access to them, and it wouldn't be hard for one of them to frame me."

"We're looking into all of them," Wooley says. "It's not our fault more evidence pointing to you ends up at our station."

"And why do you think that is?" I ask. "Because someone wants you to think it's me!"

"If it makes you feel better," Chaz says, "you're not the only member of your group connected to a murder."

"What?"

Wooley pulls a small spiral notebook from his jacket pocket and flips open the cover. "Marley Theroux. She's in the group, right?"

"Yes," I say, holding my breath.

"Her brother was murdered over a year ago."

"What?" I move closer to the table, desperate to read through his notebook and learn all the details.

"Yep. Brandon. He was bludgeoned to death leaving a bar."

As though in slow motion, I sit back, the pieces falling into place before me. That's the first murder Marley investigated. The one she believes put this chain of murders into motion.

"I do know something about that," I say.

Chaz looks at me, surprised.

"You two might think I'm crazy, but Marley believes the connection between the group's stories and murders happened long before any of the crimes you're talking about. She believes it started with his death."

Chaz pulls out the chair across from me and sits, pulling out his own notepad and pen. "Explain."

I start over, telling them the entire story from the beginning.

The real beginning, according to Marley. I'm not the only person who believes this far-fetched theory. Marley does, too. It's the reason she joined the Mystery Maidens in the first place. Two other murders that linked back to the group before anyone started messing with me.

The detectives remain quiet as I talk, writing down increasingly confusing and far-fetched information. It's clear they're not making sense of things any better than I have these past couple of weeks. All I know is that these murders are no longer only connected to me.

They're personal for Marley, too.

THIRTY-FIVE

The curb beside Marley's apartment is near deserted. It dawns on me Thanksgiving is right around the corner; most students must be getting a head start on the holiday. Mom hasn't mentioned me joining her in New England again. I wonder if she isn't relieved I turned down her invitation. Nothing more stifling than a not-so-happy family gathering around a stuffed dinner table.

I exit the car, leaving behind worries about my family and the approaching holidays. I'm here to confront Marley. All along, I sensed there was something she was withholding, and I finally know what that is. She's not some true-crime junkie who stumbled upon a strange string of murders. Her brother was the first victim, which makes her just as invested in this as I am, maybe even more so. There's an accompanying sense of relief, too. Maybe all this bloodshed and loss isn't targeted at me alone. Layla's death and the black hearts play a substantial role, but whoever is doing this must have other motives.

Marley's balcony is empty. I suppose I have the chilly November weather to thank for that. I buzz her number at the apartment's entrance, hoping Marley hasn't packed up and left town like the rest of her classmates.

After several seconds, a voice rises from the intercom: "Yeah?" I recognize it instantly.

"Marley, it's Becca," I say. "We need to talk."

A beat passes, and I wonder if she's going to ring me in or ignore me entirely. The intercom remains silent, but a few seconds later, there's the blaring buzzer of the front door unlocking.

I climb the steps to Marley's third-floor flat. The building has clearly been renovated, oily iron edging the exposed brickwork in the stairwell. There aren't many units in the complex, fewer neighbors than even I have. As I rap against the front door, I wonder, does Marley have roommates? Does she live alone? There's so little I know about her, and the few details I do have could all potentially be lies.

The door swings open. Marley stands in the doorway, her hair in a disheveled bun atop her head. Dark circles rest beneath her eyes, dulling her otherwise youthful skin. For the first time since I've met her, Marley isn't lighting up the room. Was she ever that effervescent, or was I only wanting her to be?

"Why are you here?" she asks, her voice as dull and dry as the rest of her.

"We need to talk about Brandon," I say.

It's important to use his name, I think. We're no longer dealing with fiction. No longer dealing with people far removed from our real lives, on the other side of a computer screen or in a newspaper article. Brandon was her brother, and Marley believes he was murdered by the same person who threatened me and committed the copycat killings. I want to know why.

She turns, leaving the door open, a silent invitation to enter. Inside, her apartment is as chic as I might have suspected. Gilded framed portraits of musicians litter the living-room walls. Beneath her television is a vintage record player, a massive collection of discs displayed under it. Her furniture is minimalist, all clear glass and sharp edges. The only thing that seems out of place in this perfectly curated apartment is the melancholy resident.

"When did you talk to the police?" she asks, sitting in one of the narrow chairs in the living room.

"Last night," I say. "Whoever is behind this sent them more evidence tying me to the murders."

"And are the police buying it?"

I shrug my shoulders, wandering over to another chair in the room. I sit, struggling to make myself comfortable. "Hard to say. They can't deny the information that's in front of them, but I do think they're starting to question why everything's been given to them. All that's missing is a tidy freaking bow." My smile fades quickly. "Anyway, they now have a copy of *The Mistake*. They know about Layla's death. When they dug into the group, they found out about your brother."

Marley stares out the window overlooking her balcony, the same place where I found her that night after the bridge. She looks at the street below with longing, never once acknowledging anything I've said. Finally, she speaks.

"My brother was my hero," she says. "A cliché, I know. Sounds like the type of thing a person would only say after their brother was brutally murdered. For me, it was true, from the time we were kids. Whatever Brandon did, I was only a few steps behind him, trying to copy his every move.

"He was smart. Like, freakishly so. He understood how to write code at a young age. Won loads of awards at school. I was known around our community as Brandon's little sister, but that never made me bitter. I was proud to be his sister. Proud just to grow up in the same world as him. Everyone who knew him felt that way, convinced he would do really great things one day."

"He lit up the room," I say, the words escaping before I have the chance to stop myself.

She laughs painfully. "He really did. Why is it always the best people that get taken too soon?"

The way she describes her brother, I can picture him. His smile, his impact on Marley. In many ways, he sounds like Layla. Their interests were different, their personalities unique. It's the effect they had on those around them. A special type of magic.

"Because he was so smart, he got a full ride to WU," Marley continues, her voice hardening. "He was two years older than me, and I knew the moment he received his acceptance letter, I'd follow him. That was the plan, anyway. Until he went barhopping one night during his freshman year and never came home." Marley looks up, her glare piercing something inside of me. "You know what happened next."

We went over each gruesome detail when Marley met me at the pizzeria. Brandon was the first death in a string of killings pulled from the Mystery Maidens' stories.

"Why didn't you tell me he was your brother?"

"I had to treat his death like I would any other mystery. Be objective. That meant locking away the memories of Brandon, my brother. It's the only way I can obsess over this day in and day out without losing my mind."

I study her now, her sallow complexion, her ill-fitting clothes. She's been trying to separate the case from her personal life, but it's taken its toll, stripping away her energy. It's likely why she ditched me at last week's meeting; it was all becoming too real. She's talked to the police multiple times now, Brandon's death likely being brought up. The fact that her brother died, was possibly the first victim of the killer, is impossible to ignore.

"So, there's no podcast?"

She laughs. "No podcast. That's just the story I came up with. It's easier than admitting the truth."

"You joined our group because you believe one of the members killed your brother?"

"Yes. Everything else I told you is still true. I first noticed the similarities between the murders and the short stories in Victoria's creative writing class. I put together that those stories came from the Mystery Maidens group." She crosses her arms over her body as though protecting herself. "Now you know why it was easy for me to catch the similarities. When I first read the story, all I could picture was my brother's murder. For about a week, I convinced myself it was coincidence. Just the grief talking. But when I read the second story about the man strangled in the park, I thought, what are the odds?"

If the murders had stopped there, I would have likely blown her off. Anyone would. But that was before someone slashed my tires and hacked into my email. Before someone started leaving printouts of my short stories at crime scenes. Before Jessica Wilder and Darryl Nease were murdered.

"I believe you," I tell her. The words float between us, settling around Marley like a blanket.

"Thanks," she says. "Even though I wasn't the only one holding back. The police told me about the black hearts."

My stomach sinks. "What did they say?"

"That someone has been sending you strange messages for years. And you think it's the same person who is behind the murders."

"Layla had a black heart tattoo. After she died, I started getting them sent to me from some kind of stalker. They've been tied to all the crimes that happened in recent weeks."

"How could you think I was ever behind this?" she asks. "I would have been in grade school when Layla died."

"I don't know. I thought it was possible you were working with someone else," I answer honestly. "Sometimes I wondered if I wasn't chasing two different criminals entirely. One thing is for sure, the black hearts are connected to the group now. There was one attached to the *The Mistake* manuscript that was sent to the police."

"If the police told me about your stalker, and that you were the one who went to them, they probably told the others, too."

"They've talked to everyone?"

"I'm assuming. Now everyone in the group knows about your theory, including whoever is behind it."

I cross my arms, thinking. Now that everything's out in the open, the stakes are raised. The possibility of unmasking the killer is better than ever.

"I told the police your theory that the killer was active before I even joined the group. We need to be upfront about everything if we want to put a stop to this," I say. And if we want to get justice for the many lives lost. Marley's brother, Brandon. Rudy Raines. Jessica Wilder. And now, Darryl Nease. With each name added to the list, the burden of guilt gets heavier. "I was surprised you hadn't already told them."

"We both know how ridiculous it sounds, that someone in the writing group is a cold-blooded murderer, but isn't truth stranger than fiction?"

"In my experience." I look outside. A blackbird lands on the iron railing, blending into the drab setting. It rustles its head a few times before spreading its wings and flying off. "We need to decide what we're going to do. It doesn't matter what the police think."

"I don't know what to do." She leans back, her shoulders slumped. "The one thing I do know is that whoever is doing this hasn't yet figured out I'm Brandon's sister."

"What makes you think that?"

"We have different surnames," she says. "I started going by my mother's maiden name after Brandon died. Being known as *that dead guy's sister* carried too much stigma."

"Still, whoever is behind this could have known."

"I really don't think they've given a second thought to

Brandon since he died. Or Rudy Raines for that matter. For the past couple of weeks, all the focus has been on you." She clenches her jaw, and I realize there's an extra layer of motive for Marley: she believes this is the only way to bring her brother's killer to justice. "It all ties back to Layla."

"But why?" I ask.

"I don't know," she says. "I think the only way to really answer that question is to go to the group and ask."

THIRTY-SIX

When I arrive at McCallie's Pub, it feels as though I'm approaching a firing squad, not a group of friends. Everyone is there. They've staked out our familiar booth in back, each person sitting around the table to form a letter C. I stand at the table, cringing at the awkward hush that falls over the group.

"We should talk," Victoria says, stating the obvious.

"I know," I tell them. "Let me explain—"

"Did you actually tell the police you think one of us is a murderer?" Danielle cuts in.

"And that you think we're using the stories from group as inspiration?" April adds.

"It sounds ridiculous," I say. "I know—"

"You realize I could be placed on formal reprimand for getting involved in a criminal case," Danielle says.

"Likewise, the university could be at fault for being affiliated with our group," Victoria says. "The whole reason I started Mystery Maidens was to connect emerging writers."

"And my kids," April says. She doesn't expand further, but I know what she's implying. In a custody battle with her soon-to-be ex, the last thing she needs is to be accused of committing a crime. The others don't know about April's personal life, but I do because she trusts me. They all trust me, in some capacity, and I've broken that trust.

The entire time the group members lay into me, Marley sits in silence. Whenever she opens her mouth to speak, another person cuts in. All she can do is stare back at me with pitiful, worried, eyes.

"Let's give her a chance to talk," she says at last.

I go to sit in the booth, but none of the group budges. I grab a nearby chair and put it at the end of the table.

"I can only imagine how upset you all are," I begin. "But someone is targeting me, and as upsetting as it is to say, all signs point to it being someone in this group."

"Targeting you how?" Danielle asks. "And why?"

"Well, first my tires were slashed. Just like in April's story. Then a person was hit by a car right outside my apartment, like in Victoria's story." As I speak, everyone listens along, unconvinced. "After I shared *The Mistake* with the group, Jessica Wilder was murdered in the exact same way."

"Right now, it sounds like you're rattling off a bunch of conspiracy theories," Victoria says. "None of that is directly linked to you."

"You're right," I say. "At first it wasn't. And I knew how crazy the whole thing sounded, so I wanted to test my own theory and see what might happen. That's why I wrote *Murder at the Bridge* and shared it. And guess what happened? A man died that same night, and the police found a copy of my short story in his pocket."

Despite the women's simmering anger, everyone seems to sit up a little straighter. They might feel betrayed, but no one can insist it's only a coincidence when my story was found at a crime scene.

"When the police talked to me, they were acting as though

you were a suspect," Danielle says, her gaze analytical, even a tad suspicious, "not a victim."

I exhale. "The police have video of me on the bridge. Between that and my story being found in the victim's pocket, I think they're working off the theory I've snapped."

"Maybe you have," April says. "I mean, you were quick to tell the police you thought we were involved. Maybe it has been you this whole time."

"It's not like I wanted to go to the police, but come on! We read and write this stuff for a living. How many times have you been reading a book, and you scream at the protagonist to go to the cops? That's what I did, and they didn't take me seriously, until another body turned up."

"It's suspicious that there are now two deaths linked to our group," Victoria says, still homing in on this point. She cuts her eyes at me. "And they're both stories you wrote."

"Which brings me back to my original question," Danielle says, recapturing my attention. "Why you?"

I take a deep breath, my gaze fixed on the table. "After Jessica Wilder was killed, the newspaper ran that article about a similar attack that happened ten years ago. Remember? We talked about it during group." I force myself to look up, to meet each of their eyes and really look. "The victim's name was Layla Williams. What I didn't tell you... is that she was my college roommate."

"Layla," Victoria repeats slowly. "That's the name of the woman who dies in *The Mistake*."

"Yes." My voice is shaking, but I force myself to hold it together, to continue this conversation, wherever it may take us.

"You were living with her at the time she was murdered?" Danielle asks, tilting her head slightly.

"Yes." I force myself to keep going. "I was with her that night at the bar. Before she was killed."

"So everything you'd written in that story," April says,

pausing as though it's too ridiculous to speak aloud, "it all really happened?"

"Yes. What I said about having a nightmare was true. I wrote *The Mistake* to try and process what I was feeling, and I believe that's what started all of this."

"You've written about real experiences before," Victoria says, staring right through me, no doubt referencing the near-assault I told her about, "but your friend was murdered. Don't you think that was crossing a line?"

"I don't know. I—"

"Why would you write about something like that?" April asks, not even hiding the disgust in her voice. "Something so personal."

"And dark," Danielle adds. "We all weave in parts of our real life with our fiction, but writing an entire story to share with us—"

"She already told you why she wrote it," Marley jumps in, trying to defend me. "She didn't mean for it to go anywhere."

"Clearly, it's triggered someone," Victoria says, looking around the table at the group of women she brought together, then back at me. "You told the police you think it triggered one of us!"

"That *is* what I think," I say, lacking a better response. Their defensiveness and outrage is warranted, but it doesn't change my suspicions. One of them must be responsible for the copycat crimes. There's no other way. "I didn't intend to start some crime spree."

"Not to mention you've thought this for weeks and been coming to meetings like everything is fine," Danielle adds. "Did you ever consider you might be putting us in danger?"

I sit up straighter, desperate. "I was careful. I told the police—"

"We already know what you told the police," April cuts me off.

"I don't know if you're crazy or just completely careless." Danielle stands, putting on her coat. "Either way, I think you should stay away from the rest of us."

"Guys," Marley chimes in. "She's trying to explain."

"I think we've heard enough," April says, sliding out of the booth. "Danielle's right. Stay away until this gets sorted."

"Needless to say, no more meetings," Victoria says, packing her things. "Thanks to Becca, the police are looking into all of us, and we don't need to give them any ammunition."

One by one, they storm away from the table until Marley and I are the only ones left. From where we sit, we can see the trio of women still deep in conversation on the sidewalk, breathy clouds exiting their mouths, hands gesticulating wildly. Another moment passes, before they head down the street.

"Are you ready?" Marley asks me, a conspiratorial glint in her eye.

"I've got April," I say, standing. "Are you sure you can track the others by yourself?"

"They live on the same street. If one of them takes off in a different direction, I'll let you know." She pulls out her phone, tapping at the screen. "Is your location working?"

"Yep. I checked before the meeting started." We agreed to share locations on our phones. Keeping eyes on everyone, including each other, is the only way to stay safe. "Make sure yours is on, too."

We're outnumbered. That's one of the many barriers Marley and I ran into when we concocted the plan to follow the rest of the group. Regardless, this is our best opportunity to find out who is behind the murders. Now that we've confronted all of them, whoever is responsible will no doubt act erratically. We'll follow each of the members, watching their every move until we figure out the truth.

April crosses the street while Danielle and Victoria head in the direction of downtown, followed by Marley. I hustle to the front of the restaurant, tracing April's footsteps, making sure to keep enough distance between us that she won't know I'm following her.

THIRTY-SEVEN

As I predicted, April uses the free parking spots by the library. She'd rather walk an extra block than fight for the frenzied meter parking closer to McCallie's. I thought I spotted her car there before the meeting, which is why I used a meter across the street. I'm able to get into my car and follow her without being noticed.

We leave the stop-and-go traffic of downtown, merging onto the highway. She's headed home, I think. I remember this route from when I visited her last week. However, when April passes her street without turning, my curiosity grows.

"Where are you going?" I say aloud to the empty car.

My phone begins to ring. I connect it to the overhead system and answer.

"Where are you headed?" Marley asks. Her voice is breathy and close, like her mouth is nuzzling the receiver.

"I'm following April," I say. "She's not going home. We just passed her street."

"I'm still on foot," Marley says. "Victoria and Danielle are together. It makes me suspicious."

"They live close to one another," I say. "They probably do this after every meeting."

"They haven't noticed I've followed them," she says, confidently. "I don't know what I'm going to do when they split off."

"Just keep watching," I say, turning on my car blinker. Up ahead, April has taken a left at the light. She's heading down Washington Street. In my head, I try to piece together where she might be going. All I know is that's the part of town where the police station is located.

"What are we supposed to be looking for anyway?"

Marley sounds frustrated. At least my chase is taking place in the heated comfort of my car. She's stuck on the streets, no idea where she's headed, or what she's looking for. The fact she's tailing two people will make her task harder. If one of them is the killer, they aren't going to do anything suspicious until they are alone.

I'm convinced whoever's responsible for this crime spree will act. We've exposed their pattern to the entire group now. Not to mention, the police have now cornered all of us. At the very least, there must be some evidence they have to hide, some action that must be taken, and we're hoping either Marley or I will catch them doing it.

"They've stopped walking," Marley says. I can hear the sharp intake of breath, can almost imagine her trying to duck behind an old building or lamppost to hide.

"What's happening?" I ask. My eyes are glued to April's bumper, which is still moving slowly down Washington Street. There's only one car between us, and I hope it's enough to keep me concealed.

"Still just talking. Now they're..." She pauses. I can hear her raspy breaths. "They're hugging. Danielle is going inside a building."

"What kind of building?"

"I can't see. Not until Victoria starts walking again. She's just standing there."

April's car comes to a stop outside a large apartment block. It looks familiar and forgettable, the way most complexes do. I'm not sure whether I've ever seen it before. I park against the curb on the other side of the street, watching as April exits her vehicle.

"Okay, Victoria is walking again," Marley says.

"April has stopped," I say, watching her like a lioness watches its prey. "She's at an apartment block off Washington Street. She's out of her car, but she's not gone inside."

Instead, she leans against the car. April's head is raised, staring at the drab building. Even from where I sit, I can pick up on her sad expression. There's an emptiness in her eyes, a look of despair. Is her guilt finally catching up to her? Does she realize it's only a matter of time before the twisted game she's constructed comes crashing down?

"Looks like Danielle went inside her offices," Marley says, apparently reading the inscription on the front of the building. "Gates and Hamblin Associates."

"I forgot her office was on that street," I say. "What's Victoria doing?"

"Still walking towards her apartment." Her words run together, tense with indecision. "What should I do? Wait on Danielle or follow Victoria?"

"Follow Victoria," I say. "At least see if she heads home. Danielle can't do too much at work."

Truthfully, I'm too preoccupied to think about either one of them. I'm watching April, trying to figure out why she's here and what she's doing.

The double glass doors to the apartment building open. A man walks out. He's wearing a dark trench coat, hands in his pockets. He stands directly in front of April, and the two of them begin to talk.

It dawns on me that even if one of these women is behind

the killings, they may be enlisting the help of someone else. It's a lot for one person to carry out on their own. Could April have asked this man to help her? Plant evidence at times when she was elsewhere to better establish an alibi?

The questions shoot off in my brain like a firing squad, and then the double doors open again. This time, two small children come running out, one toddling as though he just learned how to walk. They rush past the man in the trench coat and into April's arms.

Her children. I'm not familiar enough with either of them to know their faces, but April's expression confirms it. The worry and apprehension on her face disappears, replaced with joy. She bends down, kissing each child on the top of the head.

It must be her night with the kids. April told me she'd been separated from her husband for some time. This must be where he's staying, which explains the worried look on her face. I can't imagine what it must be like to be a mother and have your children out of your sight, to move them from a swanky house in the suburbs to a dingy apartment downtown.

The kids turn and hug the man in the coat. Chase, their father. April opens the door to the backseat, and they jump inside.

"Are you still there?" Marley's voice sounds irritated.

"Yeah," I say, putting the car in drive. "It's not April."

"How do you know?"

"She's picking up her kids from their dad's. Even if she was behind this, she wouldn't do anything with her kids around. We need to keep watching the others."

"Okay, so that's one off the list," she says. "I still have no idea where Victoria is going. I'm pretty sure we passed her building a couple of blocks ago."

"That's good," I say, driving back in the direction I just came from. "Maybe she's going to meet someone."

"I'm getting a bad feeling," she says. "The roads are thinning out. There are barely any people around. She's going to see I'm following her."

"Just stay on her," I say, merging onto the highway. "I can make it back to Danielle's office. We'll have eyes on both of them—"

A high-pitched, heart-stopping scream rings through the phone. The sound startles me so much I slam on the brakes, almost causing the car behind me to rear-end me. From behind, a horn blares.

"Marley, are you there?"

Nothing. The staticky rustling of the line, still connected, but no voice at the other end.

"Marley, did something happen?" I shout. "Answer me."

The sound on the line changes. Becomes clean and crisp, like someone is holding it up to their ear. There are the heavy exhales of someone breathing—

Click. The line is disconnected.

My nerves rattle, my heart pounding. Marley was still following Victoria when she let out that scream. Could Victoria have seen she was being followed? Could she, or someone else, have attacked Marley? If they did, the person would have looked at her phone afterward, and seen she was talking to me.

Every car on the road seems to move at a snail's pace as I slam my horn, swerving in and out of traffic. Hurriedly, I type in Marley's last known location into my GPS. She's eight minutes away, only a few blocks from Victoria's apartment complex.

In my mind, that terrifying scream rings out again and again. She's in danger.

Last time a friend was at risk, I walked away. I knew the world was a scary place. My own experience with Michael had taught me that, but I was too insecure and afraid to fight for my friend's safety, and that mistake cost Layla her life.

Now, I know better, and I'm not going to let Marley fight this battle on her own.

THIRTY-EIGHT

The world feels like it's tilting, time a foreign construct, as I race to Marley's location. I slam on my horn, urging cars to move out of the way. Heat pumps into the vehicle, droplets of sweat dripping down my neck, but even messing with the temperature dial feels like a waste of precious seconds. My vision zeroes in, focusing on the road ahead.

Four minutes until my destination.

I re-enter downtown and its crosswalk-littered streets. As much as I need to go fast, I'm afraid I'll hit someone if I don't slow down. I pump on the brake, my body aching. A group of college students walk aimlessly across the street. I blare my horn again, and they jump back just in time for me to zoom past.

Three minutes until my destination.

I'm not even sure where I'm headed. Somewhere in the vicinity of Victoria's apartment. That's where Marley was when I heard that awful scream, the echoes of which reverberate in my mind. How long does it take to murder a person? Strangle the life from their body? Crush their skull? What if I'm too late?

Two minutes until my destination.

My surroundings are becoming increasingly familiar. I've

just passed McCallie's Pub, the starting location of today's stupid mission. To the left, a police car sits against the curb. Instinctually, I hit my brakes. The car must be empty because it doesn't pursue, but that gives me an idea. I fiddle with my phone, my shaking hands almost dropping it, and dial 911.

One minute until my destination.

The phone rings twice before it connects.

"Whitaker 911," the operator says.

"A woman is being attacked," I say, searching the streets for a place to park. "Send help."

"What is your location?"

I step out of the car, my stomach dropping when I realize where I am. I'd been so determined to get here, seeing the address didn't strike a chord. It's changed since the last time I was here. My old apartment building torn down, an unfinished structure in its place.

"The construction site on Magnolia Avenue," I say. My eyes scan the brickwork, looking for the correct address, while my mind recalls old memories. Layla and Crystal and I on moving day, unloading our cheap belongings. Waltzing down the sidewalk to the restaurants and bars nearby. This is where we lived together, the last place Layla ever lived.

"Who is being attacked?" the operator asks. "Calm down and give me some details."

I'm out of breath, struggling to handle a conversation and open the front door to the building. The door is unlocked, but it's so heavy, it takes all my strength to pull it open.

"The victim's name is Marley Theroux," I answer, once inside. "I don't know what's happening."

"What is your name?"

I'm inside. The entranceway is empty and made of stone, reminding me of being inside a cave. To my left, I see a series of boxes inscribed with names and numbers. This is a storage facility, with countless units on the inside. Even if Marley and Victoria are here, it could take hours to find them.

"Ma'am, what is your name?" the operator repeats, her voice increasingly agitated.

"It's a storage facility," I say. "Send help."

"You need to stay on the line—"

I end the call before she can finish her instructions. There's no more information I can provide at this point, and I must use every minute between now and when the police get here to find Marley.

I pull up my location app, the blue circle showing Marley is in this exact location. She's here, but where? Luring her here was intentional. Another way to send me a message.

"Marley?" I call out, my voice echoing. It's a long strand of locked metallic units. It's like I'm underground, hunting through catacombs, and I'm not sure which one might be Marley's tomb. "Victoria?"

Marley was right, and Victoria is the one who was behind this. I suppose it makes sense, seeing as Victoria was always the biggest literary critic of the group. She's spent so many years reading and writing crime stories, life began imitating art. But still, why? Has she completely lost her mind? Did working alongside Layla's parents send her over the edge?

My footsteps thud against the concrete floors as I run the length of the storage containers. Each one is closed and locked; Marley could be right on the other side of a metal awning, and I'd never know. At the end of the hallway, another row continues on. I turn the corner, and that's when I see her.

Marley is sprawled out on the concrete, blood trailing from behind her ear.

"Marley!" I bend to her, placing my hand on her neck. There's a faint pulse—

"Don't move."

The voice is behind me, the echoing sounds of the order

freezing me in place. I pull back my hands, Marley's blood staining my fingers. I raise them slowly, showing I'm unarmed.

"Victoria?" I call out.

"Nope," the voice says, smug and indignant.

Slowly, I stand and turn around.

Danielle is standing in front of me, holding a hammer at her side. The bright fluorescent lights illuminate her and the weapon completely. There are dark red stains on the metal.

"You're behind this?" I say.

"You'd figured out it was one of us," she says. "Why so surprised it's me?"

I could never figure out why any of them did this. For the past ten minutes, I was convinced it was Victoria. That's who Marley had been following when I heard that terrifying scream.

"You're not as smart as you think you are," Danielle says, gesturing the hammer toward Marley. "She isn't either."

"It's been you this entire time?" I ask, my voice pleading.

"I thought you would have figured it out by now," she says. "I've left you enough clues."

"The black hearts." All the images flash through my mind, but still nothing makes sense. "Why are you doing any of this?"

"It's about Layla!" Danielle roars, raising the hammer in a murderous rage. "By now, you should know this isn't about some stupid writing group. It's about *her*. Everything has always been about her."

"You knew Layla?" I stare at Danielle's face, trying to understand. Danielle and Layla exist in two different lives, the one I lived before my roommate's death, and the one after. How could the two of them have ever intersected?

"She was my best friend," she says. "And she died because of you. All these years later, you still can't give her the attention she deserves."

"I don't understand." At first, I'm not sure if the words are spoken or merely thought. Confusion and fear mingle, making a mess of my mind. All I can piece together is that Marley is wounded, Danielle is holding a hammer and this all somehow relates back to Layla.

"I didn't know you were friends," I say. "I don't remember you—"

"You wouldn't! I wasn't friends with *you*," she says. "Layla was my best friend all through high school. We went to different colleges and grew apart. You think she was only your friend, but she was mine first. And you just left her."

"What happened to Layla was a tragedy," I say. "If I knew what was going to happen, I never would have left."

"Woulda. Coulda. Shoulda. People like you are just as bad as the monsters out there. You pretend to be someone's friend, and then abandon them when they need you most. Imagine what that night was like for Layla."

"I do all the time."

I think of the fear, the sense of abandonment she must have felt. Only recently, I expressed all those emotions in the story I wrote. *The Mistake.* If there's anything I could take back, it would be my actions the night she died.

"What you're doing now makes no sense," I say. "Killing those people had nothing to do with Layla."

"It was that awful story. The moment I read it, I knew. You didn't even care enough to change her name. For a while, I thought I'd gotten control over my anger, but when I read that, it all came rushing back. I needed to punish you for what you did, and what better way than to use your own words against you?"

On the ground, Marley starts to tremble. She's alive, but when she wakes and sees the situation, her terror will renew. I worry for her safety, and mine, too. No one can predict what Danielle might do next.

"This didn't start with my story," I say, desperate for more answers. "What about the other two men? Brandon, the man bludgeoned to death in an alley. And Rudy, who was strangled and left at a playground. Just like in the stories from group."

"Oh. Those." The nonchalant way she responds sends shivers down my spine. "In the years after Layla died, I struggled. I kept replaying that night repeatedly. Seeing her sitting at that bar, talking to *him*. If she hadn't been so focused on some guy, she'd still be alive today.

"I was able to keep my anger under control while I was in school. When you have a heavy class load, you don't have time to feel anything, even grief. I think that's why I was able to control it for so many years. No choice.

"Once I got a job, it's like I finally settled into what my adult life was. What my life without Layla was. For the first time since she died, I'd go out into the world, and I really felt her loss. She'd never be with me again, and every time I saw a group of girls together or guys alone at the bar, I felt her absence.

"Writing helped. I wrote stories to try to process what I was feeling, just like you said you did with *The Mistake*, but this anger inside kept growing, getting out of control. It wasn't long after I'd written that first story, I went out to a bar, and saw Brandon."

"Marley's brother," I say, my heart hurting for her, even though she can't hear.

"Never knew that tidbit," Danielle says, taking a look at Marley on the ground. "He looks like Michael Massey, did you ever notice? When I saw him at the bar, I watched him half the night, thinking of how much he resembled the man who'd been with Layla. The story I'd written was fresh in my mind, and I kept thinking, this guy would make the perfect victim.

"I don't know what came over me. It's like I couldn't tell the difference between what was real and what was fake, between the past and the present. I followed the guy out of the bar, retracing the similar path the victim would have taken in my story. He cut down an alley to take a piss. Disgusting little creep. Before I knew it, I had a two by four in my hands and I was bashing him over the head with it."

"You murdered an innocent man," I say.

"But I wasn't attacking Brandon, don't you see? In my mind I was attacking *him*. The man who took Layla from me."

"What about the second murder?"

"After that, it's like I had this urge inside, but at the same time, there was this other voice in my head. The real me, telling me that if I wasn't careful, I'd end up in jail, no better than Michael Massey. For a while, that was enough. Then, April shared that story about the cheating husband during Mystery Maidens. I get so disgusted thinking of all the pathetic men out there who walk over us women, like it's their birthright. The story stuck with me for a while.

"Not long after, I went to a bar and struck a conversation with some guy. Rudy. I could see the tan line of the wedding ring on his hand, knew he was a scumbag, just like the character in her story.

"When we left together, he thought he was going to get laid. We ended up at the park not far from where he lived. He started unbuckling his pants. I used his own belt to strangle him to death."

I struggle to shake away the images in my mind. It's important to keep Danielle talking. I have to understand why she did all of this. Any of it. "And then you just stopped?"

"You came to me. I couldn't believe it. I'd been keeping tabs on you for years, of course. Sending you the black hearts whenever I thought you needed a reminder of what you'd done. Out of all the lawyers in Whitaker, you show up at my doorstep asking for help."

"A black heart is what lost me that job in the first place," I remind her.

"I know. I remember putting it in the tip jar," she says. "Just like I broke up your relationship before that. You should be thanking me for that one. Jasper was a lousy lay."

I clench my jaw, trying not to react. For years, the black hearts have been shrouded in mystery. Now I imagine Danielle's face at each scene, in every scenario.

"So, you decided to be my friend instead?" I ask.

"I'd spent years trying to ruin your life. Not just with the hearts. Before that, I'd followed all the details of Layla's case, remained in contact with her family. I was one of the people who urged her parents to file that suit against you and Crystal. Sure, it didn't go anywhere, but maybe it will make people think twice before leaving their drunk friend alone in a bar with a man she barely knows.

"But ruining your life hadn't done much for me, had it? I was still so angry inside. I was still *hurting* people. When you sat in my office that day, I thought it was time I take a different approach. I decided to forgive you."

"Forgive me?"

"Nine years had passed at that point. I knew I had changed, for better and worse. I thought maybe you had, too. And it's not like the black hearts hadn't done enough damage over the years. Your life was rather pathetic. I chose to tell you about the writing group, tried to get to know you on a different level. I never even let you know how much you had taken away from me. As it got closer to the anniversary of her death, I sent another black heart to your apartment, just to keep you on your toes. Still, I truly believed I'd moved on from what happened.

"And then you wrote that story."

My heart thuds against my chest. "It was a mistake. I'm sorry. I never meant for anyone else to read it."

"Then why did you share it? I'm telling you, reading that story made me feel like I was right back in that moment. There at that bar."

The way she says this comes out strange, reminds me of what she said earlier, about seeing the man with Layla.

"You weren't there that night," I say. "How could you be right back in that moment? How could you see her sitting at the bar with him?"

Her face stills, the same way it did earlier when she was caught in a lie.

"Oh," Danielle says. "I guess you don't have the full story about that either."

THIRTY-NINE

Danielle leans against the brick wall, her slumped shoulders speaking to exhaustion, but the weapon she grips tightly still serves as a threat. I watch her closely and listen.

"I was heartbroken when Layla decided to go to another school," she says. "I always thought we'd stick together. Maybe even room together. I couldn't understand why she'd ruin our plan and do her own thing."

Her face changes, shedding years of maturity, and for a moment, she appears younger, the lines across her forehead and around her eyes gone. I can almost imagine that version of herself, before time and tragedy changed us both.

"We stayed in touch as best we could," she continues. "We'd catch up over winter and summer breaks. Made plans to meet up on weekends. Of course, it was always easier for me to shift my schedule around. I never made the connections she did at college. Layla was my only true friend. I was always willing to make time for her."

The last few sentences come out as an accusation, as though Crystal and I did something wrong by befriending Layla. We weren't trying to take her away from anyone. In fact, I barely remember Layla talking about her relationships back home. There could have been the odd weekend she met up with an old friend and didn't tell us. I recalled all the times she'd return from a visit and seem bothered. Maybe it wasn't a complicated home life that was causing her problems, but an obsessive friendship. This fact raises my guard against everything Danielle is about to say. How much is the truth and how much is a carefully created narrative?

"I was going to visit her at WU," Danielle says, recapturing my attention. "I knew Layla was busy with exams, and I told her I'd be happy to hang around until she finished. Then we could spend all our time together, just like the old days. She'd blown me off for several months in a row, and I was starting to think she was avoiding me. The real Layla would never do that, not to her oldest friend. She was just so distracted with her life at school. Every time I tried to make plans with her, there was always an excuse. She said we should wait until after the semester was over.

"What she didn't know was that I'd already driven to Whitaker. The last thing I wanted to do was get back in my car and go home. I figured I'd surprise her. Once she saw I'd come all this way to visit her, she'd be happy to take a few hours away from her studies."

Danielle looks down, rolling the hammer between her hands. It's visibly painful for her to tell this story, and for a moment, I pity her. I've spent the last decade revisiting that awful night, trying to work out where I went wrong, what I could have said differently. When she lifts her head, there's a hardness to her stare, her eyes almost completely black.

"I was on my way here. To this very apartment building," she says. "I was going to surprise her. Imagine my shock when the three of you came out, dressed to the nines and ready for a night on the town. Layla was too busy to hang out with me but had all the energy in the world for her *new* friends."

Like a movie replaying in my mind, I envision us. The smell of hairspray rising from Crystal's stiff updo. The cold chill in the air. Layla's flushed cheeks. I'm back in that moment, on our last night together, watching as three young women stumble down the sidewalk, our unified laughter echoing through the streets.

"I figured you two pressured her into going out," Danielle says, halting my imagination, forcing me into her story. "Sure, she looked happy, but she was just trying to please. Like she always did. There's no way she would have ditched me for the two of you, not when she got to see you every day.

"I followed you to that awful bar. I don't know how Layla could stand it for a second. All those gross frat boys everywhere and the vulgar music. It wasn't the type of place we would have ever gone. I decided I'd wait a little longer, surprise her there and we could leave together."

I revisit the scene at the bar. The three of us huddled around the sticky countertop, fighting to get the bartender's attention. Only now, I imagine Danielle lurking in the back, watching and dissecting our every move. I never knew she was there, and inserting her into the scene now makes my body shudder with fear.

"Except, the longer I waited, the more I realized Layla was having fun. She was enjoying herself," Danielle says, her words filled with hatred. "Even after the two of you wandered away and left her with *him*."

"We *were* just having fun," I say, the words out of my mouth before I've thought them through.

This is the part of the night that's most painful for me to remember. The actions I took before leaving Layla alone. Even now, I wish I could somehow scrub the memories from my mind, imagine a situation where I grabbed Layla by the hand and urged her to come home with us, but I didn't do that, and I've lived with my guilt ever since.

"Fun? You were getting wasted. Not even spending time with one another. I don't understand it, how people somehow think they're close to someone else because they get shit-faced together. That's not quality time. That's not friendship. It was obvious just by looking at the three of you that you weren't really her friends."

I open my mouth to speak but stop myself. My eyes land on the weapon, and I'm reminded that Danielle is still a threat. But her analysis is wrong. She's basing her idea of our friendship off a few glimpses of us in a bar on one night. She never saw the way we comforted each other after breakups, the way we revved each other up to get through challenging courses. She never saw the laughter, the love. Danielle's reduction of our relationship angers me, even if it's only intended to make her own connection to Layla superior.

"I decided I'd wait until you headed home to confront her," she says. "I watched as you and Crystal stumbled to the entrance, waiting for Layla to join you. But she just stayed there, talking to *him*. It was a whole other layer of betrayal. She wasn't just choosing her fake friends over me, but now a complete stranger!

"Finally, she got up to leave. I thought maybe it was for the best. She'd ditch this guy and I'd be able to catch up with her. Just the two of us. Maybe we'd take off and have our own fun. As I followed them, my anger continued to build. I kept thinking of how I kept putting Layla first, only for her to put everyone else in the world above me. By the time he took off and left her alone, I was fuming."

I raise my eyes suddenly, the scene playing in my mind jarred. For years, I've imagined it. His hands around her neck. The fear she must have felt when she realized no one was around. The way he callously left her body in the gully, as though she was no more than a discarded cigarette butt or other piece of trash.

"You said he took off?" I ask, trying to clarify. "Layla was alone?"

Danielle raises her eyes to meet mine, the intensity of her stare sending fear, cold and sharp, through my entire body.

"Yes," she says. "He left, and it was only the two of us."

"But then, how did he—"

I imagine Layla turning around, still smiling from her night. She sees she's not alone and takes a step back, fear shooting through her, only to see it's not a stranger behind her. It's Danielle. Her friend.

"I asked her why she lied," Danielle says. "I wanted to know why she'd cancelled our plans together. Clearly, she wasn't studying. And she couldn't say her friends talked her into going out. You were long gone by then. Even the man from the bar was gone, and it was only her, and I wanted to know why she lied.

"She became angry that I'd followed her. That I'd been hiding out all night watching. I told her I'd come to Whitaker to surprise her, but that was before I realized she was ditching me."

I imagine Danielle and Layla arguing. How invasive it must have felt for Layla to know one of her oldest friends had stalked her all night. I imagine Layla's eyes cutting from left to right, searching for a witness, but finding herself alone.

"She told me I was smothering her. That she'd chosen WU to put some space between us, and that I was disrespecting her boundaries by showing up unannounced. She even said I was scaring her!

"We both started shouting. I hadn't come all this way to listen to someone who didn't understand what real friendship meant. I felt so hurt, so rejected. I ran toward her."

The scene in my mind changes. It's not *his* hands around Layla's neck, it's not *his* voice shouting—it's Danielle's. It was always Danielle.

"You killed Layla," I say, the accusation leaving my mouth in a whisper.

"I didn't realize what I'd done until it was too late," Danielle says. The darkness in her eyes recedes, replaced with sorrowful tears. "I was just so angry, you know? I felt betrayed by my only friend. Next thing I know, she was just lying there, mouth open, eyes wide, silent."

"You murdered her," I say, trying to force the image of Layla out of my mind. "For no reason at all."

"I had a reason!" Danielle corrects me, her voice charged. "We were supposed to be there for each other. She discarded me, and I couldn't let that happen."

"You let another person take the fall," I say. "He's been in prison for nearly ten years—"

"He wouldn't have taken the deal if it weren't for those other accusations against him," she says. "I've lost sleep over the past ten years, but never over that."

"You killed Layla. My best friend! And then had the nerve to use her death against me. And Crystal. You urged her parents to file that civil suit against us."

Danielle is standing straighter again now, fueled by her own sense of justice.

"If you hadn't gone out with her that night, none of this would have happened. If you hadn't left her, she'd still be alive. You're to blame just as much as everyone else," she says. Then quieter, "I was just helping her parents see that. It's what real friends do."

The past ten years have been a puzzle, but finally the pieces are falling into place. The way Layla's mother described her daughter's close friendships from childhood. The way Danielle talks about Layla now, as though she only saw her yesterday.

The strange behavior Layla exhibited whenever she came back from a visit home, acting like something bad had happened, but not wanting to talk about it. I realize now, long before Danielle became my stalker, she'd been fixated on Layla, and it's that infatuation that led to my friend's death.

FORTY

My heart is beating so furiously I can feel it in my throat. My eyes sting with tears, and yet, when I open my mouth to speak, nothing comes out. I'm heartbroken for Layla and what her final moments must have been like. I realize now it's so much worse than I imagined. She wasn't lured by a stranger, killed by a sexual predator.

She was murdered by one of her best friends. I can't imagine the fear and betrayal she must have felt. I made a mistake leaving her behind that night, but I no longer carry the burden of her death. Michael Massey wasn't the real threat that night. It was Danielle.

"I thought I'd moved past this," Danielle says. For a moment, I forgot she was still here. I was too far into the past. "I really did. There were the two guys last year, but those were flukes. I'd carried on with my life. I'd even forgiven you. Until you had the audacity to write that awful story about Layla."

"You murdered her!" I remind her, my anger giving me the courage to speak. "Do you realize how delusional you sound? You're claiming to be her friend, when this whole time you were the one who killed her."

"No one can prove that," she says, defiantly. "Just like the civil suit couldn't prove you were at fault. But now? There are multiple dead bodies with ties to you and the stories you wrote. You're finally going to reap what you sowed all those years ago."

"You can't—"

Moaning sounds interrupt our exchange. On the concrete floor, Marley begins to stir.

"Where am I?" She's raising herself onto her elbows, touching the back of her head. Blood stains her fingers and she gasps. "What happened to me?"

"You were attacked—" I explain, but before I can finish, Danielle cuts in.

"Becca knocked you over the head!" she shouts. "I saw the whole thing."

"She's lying," I say. "You know that. I was on the phone with you."

"She was following you," Danielle says. "That's why I came here. To help protect you."

Marley winces. I wonder if she can even understand anything that's been said. "I think I should go to the hospital." She tries to stand but tumbles back to her knees.

"We have to get out of here," I say, looking at Danielle. "Please let us leave."

"I'm not letting her go anywhere with you," she says. "You're a murderer! You're the one behind all this!"

"She's lying."

"I don't care who's lying," Marley says, her words beginning to slur.

"Danielle is the person we've been chasing all this time. She killed Layla," I say. Then more desperately, "She killed your brother!"

"You can't believe her. She—"

Danielle is interrupted by the screeching sound of the

heavy door hitting the cement wall. Two officers raid the storage facility with their guns drawn.

"Hands up," one of them shouts, while the other hunches forward.

I obey, as does Danielle, dropping the hammer on the ground. Marley is still sitting, her hand on the back of her head, dazed.

"It was all her," Danielle cries, pointing at me. "I saw the whole thing. She attacked my friend and just admitted to killing two other people."

"She's lying!"

"Everyone on your stomachs," the second officer says, ignoring us. "Place your hands on the back of your heads and remain still."

Again, we obey. The officers move around us, placing handcuffs on our wrists. The metal feels heavy and cold, digging into my skin. On the ground, all Danielle and I can do is stare at each other, a silent face-off.

"Do you know who attacked you?" the first officer asks Marley.

She shakes her head. "I don't remember anything."

I can't fault her for not having my side. She genuinely doesn't know what happened, and I'm briefly happy she doesn't yet have to face her brother's killer. When Danielle catches my eye, she smiles greedily. She believes there's no proof against her. All the evidence points to me, and even Marley is too out of it to come to my defense.

"Can someone tell us what happened here?" the second officer says, his weapon at his side.

"I already told you," Danielle says. "Becca admitted everything. She attacked my friend."

The officer looks at me, waiting for my answer.

"Check my back pocket," I tell him.

I'm still face down on the ground. He pats around my lower body, pulling out my cell phone.

"This yours?" he asks me.

"Yes. If you let me unlock it, you'll be able to hear everything that happened."

"What are you talking about?" Danielle says, angrily.

Being a crime writer, albeit unpublished, does have its advantages. I've made a lot of stupid mistakes in the past couple of weeks, but I've kept a few tricks up my sleeve. Just as I did that night I met Marley at the diner, I started recording on my phone after I disconnected the call with 911.

I wanted to ensure that if whoever was behind this confessed, I'd have it on tape.

The officer uncuffs me long enough to unlock my phone. The second officer watches me closely, his hand on his service weapon just in case. The app is still running; all I have to do is hit the playback button to listen to everything Danielle said in the past ten minutes.

When she hears her voice on the recording, she closes her eyes, resting her forehead against the cement. It's all over now, and she knows it. Warm tears swell as it sinks in, I've finally broken free from the black hearts and my tormentor.

The world will soon learn Danielle was behind the copycat crimes for which she tried to frame me. They'll hear the truth about what happened to Brandon Davis and Rudy Raines, Jessica Wilder and Darryl Nease.

And most importantly, they'll know she was the one who killed Layla all along.

FORTY-ONE

ONE YEAR LATER

I close my eyes and try to breathe.

My stomach is a bundle of nerves, heat climbing the back of my neck. Within the cramped confines of the bathroom stall, I try to escape into my mind. *You can do this*, I tell myself. *You've already done it*. But it doesn't matter how much has changed in the past year, feelings of insecurity plague me.

Someone raps against the stall door.

"Becca, are you in there?" Crystal asks. "They need you up front. It's about to start."

"Coming," I say, keeping my voice level. I count to ten, try to take control of my nerves. *This is what you wanted more than anything*, I tell myself.

When I open the stall door, she's standing there, waiting for me.

"It's going to be great," she says. My friendship with Crystal has been tested more than most, and she's still here. That's a victory within itself. Once she found out what happened, she came rushing back into my life, and she's been by my side ever since.

She pushes open the bathroom door and we enter the main

area of the store. Shelves with books line either side of us, showing the names of authors I've always admired. As I walk through the corridors, I can't help thinking about everything that's brought me to this point.

My love of reading and writing, which started when I was in middle school, the way I was able to escape into fictional stories when the hardships of adolescence became too difficult. And then, in the blink of an eye, it seemed, I was grown, a student at WU embarking on real friendships, Crystal and Layla at my side.

The open doors to the conference room provide a glimpse of the audience inside. Rows upon rows of readers ready to fire off questions about the book. About what happened. I spot my mother sitting in the front row. A few seats down, I spy April and Victoria playfully gossiping as they wait for the event to begin. The sight is overwhelming, and I take a step backward.

"Don't be nervous." Crystal grabs my shoulder, keeping my balance. "Everyone loves you."

Everyone being the loyal readership we've gained in the past year, all thanks to the nonfiction release, *How a Fake Murder Caught a Real Killer: A Tale of Grief and Obsession* by Becca Walsh and Marley Theroux. I focus on the banner at the front of the room which features the book cover I dreamed about for so long. It's shades of black and red and navy blue, the title written in white, bright and bold.

"Becca?"

I turn to see one of the bookstore attendants approaching, clipboard in hand. "The moderator is going to speak for about ten minutes before we get started. Marley's waiting in another room. Would you like to join her?"

I flit my eyes to Crystal once more. She's nodding and smiling. "Good luck," she says, before entering the conference room.

I follow the attendant through the back of the bookstore, trying to keep my heart from beating too fast. She opens a nondescript door. Inside, Marley is sitting in a foldable chair, her feet propped onto a table.

"I wondered if you'd gotten lost," she says. "You look like a nervous wreck."

"It's our first big event," I say, lowering myself into the chair across from her.

"We better get used to this. We have four more readings before the holidays."

How a Fake Murder Caught a Real Killer has been a runaway hit. Marley and I started writing shortly after Danielle's arrest, and an agent swooped up our proposal before we were even finished. Marley is set to start a true crime podcast, after all, and *Night Beat*, my first novel, is scheduled to release next spring. A year ago, I never would have imagined this level of success.

"I'll let you know when it's time," the attendant says, leaving the clipboard on the table between us. "Here are the moderator's notes if you want to look over them."

Alone in the room, the reality of everything that's happened in the past year begins to set in. When I think of the night Layla died, it's difficult to separate what I thought happened from the truth. For years, I blamed Michael Massey. I blamed myself. I imagined her death hundreds of times, never knowing the real culprit was someone else entirely. There's no way I could have saved her, I realize, not when Danielle was, unknowingly, watching her every move.

On the day of her arrest, I handed over the recorded confession to Chaz and Wooley as soon as we made it to the police station. Turns out they'd been keeping tabs on me, would have likely arrived even if it wasn't for my hurried call to 911. The detectives claim they were only trying to keep me safe, but I still believe I was their number one suspect, until I captured Danielle's confession on tape.

The recording in hand, they were able to switch their sights to her. It didn't take them long to find additional evidence tying her to the location of Jessica Wilder's murder, and she never presented a convincing alibi for the night of Darryl Nease's death. Technical data even shows when she likely hacked into my email account to send those messages. The list of evidence against her is long, and after years of tormenting me with the black hearts, I feel a sense of relief knowing she's behind bars.

Of course, Danielle's arrest means Michael Massey has a chance of being released. The justice system moves at an even slower pace than publishing, so I'm not sure when that will be, but he has a hearing coming up soon. I'm conflicted about his fate. Part of me pities the fact he spent a decade in prison for a murder he didn't commit; however, when I consider the testimony of his living victims, or dare myself to recall the night I was nearly assaulted at the frat house, I'm convinced he is where he needs to be.

"Did you read over the moderator's questions?" Marley asks.

My throat is dry when I try to speak. "Yeah. I did."

"What's going on with you?" she asks, sensing my uneasiness. "You look like you've seen a ghost."

I stare at her. Marley has always reminded me of Layla, ever since that first meeting, but looking at her now, all I can see are their differences. It was never the event in front of our readers that had my nerves all twisted. It's the conversation I'm about to have now with Marley, my collaborator and friend.

I pull the clipboard on the table closer to me, flipping through the same series of questions I studied last night in preparation for the day's event.

"I've been thinking a lot about the timeline. The murders of Jessica Wilder and Darryl Nease. Do you ever feel guilty that we're profiting off their deaths?"

"We're profiting off our own experiences," she says, firmly. "Remember, we lost people, too. Layla and Brandon. Besides, a portion of the sales goes to charities. We should be proud of that."

"I am." I stop when I see the question that's been keeping me up at night. The one that's been impossible for me to answer after all this time. "Check out question twenty-three."

I shove the clipboard closer to her, and she reads. Of course, she would have already seen it. We were both given a copy and asked to comment on anything we did or didn't want mentioned.

Marley sits upright, pushing the clipboard back to me. "I scratched that one out. Don't worry about it."

"It's been bothering me though."

The question reads: *Any idea why Danielle chose not to leave a black heart at the scene of Darryl Nease's death?*

I sit back, looking straight at Marley, and ask, "Why did you scratch that one off?"

"We have a limited amount of time. We can't get to every question, especially if we want time for readers to ask their own." She pauses. "And there was a black heart at the bridge. It was left with the article about Layla's death, remember?"

The fear of finding that article still feels fresh. It was the first time I made a solid connection between Layla's death and the hearts and the copycat crimes. The first time I acknowledged all the horrors writing that story had brought to life.

"Danielle left that before I arrived at the bridge. Before I came looking for you and we talked at the diner. Long before Darryl Nease was pushed."

"So?"

"His body was found with a copy of my story," I remind her.

"Right. Just like a copy of *The Mistake* was sent to the police station."

"There was a black heart with that," I say. "No black heart was left at Darryl Nease's crime scene."

"The man was found in a river. No telling what evidence

was lost." She crosses her arms over her chest, kicking her feet back on the table. "What are you getting at, anyway?"

"When we met at the diner, I told you my suspicions about what had been happening. The copycat crimes. Jessica Wilder's murder mimicking *The Mistake*." I pause, watching her closely. "I never told you about the black hearts."

"So?"

"Danielle had been sending me the hearts for years. She left them at every crime scene, even when she slashed my tires. Why wouldn't she leave one there?"

Marley doesn't answer. She's no longer looking at me either. She's staring ahead.

"Marley, where did you go after we left the diner?"

"Home."

I have no way of knowing if that is true. The narrative of what happened to Darryl Nease has already been decided for us. His death was lumped in with the crimes Danielle committed, and no one, not even me, questioned it.

And yet that one loose end won't leave me alone.

"You didn't know about the black hearts until after he died," I say. "That's why one wasn't at the scene."

"What are you suggesting?"

"If Danielle killed Darryl Nease, she would have left a heart behind. It makes me think maybe we got it wrong. Someone else killed him." I pause again, hoping she won't make me say out loud what we both know I'm thinking. "I just can't figure out why."

She places her feet on the ground, moving her body closer to the table. When she looks at me, the sunny, bright expression behind her eyes is gone.

"At the diner, I urged you to go to the police. You refused. You thought there wasn't enough evidence. That they wouldn't believe you. No one was ever going to listen to my theory that someone was killing people based on fictional stories. I needed the police to investigate Brandon's death. I needed something to grab their attention."

My chest heaves up and down as I try to control my breathing. "Marley, did you go back to the bridge after our conversation that night?"

She lowers her eyes further, her voice low and hard to hear. "I already had access to the shared drive, you know. Victoria added me in before you ever told me about it. It was easy to print a copy of your story, to present a solid connection between a man's death and what you'd written. But you're right. I didn't know about the black hearts."

That's why one wasn't found at the scene. Marley never knew to leave one. Danielle may have been responsible for everything else, but not for the murder of Darryl Nease.

Marley did that.

"He was an innocent man that had nothing to do with any of this." Tears fill my eyes, fall down my cheeks.

"He had no family. No one to worry about him—"

"You don't know that!" I shout, my body beginning to shake with anger.

"I missed Brandon so terribly, and all I wanted was a reason for someone to take a closer look at his case. I needed you and the police to believe this was real!"

Thinking back, the murder at Banyon's Bridge happened right before our meeting at the Pizzeria, when she was complaining about lack of sleep. She missed the next Mystery Maidens meeting, but it wasn't because she was paranoid about how dangerous the situation had gotten. She was spiraling over the fact she murdered an innocent man.

"And look what happened as a result," she says, spreading her arms wide. "We've brought closure to multiple other families. Danielle is behind bars. Both our lives have changed for the better."

Two quick raps on the door, and it opens.

"It's time," the coordinator says, standing in the doorway. "Are you ready?"

Marley is motionless, staring at me. "Becca, are we good? I need to know you can do this."

I stand slowly, walking through the open doorway and waiting for Marley to follow. When she does, she sees that Chaz is standing beside me, and freezes. Unbeknownst to her, he'd been waiting outside the door the entire time. Listening.

"Becca, please don't do this," she pleads, her voice quivering when she spots the glint off the handcuffs Chaz holds in his palms.

"All I'm doing is telling the truth," I say, refusing to give Marley a second glance. "The audience is waiting."

And I have one hell of a story to tell them.

A LETTER FROM MIRANDA

Dear reader,

Thank you for taking the time to read *The Writer*. If you liked it and want information about upcoming releases, sign up with the following link. Your email address will never be shared and you can unsubscribe at any time.

www.bookouture.com/miranda-smith

Out of all my novels, I really wrote this book with readers in mind. As a reader myself, I know there's nothing better than getting lost in a story, and I've been lucky to get feedback from different readers in recent years. My husband was the one who suggested I write a mystery centered around a book club, mainly because several groups have reached out about featuring my books. I tweaked that idea, deciding to write about a group of writers instead. There was something terrifying about the idea of life imitating art! I hope that longtime mystery and crime readers will appreciate the little nods to the genre throughout the book. This one was so much fun to write!

If you'd like to discuss any of my books, I'd love to connect! You can find me on Facebook, X and Instagram, or my website.

If you enjoyed *The Writer*, I'd appreciate it if you left a review on Amazon. It only takes a few minutes and does wonders in helping readers discover my books for the first time.

Thank you again for your support!

Sincerely,

Miranda Smith

 facebook.com/MirandaSmithAuthor

 x.com/msmithbooks

instagram.com/mirandasmithbooks

ACKNOWLEDGMENTS

There are several people I'd like to thank for their support in completing *The Writer*. To my editor, Ruth Tross, your feedback is essential to taking a random idea and turning it into a complete book. Thank you for your guidance and continued faith in my writing. Thank you to the rest of the Bookouture team for all you do, especially Sarah Hardy, Kim Nash, Jane Eastgate and Liz Hurst.

To anyone who has read this book, thank you for taking a chance on my writing. This is my tenth published book, but I'm always hoping to reach new readers. I've been fortunate to meet several of you in person over the past couple of years at different events, which has been lovely. I'd also like to thank the book bloggers and reviewers that shout about each new release online. None of this would be possible without all of you!

As always, I'd like to thank my family for their love and encouragement. Much love to Harrison, Lucy and Christopher. *The Writer* is dedicated to my husband because he gave me the idea for the premise. Chris, it's always fun coming up with hypothetical crimes together! I love you.

PUBLISHING TEAM

Turning a manuscript into a book requires the efforts of many people. The publishing team at Bookouture would like to acknowledge everyone who contributed to this publication.

Audio
Alba Proko
Sinead O'Connor
Melissa Tran

Commercial
Lauren Morrissette
Hannah Richmond
Imogen Allport

Data and analysis
Mark Alder
Mohamed Bussuri

Editorial
Ruth Tross
Melissa Tran

Copyeditor
Jane Eastgate

Proofreader
Liz Hurst

Marketing
Alex Crow
Melanie Price
Occy Carr
Cíara Rosney

Operations and distribution
Marina Valles
Stephanie Straub

Production
Hannah Snetsinger
Mandy Kullar
Jen Shannon

Publicity
Kim Nash
Noelle Holten
Jess Readett
Sarah Hardy

Rights and contracts
Peta Nightingale
Richard King
Saidah Graham

Printed in Great Britain
by Amazon

40591631R00169